MURDER IN THE MEDINA

A BLAKE SISTERS TRAVEL MYSTERY

CARTER FIELDING

Published by Carter Fielding Press
5237 River Road, #304
Bethesda, MD 20216

Editing, design, and production by Bublish, Inc.
ISBN: 978-1-64704-417-6 (Paperback)
ISBN: 978-1-64704-416-9 (eBook)

**For information about the author and her projects
please visit:
www.mcarterfielding.com**

To loves lost or yet unfound,
love does endure.

Carter

FINLEY BLAKE WASN'T SURE WHAT to expect when she walked through the doors of the nondescript brownstone on West 23rd Street that housed the offices of *Traveler's Tales* magazine. She had decided after six years of fifteen-plus-hour days at that major league consulting firm that she had had enough and needed a break. Partner had its benefits, but it wasn't worth the burnout she was experiencing. Maybe it wasn't burnout, just boredom.

So, there she stood looking at a sea of cubicles surrounded by a wall of glass-fronted offices. She prayed that she would be given an assignment soon. Living in a cube wasn't her style. She sighed heavily. Out of the frying pan and into the fire, as her granny used to say.

"Excuse me, I was looking for Dan Burton?" Finley hesitantly asked the only person who wasn't screaming into a phone or lost deep in their headset.

"Alisha should be back in a minute," was the reply from a smartly dressed woman in her late twenties who walked by without a backward glance.

After ten minutes or so, the receptionist, or the person Finley thought might be the receptionist, returned to the stark Formica barricade that was her desk.

"May I help you?" A middle-aged woman in a bright green and yellow sari asked in a voice that could barely be called a whisper.

"I have an appointment with Dan—" Before Finley could finish the sentence, she was wrapped in a hug from behind by a giant of a man who towered over her.

"Finley, kid, what've you been up to? Come on back. Alisha, can you get us some coffee? Finley likes hers strong and black if I remember correctly. And I'll have my usual. We'll be in my office. And hold all my calls for the next half hour or so!" His rapid-fire cadence ricocheted off the walls as he led her to his office down the hallway.

"So, fill me in on your life. You said you were looking for something different, something daring. Well, here it is. Travel. Adventure. You'll have it all!" Dan continued in an overenthusiastic voice that made her feel like she was listening to a snake-oil salesman, and she wasn't buying the schtick.

Dan's sandy curls flopped over his eyebrow as he rounded a doorway and turned to show her a chair in his overstuffed office. He was a big guy—well over the 6'3" he claimed to be when asked his height—with a barrel chest and arms that were visibly muscular. He used to be a rugger in college and must still be playing. If not, it was a waste. An affable man with a quick wit and a machine-gun mouth, he was also one of the brightest people Finley had ever met.

The two had met during the first week of law school and often sat side by side during their first year because of their last names, Blake and Burton. But after that, their paths diverged. She focused on international corporate law and he on First Amendment issues. Yet, somehow, they kept in touch, running into each other at friends' houses or professional events over the past decade.

He was one of the first people she called when she had decided to leave the firm. He also had left law behind, as had she, but he

2

had managed to recreate himself a couple times professionally before settling into journalism. She thought he might share his experience making those transitions.

Besides, he always seemed to know how to lay the issues out, evaluate options, and make a decision quickly. And she needed to do that quickly. She had some money tucked away that would last her a while, but the indecision and uncertainty that surrounded her change of career made her antsy. She was afraid that she would back out and rescind her resignation, going back to the familiar because it was familiar, and not because she liked what she was doing.

"So?" Dan's question was hanging in the air when Finley finally rejoined the conversation.

"I need a change. Life is too short, and I feel like I'm coasting. So I'm ready to travel to far-off places, do interviews, take pictures," Finley started. "Tell me what you need. What angles work best with your audience?"

Finley's time writing for *Vanity Fair* right out of college—before the law school bug had bitten—was what got her the interview, but it had been a tough sell, even as a freelancer. She would be on a six-month probation: bring in sellable stories in that time or get cut. Dan was honest. Her background was impressive, but all his magazine cared about was getting stories that readers liked. Give him that, and she might find a regular outlet for her work.

"Look, we had a staff writer pull up sick for an assignment in Morocco. We could cut the story and put something else in, but this might be a good one for you to cut your teeth on. Small story, so small budget, but see what you can do. I managed to find you an advance—not normal for freelance, so don't expect it next time," he growled good naturedly.

"What's your deadline? And when do I leave?" Finley asked, gently touching the passport that was always in her handbag. Past experience made that necessary, and the same went for the bag that was always packed in her front closet, ready for the client who demanded that she be in Zurich or Hong Kong the next day.

"Will two days be enough for you to make arrangements and get over there?" He pulled out the file that the *Tales* writer had compiled with ideas, background, possible interview subjects, and regular contacts. Things to get her started. She could take it from there.

"Morning, Miss Blake," the doorman, Mr. Byrne, a middle-aged man of fifty or so with a strong Brooklyn accent, pulled open her building's large brass door. He had been the doorman for as long as Finley had been in the building, almost five years now. "Finally stopped raining. Looks like it might be a nice day, after all."

"Indeed. Good morning, Mr. Byrne. Mail here yet?" Finley asked.

"Carrier's filling the boxes right now," Byrne replied.

"Good deal. By the way, I'll be away for a while, so I'm going to have a hold put on my mail. If anything else comes, can you keep it behind the desk?" she said.

"Where're you off to now, Miss Blake? If you don't mind me asking," the doorman queried quietly. He knew that she used to travel a lot for her previous job, but he also knew that she was making a career change and wasn't sure what this new career was.

"Morocco!" Finley replied. "It's been a while since I've been there and I'm looking forward to going back." Her thoughts were drawn back to a time not too long ago when Morocco—and a certain gentleman there—held a special place in her heart. But that time had since passed. "You'd really like it there, I think, Mr. Byrne. Good coffee. Great food. Warm sun."

"Morocco. Makes me think of *Arabian Nights* and all that exotic stuff," replied Byrne, shaking his head. "I think I'll just stay right here in good old Manhattan."

"You don't know what you're missing. See you later," Finley answered as she headed across the lobby to the elevator.

Byrne skirted around the desk and hit the elevator button, holding the door back once it had opened until she finished grabbing her mail from her box. Finley stepped into the elevator and pushed the number nine for her floor.

The apartment was warm; sunlight poured in through the bank of windows that ran down the street side of the wall. The adjacent wall, which faced the alley, had fewer windows but more wall space for the artwork that Finley had collected over the years—art that held memories of places and people. She walked to the dining table to drop her bag and the junk mail that had been in her mailbox. She looked around and sighed. She was going to miss the comfort of the place, even as she looked forward to this new adventure.

While she pulled her suitcase from the upper shelf of the front closet, Finley asked Alexa to call her sister. Whitt, her baby sister by six years, lived in Manila, working in development banking. The two saw each other a couple times a year, or sometimes more when they figured out how to arrange their work assignments so that at least part of their projects were in some proximate parts of the world, and they could wrangle a weekend in a spot between their locations.

Sometimes it was Dubai for a couple hours during a layover, or better still Doha where the stop could give them as much as ten hours to catch up. Last time, it had been a whole three days in Istanbul, a city Whitt loved and knew well. Finley was hoping that Whitt had a trip planned that would take her near enough to Tangier so that they could grab a few days of girl talk.

"'Lo!" came a dusky voice, muffled by sleep.

"Sorry, kid! Hope I didn't wake you."

"Nope, it's only eleven here. I must've nodded off." Whitt yawned into the phone. "Sorry. What's up?"

Finley explained the Moroccan assignment with *Traveler's Tales* and the timing. She had already told Whitt about her need for a career change, the opportunity—however temporary—that Dan had offered, and her concerns, her uncertainty. Whitt was encouraging, assuring her of her ability to make the change and talking about all the places they could travel to together.

"So, you stuck in the office, or are you on the road?" Finley asked.

"I'm off to Tbilisi the week after next for meetings with the Central Bank. When are you heading out?"

"The day after tomorrow. I need to book my flight and hotels today and see if I can set up a few calls for when I land. The person I'm standing in for has done a lot of the grunt work, so I think I'm good to hit the ground running," Finley ventured hopefully. "You up for a little adventure? A bit out of the way, but still good fun."

"Let me see what I can do." Whitt answered, sounding wide awake. She was up for the challenge. It would mean that she would have to do all the preparations for her trip to Georgia as well as book a flight to Tangier in the next day or so. Her meetings weren't for another ten days, so she could use some of her vacation rollover that was accumulating. It would be great to see her sister after five months apart. More importantly, it would assure her that Finley was doing okay and that her decision to leave consulting was a good one.

"I'll shoot you a message with my flight info. I think it'll work," Whitt relayed before dropping off the call and pulling up Expedia. "This is going to be fun."

2

FINLEY HAD BARELY ENDED THE call before another notification popped up on her phone screen. She would have recognized the ringtone even without the picture of the Kate Hudson doppelganger with a perfectly styled blowout.

"So how did it go?" asked Mona Allen, aka Mooney, her closest friend since she returned to New York over three years ago.

She and Lydia, Finley's classmate from law school and former colleague at the firm, had been roommates for years, but Finley and Mooney never actually met until three years ago. Back in New York after two years in Morocco, Finley had felt adrift, unmoored by the change in so many parts of her life. Mooney had been the perfect antidote to the confusion. She was a doer, a mover. Smart, pretty—no, make that gorgeous—and she knew her stuff. A top-tier event planner, she had the heavyweights of the city begging to be on her invite list, and she worked it like a master puppeteer. Hers was a golden contact list, the stuff of king makers.

And despite all that power, she chose Finley as her friend. Since their introduction at an impromptu Friday night happy hour, the two had been inseparable. They commiserated stumbles over Kamikazes and celebrated triumphs with Taittinger.

"So, tell me all," Mooney gushed. Finley could see Mooney pouring herself a cup of matcha. *How she can drink that stuff is beyond me*, Finley thought. *Tastes like green plaster. Sour, gritty—and green.*

"It looks like I got an assignment," Finley said. "Morocco."

Finley had moved away from her screen and was roaming around the room, pulling out pants and tops and shoes that might work. She was trying to think through where she might go and the associated weather and travel conditions. The itinerary that she and Dan had reviewed included mainly city locations, so she didn't need her hiking boots.

"Morocco! You lucky bugger. What're you taking to wear?"

"Mainly linens and cotton. And a few shawls. It'll be rather warm during the day with that quick cooldown at night."

"Don't forget something dressy. You never know what you may get invited to. As pretty as you are, I wouldn't be surprised if some handsome sheikh whisked you off into the desert on his trusty steed."

"Mooney, you read way too many cheap romance novels," Finley stuck her head back on camera. "And if I'm wearing something sexy, I don't want a damn horse snorting all over me!"

Mooney chortled. She remembered a time when Finley couldn't even make smart-mouthed jokes—when even smiling seemed like it would hurt her face. Mooney wanted to ask whether Finley was going to see Max, but she didn't quite know how to raise the question.

Finley pulled out her packing list and ran over the items that had yet to be checked off. They were mainly things that she needed to get from 47th Street Photo. She could do that tomorrow. Maybe she and Mooney could grab a drink and a light dinner after.

"I need to get another lens for my camera, so I'll be down in your neck of the woods in the afternoon. Want to go for a drink when I'm done?"

"Sure. Shall I bring Logan?" Logan Reynolds was a client of Mooney's that she had been trying to set Finley up with for ages. The first few meetings had gone well. He was interested at least, and Finley hadn't run out of the room, but Mooney wanted to proceed with caution.

"Fine with me. I don't see why you're trying so hard to get me paired." Finley set down her computer. She smiled, shaking her head at Mooney's persistence.

"Besides the fact that he is one, beautiful, two, brilliant—and three, loaded?" Mooney enumerated.

"Yeah. There are lots of guys in New York that fit that description."

"And also very FOF—fond of Finley?"

Finley paused. She hadn't done much dating since she got back from Tangier. She immersed herself in work, traveled a bit with her sister and with Mama. But she hadn't gone out with more than a handful of guys. She never really liked the process. *I am always too tall or too opinionated or too something*, she thought.

"Let's stay focused. I need to get organized. I have one day to get this all done," Finley picked up her computer and began to show Mooney what she was planning to pack.

"Where are your heels?" Mooney asked. "You need at least one pair of drop-dead stilettos. You can dress up anything with those."

"Where would I be going that would require stilettos? This is a work assignment, not vacation."

"I know, but you never know. They aren't going to take up that much room," Mooney peered at what was laid out on the bed.

Finley grabbed her computer again, walked into her closet, and scanned her shoe rack so Mooney could see.

"Those!" Mooney was pointing at something through the screen.

"Which ones are 'those?'" Finley had moved the camera back so that Mooney could point again.

"Those, the multicolored ones. They'll go with everything, so you only have to take one pair."

Finley grabbed the shoes and a mesh evening bag and closed the closet door. "You're cut off! My bag will be over the weight limit if I let you keep shopping in my closet for more things to take with me."

Mooney feigned a pout and took a sip of the wine that had been sitting off camera beside her matcha. *The girl is a study in contradictions—matcha and wine. Luckily, I get to see both sides. Whatever works for you,* Finley thought.

"Are you going to see him?" Mooney had decided to just spit out her question rather than keep dancing around the subject.

So that's why she needed wine! Finley thought about playing dumb, but decided that if Mooney could ask, she could at least give her some sort of answer. Mooney had known her only a short time when they became friends, but she understood Finley's pain and helped her work her way through it.

"I don't know if he's still there. So, I guess the answer is 'I don't know.'" Finley stopped arranging clothes on the bed and looked at Mooney on the screen.

"That's fair," Mooney said. "You're strong enough now to be civil if you do see him."

"I am a Southern woman. I am always civil," Finley feigned mock indignation. *Even until the very moment that I draw and quarter him.*

"Look, I've got to go, but I'll see you at Cork at about six o'clock tomorrow night. We can talk more before the crowd comes." Mooney pointed her empty wine glass in Finley's direction. "And I'm making sure that Logan comes, so wear something cute!"

Finley nodded and clicked to end the call. *Since when do I run errands in anything cute?* she pondered. *Maybe I will just buy something after my errands and wear it to drinks! Kill two birds with one stone. Something new for the trip and something cute to satisfy Mooney.*

The next day, she ran through her list, ticking off the myriad things she needed to take care of before she left. She had put in some dry cleaning that needed to be picked up. Her black silk pants were among the items in there. She needed travel-size containers of everything: Lysol, Handi Wipes, toothpaste. She checked the pre-packed Ziplocs that populated her suitcase pouches and realized that she was running low on several items. She had already made two trips to CVS and noted on her list a few things that would warrant yet another trip. Finley decided that she could stop by the Duane Reade near the photo shop instead.

When she reached the photo store later in the day, she was shopped out. Unlike Mama and her sister, who both loved to peruse, Finley was a purposeful shopper. She made a list and made a point of picking up only what was on the list. Somehow that method made the end of the shopping spree seem closer. *Almost done,* she consoled herself. *You have the lens you want marked. They said they had it in stock. Just get it and go.*

The guy behind the counter was in a talkative mood. He pulled her lens from stock, showed her how to fit it on her camera and then started asking her questions. Finley got the idea he was trying to cross-sell her more stuff than he was being friendly. *Whatever it is, it isn't on my list,* she thought to herself.

"Heading to Central Park to take advantage of the good weather this weekend?" he asked.

"Nope, heading overseas tomorrow, so I'm going to miss it," she said.

"Where're you headed? For work or play?"

"Morocco, and for work," she informed him matter-of-factly.

"Great. So, what sort of filter are you using?" he asked. Finley hadn't thought of additional filters. She wasn't used to needing them except for special effects. But with the glare off the sand and the whitewashed buildings, she thought she should reconsider.

"What would you suggest? I'll be in cities most of the time, so not out in the sand per se, but the sun is likely to be bright against the buildings."

He pulled out a couple of neutral density filters that she hadn't used before and some polarizing ones to add to her own collection. They were all ones he thought might work well given the landscape and cityscape she had described. He also suggested a few ways she might think of using them under different conditions. While he was wrapping up her purchase, she wandered the side aisles, picking up another telescoped tripod and some lens cleaner as she passed through. She thanked him for the tutorial, stuffed her purchases in her backpack, and headed out to do the kind of shopping she hated the most—clothes shopping.

She walked the few blocks to Saks and pushed the heavy revolving door to enter. If it were up to her, she would have stayed by the ground floor fragrance counters and never bothered with the upper levels. She couldn't begin to think of what floor had "cute" clothes on them. She normally only shopped for work clothes, and now she had a woman at Bergdorf's who called her when something she might like came in, so she could buy her Max Mara and Armani suits or von Furstenberg wrap dresses in less than thirty minutes each season.

She pushed the button for sportswear and headed up to see what she might find that would pass Mooney's cute test. She surprised herself by pulling out several possible outfits in record time. Her favorite was a pair of black-and-white striped palazzo pants and a fitted black V-neck top. Before she knew it, she had made the purchase and was headed down to buy matching shoes. She liked the way the chunky bone and silver necklace she was wearing looked with what she had pulled together. She had her "cute" outfit.

A little after six o'clock in the evening, Finley walked into Cork. The doors along the front of the restaurant had been opened completely for an indoor/outdoor feeling. Mooney had claimed their usual tall bar table in the middle of the wide opening, which offered a full view of the action along the active Manhattan street. Mooney liked it because she could see what people were wearing, a veritable fashion show at rush hour in the spring, which this was.

"Well, don't you look darling!" Mooney stood to greet her, pecking her on both cheeks before checking to be sure she hadn't left any lipstick traces. "That's a new look for you. I like it."

Finley had to admit that she liked it too. It played to her height without making her feel too tall. According to Mama, a woman might be statuesque, but she should never be tall. Finley got images of women with breastplates whenever Mama said the word "tall." *The Blake women are definitely a statuesque lot, then.* She could never tell who was taller, Mama or Whitt. In heels, they both topped six feet.

"All packed?" Mooney asked.

"All packed for what?" a voice asked from behind her. The voice belonged to an impeccably dressed man with cropped salt and pepper hair. His eyes had drawn up into narrow slits when he smiled at Finley. Behind the tiny lines that crowded around the perimeter of his eyes were two pools of coffee-colored warmth that radiated from a good heart. Finley hadn't known Logan long, but she knew intuitively that she liked him.

Logan kissed Mooney on the cheek before coming around to give Finley the same. He kept his hand on the back of her chair, standing at the midpoint between the stools. Mooney recognized the possessive stance and smiled slyly. *That's awfully familiar, but he clearly plans to stake his claim on this one*, she thought.

Logan placed his order when the waiter brought Finley and Mooney's wine. "So, who's going where?"

"Finley, to Morocco," Mooney watched over the rim of her glass as to how this might play out.

"You're going to Morocco without me?" Logan looked like his feelings were hurt. "I could book a Challenger, and we could leave tonight."

Finley marveled at the ease with which wealth made everything possible, even the prospect of a midnight jaunt to Marrakesh. "You'd be bored. I have to work."

"I'd find ways to distract you," Logan grinned. Mooney was fully committed to following this game of wits. She put her glass down and looked from one to the other as the sparring continued.

"I'm sure you would try, but I have an assignment to finish."

"All work and no play can make Finley a very dull girl. And you are too bright a penny to be dull."

Finley turned to look at Logan with a look of disbelief on her face. "You really are serious, aren't you? You would fly to Morocco on a whim?"

"Of course, if it would impress you enough to give me the time of day." Logan looked so sincere that all Finley could do was smile.

By that time, other friends of Mooney's from work and Finley's from her former firm had begun to fill the table, and this thread of conversation was lost. They all asked about her new job, the trip, and the nature of the assignment. Throughout the evening, Logan talked with others in the group, but his position remained fixed.

"You up for a quiet dinner? You look far too nice for us to just leave it at drinks. I want to show you off," Logan had leaned in to counter the noise in the bar. He stepped back to better see her face when she responded. She was conflicted. Part of her was repulsed by a man who wanted a show thing. The other part of her was flattered. *Some feminist you are, letting pretty words turn your head.*

Finley caught Mooney watching them from the corner of her eye. *This is her client, so I have to play this one cautiously*, Finley remembered. To be honest, if she hadn't needed to do her work plan for the next couple weeks, she might have taken him up on the offer.

"As tempting an offer as that is, I leave tomorrow afternoon, and I'm behind in planning for this trip. It came up rather quickly. It's my first assignment with this magazine, and I don't want to blow it," Finley held his gaze and smiled as she gathered up her backpack and packages. "Any chance I might get a rain check on that dinner for when I get back?"

"Sure, but I plan to hold you to it." He kissed her cheek. "Let me grab you a cab." He slid through the growing crowd in the bar and headed to the street. Finley kissed Mooney goodbye and threw a general farewell out to the others at the table before turning to join Logan at the curb.

"You maneuvered that one well," Mooney called out over the crowd. "Have a great trip. Love you."

When the taxi came, Finley deftly positioned herself inside the open door, thanked Logan for hailing the cab for her and quickly slid into the back seat. She wasn't up for any awkward groping or lip locking. He was a nice guy, and she would go out with him again, but she wanted to set the pace, and that pace would be slow and steady.

As she prepared to leave her apartment, Finley went through her standard mental checklist: tickets, passport, letters of introduction, credit and debit cards, cash—crisp, unmarked bills only—camera equipment, computer, phone, converters, chargers, shawl, and fan. She could manage in almost any situation if she had these things. Clothes she could buy if her bag didn't make it, but most of the things on the checklist were hard to replace. She had arranged for a car to pick her up well before she needed to be at the airport. It was habit. She preferred to get through security, head to the lounge, and read leisurely rather than rush.

When she got home last night after drinks with Mooney, there was a message on her machine. Whitt had called to say she was in, flights already booked and work arrangements underway. Finley was glad. As excited as she was about this assignment, having her sister there to ease the transition—and to share the adventure—made it less scary. And she had to admit that, for whatever reason, she felt a little unsettled.

S. **WHITTAKER BLAKE, OTHERWISE KNOWN AS** Whitt, had jumped at the chance to go away somewhere, anywhere. She regularly traveled for work—in fact, that was what kept her tied to the bank. The travel and the people, mainly her immediate team and the ones in the field. The rest of them could go to hell. The pettiness and the politics sickened her at times, but then she got on the road, heading to Phnom Penh or Mumbai or Tbilisi, and the drama would melt away like snow in the sunshine, and she could find her center.

After she had gotten off the phone with Finley, Whitt shot a message to her boss, a surprisingly prickly Australian who feared Whitt more than he managed her. She simply said that she would be taking a few days off before heading to Georgia—she didn't ask if it would be okay, she simply stated that it would be happening. The reply was, "Sure, take whatever you need," which confirmed that she had used the appropriate tactic.

Whitt would organize her work life tomorrow, pulling whatever papers and documents she would need onto a thumb drive as back up to the versions she would email herself. But tonight, fired up by the prospect of someplace wild and different, she planned on packing. As she pulled out monotoned tunics in taupes and grays to match the navy and black pencil skirts that were her work uniform for Georgia, she also laid out silk crop pants, linen trousers, and loose tops that would work for walking around the souks and flea markets in Tangier—and Marrakesh, if they could head south during this sojourn.

She thought of the silver bangles and hammered plates that she wanted to add to her already bursting collection of treasures from her travels. And a few of the blue-and-white couscous bowls. They always came in handy as serving dishes. Or, perhaps, one of the hand-painted tagines, the steepled covered dish that those rich Moroccan stews were served in. Of course, the saffron, magenta, and indigo shawls, and the etched hands of Fatima that hung in the stalls always seemed to make their way into her suitcase as last-minute gifts for an assistant or Christmas stocking stuffers. Maybe she could find an expat friend heading stateside and put these items in with their household shipment. Saves having to carry them to Georgia.

An inveterate shopper like her Mama, she endured Finley's teasing about being a hoarder, mainly because her sister always seemed awed by the special finds that she presented as gifts for birthdays and other special occasions. Finley was still wearing the rose-cut diamond studs from India that Whitt had given her for her birthday. You'd think the things had sprouted from her ears; she was never without them.

The details of her mental shopping list were interrupted by a ping on her computer. She had set the alert to sound like the "You've Got Mail" AOL chime, reminiscent of the old Meg Ryan movie. It was a sound that sent little tingles through her since it meant that David was trying to FaceTime her from Georgia. It also meant that she had to tell him she wouldn't be coming to Tbilisi early as she had originally planned.

"Hey," a deep voice said, as she moved toward the computer. It was a voice that warmed her, even before his image came on the screen. They had met during one of her trips to Georgia—an expat friend of a mutual Georgian friend. She couldn't remember which trip it was. They came up so frequently recently that they all blended into one. All she knew was that ever since that encounter, she looked forward to going to Tbilisi like she never had before despite the fifteen-hour trip.

"You there?" came the voice again. Whitt hit the video button and unmuted her mic as David came on screen. With a tanned face, a broad jaw that was framed by dark blond hair, and liquid blue eyes, he looked like a surfer boy in a suit.

"Yep. Hold your horses," she countered, adjusting the camera angle, and taking the time to get a good look at him. His chiseled face was just short of perfection, at least to her, but it was his eyes that captivated her. Pale blue with glittering flecks of gray. When she spoke, she had to clear her throat so that he wouldn't hear the catch in her breath when she looked at him. *How can someone so damn good looking be interested in me?* she wondered.

"What's with the suit and tie? You look like an undertaker," she blurted out. She then continued hurriedly, afraid she had gone too far and that he might not like the ribbing. "Don't mind me. I'm being my normal 'cheeky' self. You look rather nice. What's the occasion?"

"Had a meeting with the ministries. Tourism and Commerce. Looking to export their nut oils in addition to the wines we are handling now." They talked a bit more about the market for Georgian products in the United States and Europe, and how David's company was hoping to expand. And then some small talk about mutual friends, Georgian and foreign, who were back in the city.

"So, when do you get in? Luka mentioned that you were coming back later this month. Is that true?" He paused, "And do I get to see you?"

The questioning in his voice made her glad that she was sitting down. How could someone she had never heard of four months ago make her turn to jelly so quickly? She used to think she was made of sterner stuff. Apparently not.

"Here's the thing. Yes, I'm coming to Tbilisi," she hesitated, not sure how much more she should reveal.

When she had talked to him earlier, she didn't indicate exactly when she was going back to Georgia, so he shouldn't have any expectations about her arriving early. But she didn't know what Luka, her handler for meetings in Tbilisi—and their mutual friend—had said about her itinerary.

"But I won't get there until the evening right before my meetings start, and I have to head out immediately after. Maybe we can figure out a time to grab a drink," she finished.

"Or late dinner?" His suggestion hung in the air. She wasn't quite sure what to do with it, but she could feel her face getting hot as she started to blush. "That would be . . . um . . . Dinner would be great. Sure."

She decided to tell him about Morocco. It was one of the places on his bucket list—and it had rather good wines and oils. "I'm going to take a few days and meet my sister in Tangier before arriving in Tbilisi. She's heading there on assignment." She had mentioned Finley's new job in passing before, so he knew about the career change.

"A little out of the way, isn't it?" he asked.

"Yeah, but I haven't seen her in a few months, and it'll be fun to have some girl time." A piece of her—the closet romantic piece of her—wanted to leave off the last part about "girl time" and see if he was crazy enough to say he would jump on a plane and meet her there. But that was only in movies.

"Look, have fun, and I'll catch you when you get into Tbilisi. Let me know your flight details, and I'll pick you up at the airport." He got up and started packing up some papers beside his computer.

"Got to go. Have another call. Talk to you later and see you when you get here. Just send me the info. Take care—"

The "take care" was partially cut off by the click of him leaving the call. She sat staring at the black screen, still picturing his smile filling the frame. She liked this boy. That she could no longer deny.

Finley's flight to Tangier was the best kind—uneventful. She made her connection through Barcelona, suffering through the layover by arranging to have breakfast with some former colleagues from the firm, and even managed to catch up on sleep. Her suitcase arrived with the flight, still closed and seemingly intact. And surprisingly, the rental agency had her car ready, and it was fueled and clean.

Driving through traffic made the short trip seem longer than she remembered, but the city appeared just as colorful and curious. A wonderfully quirky port city that connected the Atlantic and the Mediterranean, Tangier always maintained its underlying grittiness, despite its efforts at gentrification.

The flair of its squared and whitewashed structures, its unending blue sky and surrounding waters, its quaint winding streets and its passageways filled with overhanging bougainvillea were no match for the cars, motor bikes, donkey carts, and the occasional camel that kept it grounded—and gritty. It was this grit that made it a bohemian haunt decades ago, attracting writers and artists such as William Burroughs and Matisse as well as a raft of other unknown eccentrics. Proximity to the cannabis fields in the nearby Rif Mountains didn't hurt either.

Finley was reminded of the story that Mama had told her about Malcolm Forbes, of *Forbes* magazine fame, holding his seventieth birthday party at his Military Miniature Museum in the Palais Mendoub, overlooking the harbor. Apparently, he had flown his guests, including Elizabeth Taylor, over on the Concorde and opened the party to any American in Tangiers that day. *Nice*, Finley thought. *Mooney, with her golden touch, could probably have gotten me on that guest list. But I wouldn't have had anything to wear!*

Finley thought through her plans for the next couple of the days before Whitt would arrive. She had the remainder of the afternoon to unpack and get familiar with the hotel, a new one recommended by Dan. Then tomorrow, before picking up Whitt, she would walk around the harbor and get acclimated, see what the latest changes were in this unique city. She had considered taking the ferry from the airport but decided she would get a better class of car at the airport car rental than from one of the rental agents in town.

Her unfamiliarity with the Medina neighborhood where the hotel was located didn't cause any problem, and before she realized it, she was coming up on the sign for Hotel Sultan, only a stone's throw from the Rue du Kasbah. She wondered whether she could see the sea from the hotel. *Maybe if they have a roof bar,* she mused. When she pulled into the tiny driveway in front of the hotel and stepped out into the evening air, she could hear the gulls and smell the briny water. *Can't be that far if I can smell it from here.*

The doorman came out dressed in a traditional *djellaba,* white with tan embroidery running around the collar and front yoke, a low fez in deep red perched on his head. Welcoming her first in Arabic, he then realized that she was probably a foreigner and switched to French and then Spanish. Her Arabic was rudimentary, but she managed a *Marhaba,* much to the gentleman's surprise. He smiled.

He took her suitcase, the golden tassel of his fez swishing back and forth, and then headed toward the door, standing aside to let her enter. The air in the darkened atrium was cool, aided by a breeze that had managed to find its way into the inner courtyard onto which the large wooden entry doors opened.

The hotel was a riad that had been converted to a guesthouse and was a beautiful example of the elaborate architecture of the region. Finley stepped from the shadows of the lobby into the bright center courtyard and looked up at the beautifully carved balustrade that surrounded the open atrium of each floor. All the rooms appeared to face into the center courtyard, which had an intricately tiled floor in cream and black. Trickling fountains were interspersed between potted lemon trees and low sofas with colorful cushions and rolls.

"Welcome to Hotel Sultan!" Finley turned to see an angular man of sixty years or so, with piercing black eyes and an uneasy smile. His features suggested that he might be Moroccan, but the slight German accent made him hard to place. In contrast to the doorman's traditional attire, the man was dressed in a well-tailored dark gray linen suit offset by a crisp pale gray shirt.

"Hope you had a pleasant journey. Are you coming from the United States?" he asked, fixing his gaze on Finley. He seemed to do this more in curiosity than challenge, but with eyes that disconcerting, it was hard to say. Before she could answer, he had escorted her to one of the divans and signaled for one of the waiters standing along the wall to offer her a cool towel and the complementary drink. A refreshing spritzer with orange and mandarin juices and a touch of fresh mint. It was a wonderful balance between sweet and tart and rejuvenating after her long journey.

Once she was settled, he continued, "I am Johannes Sayeed— owner, concierge, and jack of all trades. I am generally somewhere around. This is a small guesthouse, and we want you to feel at home. So, anything you need, just ask."

"Thank you," Finley replied, lowering her eyes to break the laser stare that Sayeed still had fixed on her. "I'm looking forward to our stay." She continued in explanation, "My sister will be joining me tomorrow." She paused and looked up to see him continuing to look at her intently.

"Are you busy this time of year?" she queried, talking to ease the awkwardness of the situation. She passed the registration forms back to him, along with a certified copy of her passport.

"We will need to hold your passport," Sayeed said, waiting for her to pass the document to him.

"I understand the need for you to have a copy of my passport to register with the police, but as I'm sure you will appreciate, I don't give up my passport under any circumstance. I have given you a certified copy of my passport and have prepaid our room. I know that you may want to have an imprint of my credit card for incidentals, but with that, you should have what you need."

She smiled and rose from the divan, waiting. Sayeed opened his mouth to protest but decided better of it and moved across the lobby to deposit the registration form and documents behind the desk and retrieve the room key.

Without breaking his stare, he passed her the key, indicated the room number on the folded envelope that he handed her, and told her that her bags would be sent up to her in a few minutes. He then smiled and pointed to the stairs on either side of the courtyard that led to the upstairs rooms.

"Your room is in the middle, so you can take either set of stairs. The restaurant is on the roof, as is the bar. The hours are noted in the letter inside the envelope, along with other information about the hotel." He gestured toward the skylight, and presumably the roof.

It was then that she noticed the enormous brass chandelier that adorned the courtyard ceiling. Elaborately designed, it followed the traditional Moroccan motif with arched panels, multiple tiers of lanterns, and delicately filigreed cutouts, easily filling the void above the large center courtyard floor. *Goodness, they must have had to reinforce the roof beams to get that thing to stay up there*, she thought.

Finley murmured another thank you and headed up the far set of stairs. She was on the third of four levels, which was actually the second floor according to the envelope. She thought that the rooms must be massive since she only saw four entry doors per floor. She hoped there was a tub as well as a shower and that it was big. She was looking forward to a long hot soak after all that travel.

As she had guessed, the suite was large indeed and very well-appointed. Someone with exquisite taste, or an incredibly good designer, had decorated these rooms. The focus of the room was a massive, curtained bed with a sumptuous bronze satin bedspread.

23

At the foot of the bed was a tufted bench covered in a lushly colored tapestry weave.

Across the room was a small sitting area with sofa and chairs, a small ornate desk of inlaid wood, and a TV. Through the door on the facing wall was an opulently tiled bathroom in rich blues, ochres, and greens. With a shower and a separate soak tub. *There is a God.*

A light knock on the door signaled her bags. She opened the door to greet a young man who carried her bag in, and then turned to bring in a tray of fruit and mint tea. As he explained the custom of mint tea and welcomed her to the Sultan, she took in the heady scent of the mint and the soothing tenor of the room. *Just what I needed. Peace and quiet. Time to think and write.*

"The remote for the air conditioner is here beside the one for the television," he pointed to the devices on the desk. "But the breeze from the sea this time of year is usually enough." He moved to the French doors that led to a small balcony and opened both the curtains and the doors. "See. Lovely, isn't it?"

Finley had to agree. "Yes, the breeze is quite nice," she said, taking in the cool air. "Are you very busy? It seems so quiet."

"We are quite busy now, surprisingly. We have a crew from a movie that is shooting here, but they are now in the bar." He beamed, clearly proud that the hotel had been graced with movie people under its roof.

"What's the name of the movie?" Finley asked, trying to remember if she had heard about a movie being shot in Tangier. It somewhat perturbed her that neither Dan nor the staff writer at *Tales* had mentioned it in the briefing materials. "What's it about? Are there any famous actors in it?"

She peppered him with questions, and he was eager to answer. He seemed to enjoy the interview even though, when she finished, she realized it had been more of an inquisition. What's the name of the movie? *Road to Tangier.* What's it about? Morocco's famous rally race from Agadir to Tangier. Is it a documentary? No, an action movie with road races and crashes and fights and love scenes. Any famous actors in it?

He named some actors from France, the UK, and the Netherlands that Finley had never heard of. Who is staying here? Mainly the technical crew. The big names were over at the Villa de France, one of the most beautifully maintained and exclusive hotels in the old diplomatic quarter. Clearly, the highfliers were willing to pay for their luxury.

She tipped him for delivering the bag—and the information—and pulled her suitcase open to start unpacking. She needed to check her messages to see if she had any meetings tomorrow morning. She was hoping to be able to figure out her angle for the article soon so she could get the grunt work out of the way early in Whitt's visit. Then Whitt could help her get the voice and tone right, and they could wander the city looking for interesting shots to go with the copy.

They could traipse all over Tangier over the next two to three days and maybe make a trip south after that. She was looking for shots of the extraordinary in the ordinary since there was almost always a compelling backstory to be shared in what looked commonplace. A trip to the Marrakesh or the High Atlas might offer some exotic landscape. Or maybe Casablanca.

THE BATH, COMPLETE WITH ARGAN oil-infused bath salts, had both relaxed and refreshed her. And the glass of wine she brought into the bathroom with her hadn't hurt either. Now she was ready for another glass of white—or maybe something a little stronger. Pulling on a pair of black linen pants and a black tunic that she topped with one of her favorite necklaces, a heavy, silver-linked lariat from Indonesia, she grabbed her bag and headed up the stairs, following the sound of voices until she reached the rooftop.

The bar area was a spacious terrace that looked out onto the harbor. She hadn't thought that they were this close to the water, the salt smell aside. The open terrace that served as both a restaurant and a bar was decorated nicely, with stylish dark wood, metal tables, and sumptuously upholstered chairs with deep cushions.

She was glad that the spacious bar matched the sophistication of the riad interior and wasn't a Tiki bar, Moroccan style. She wondered how much the hotel brought in. Clearly not enough to cover these kinds of furnishings, especially given the modest amount she was paying per night. Sayeed must have come from money or made a lot of money elsewhere. Maybe this was just a hobby. He dressed well enough to be a rich playboy who had retired in the sun. *There you go again making up stories. Can't wait until Whitt is here to play the Game with me.*

"Hello, you must have just checked in?" came a quiet Liverpudlian-sounding voice from behind Finley. A plump, young woman with twig-colored hair and an open countenance, wearing an odd lavender sack dress, faced Finley as she turned around.

"I always surprise people with my forwardness, but if you sit and wait for people to introduce themselves, you might miss an opportunity. I'm Stacey Rimmer. I'm with that crew over there." She pointed to a group of about six or seven people sitting around a couple of the tables that had been pushed together. It was clear that they all knew each other. "Please join us. We're a friendly bunch."

Stacey scurried over to the table, standing aside to introduce Finley as if she were the Queen of Sheba. "This is . . . I don't even know your name. In any event, she just registered today."

Stacey paused, with a look of uncertainty, trying to get some indication from the group that Finley was welcomed. Conversation had quieted as the people at the table collectively turned to look at Finley.

A darkly handsome middle-aged man broke the tension. "Welcome to our motley crew!" He stood to pull out the only remaining chair for Finley. "Just arrived? Where are you coming from?"

Finley surveyed the group briefly, nodded, and introduced herself. "Yes, I got in this afternoon from New York," she said, taking her seat. She realized that she had made the Manhattanite mistake of assuming that when you said New York, you meant Manhattan. If not, you would give the name of the town, like Brooklyn or Tarrytown or Albany.

She decided to shift the conversation to them. "Are all of you involved in the movie all the staff was talking about?" She leaned in a bit to engage those at the far end of the table. "Oh, I'm Finley, by the way."

The man with gray at the temples, who had held out her chair, introduced himself as Peter, in an accent that suggested that he might be upper-crust British, and then proceeded to make introductions around the table. The striking woman with bluntly cut, almost-black hair and watery blue eyes to his left was Anna Broadbent, a set designer who mentioned that she had worked in both New York and Los Angeles. She aptly understood where "New York" was.

Beside her sat a rather nondescript man dressed in a nondescript button-down shirt and rumpled khakis, who did sound for movies. The angle at which Finley was sitting made it hard for her to hear his name, and she decided not to ask him to repeat it.

Stacey had brought a chair over from one of the other tables and positioned herself at the far end of the table. She excitedly pointed to the woman next to her. "Taryn, she does amazing makeup effects," she said, elongating the word "amazing" to emphasize the point.

Peter proceeded with his introductions, adding that they were indeed the production crew for the new movie being shot in Tangier and the Sahara. He took time to give each person's job title, as if Finley had any idea what the positions meant or what each of them did.

Finley simply smiled knowingly and let him drone on while she took in each person's expression and apparent state of mind. At some point, conversation had started up again and the participants stopped only to nod when their introduction was made.

Anna broke in, interrupting Peter mid-sentence. He scowled but let her continue. She wore a smirk that revealed much about her estimation of the man across from her. "This is Allan Berger. He's supposed to be at the Villa de France with the top dogs but deigns to associate with the hoi-poloi here."

The object of her scorn was an Indiana Jones lookalike with longish salt-and-pepper hair and an ageless, craggy face that might have been handsome if he had a more welcoming disposition. Allan grunted a greeting and took a swig of his beer, eyes downcast and his head slumped almost to his chest. Finley imagined him having long existential conversations with his therapist or bartender.

"I'm Ross." The man sitting next to Finley gave her a warm, boy-next-door grin." Don't mind them. Anna likes to get under his skin. Since Peter is including our CV in his intro, I am tech supervisor. Do some work on effects as well." Before he could finish, Peter interjected, "Somewhat nerdy, but harmless."

He smiled like he knew a secret, but Finley only cared about getting a drink. She summoned the waiter and indicated to the group that the next round was on her, as she remembered was British custom, before placing her order and sending him off to get the rest of the orders. Most seemed to be well in to their second or third drink.

Ross and Peter explained that most of the crew was from the UK. The French contingent, Julien and Thomas, were out doing preproduction scouting and may join later. They chatted on excitedly about a big-name producer and director, Etienne something or other, working on the movie that Finley didn't recognize. The film, as the porter had stated, was an action film with a lot of fast races and crashes. It was not a genre she liked. It was apparently based on a local rally race that was held every year out in the middle of the Sahara.

"Have you worked on many other pictures?" Finley asked, curious about the vagabond life that crews like this lived. Maybe that was the angle for the article. She was still tossing around options in her mind. List-worthy, she would say.

Ross volunteered first. "I've been doing this almost ten years. Started doing special effects when I was in college. Dropped out and kept on doing it in Hollywood and about. Tech is the future," he said with almost childlike enthusiasm.

"I've been in the industry for over thirty years. A few years acting. Wanted to be the next De Niro. When that didn't pan out, I started in production. Discovered I was rather good with the lights, so there I stayed," Peter shared.

"So, what do you do? God, this sounds like a stale London drinks party." He sighed.

"I'm a travel writer. Nothing as exciting as producing movies." Finley tried to steer the conversation back to the movie so she could see if there was enough for an article.

She angled to keep Peter talking about the movie, but he much preferred to talk about himself and the leading ladies he had met—Susan Sarandon, Julia Roberts, Demi Moore. He may have been behind the scenes in these stories, but he prowled like a real Casanova. . . At least, that's what he wanted Finley to think.

Around her, she caught snatches of other conversations. Anna was talking about some place to get trendy fabrics cheap with Taryn, her pink highlights dancing in the slight breeze. Ross had pulled Allan out of his funk and the two were debating something geopolitical. Nondescript man had nodded off, and Stacey sat darting her eyes from one conversation to the next, never quite daring to jump in. *Nothing more to learn here.*

Finley stifled a yawn and apologized, "Sorry, I think the jet lag is getting the best of me," she said as she rose from her seat.

"What, no supper? I was hoping to continue our conversation," Peter leered, and also rose, offering her support with a hand on her elbow. *Not a very original move. Next thing you know this lothario is going to offer to escort me to my room. Fat chance.*

"I ate on the plane, and I think I have an apple in my bag. That'll hold me over," Finley added.

She had mouthed her good nights to the rest of the group and started off toward the stairs before Peter could say anything more. He stood there, his eyes following her through the arch and down the stairs. Then he quietly sat down, pondering.

FINLEY LOOKED AT HER SISTER as she approached the arrivals waiting area, pulling a large leather duffel. It was good to see her; it had been too long. She looked well, if only a bit tired. Her long legs covered the distance between them quickly.

Whitt was a good two inches taller than Finley's five foot-eight-inch frame, and where Finley had curves, Whitt was swimmer straight. Their granny, as only a granny could do, had said that none of Finley's features, okay in themselves, fit together: it was like Meryl Streep's aquiline nose was on a face with Helen Bonham-Carter's lusciously full lips, to which were added sweet doe-shaped eyes—in alligator green.

Whitt's eyes were a bright crystalline green, like Daddy's. Finley's played tricks on you, mossy green with flecks of caramel brown that made them look like algae in swamp water. The Brits might say Finley was "handsome"—a backhanded compliment, if ever there was one. Whitt, on the other hand, was classically pretty with Mama's high cheekbones on a perfectly oval face, sketched with delicate features. Whitt somehow managed to look "petite" despite her height. *Go figure.*

"Hey, kid!" Finley called over the airport noise, waving her arms to attract Whitt's attention.

"Hey, yourself! Finally! I thought I'd never get here. I didn't know I had a stop in Casablanca. Would love to see what that place looks like—Humphrey Bogart and all."

"Depends on how long you plan to stay. We can talk about a plan of action over dinner. Unless you just want to go to bed," Finley said. It was almost seven thirty in the evening, and the trip to the hotel could take another fifteen minutes—or it could take forty-five, depending on traffic. Whitt had already been traveling a good twenty-plus hours. She was likely to be dog-tired.

"Dinner's fine with me. I slept on both legs of the flight, so I'm rested." She threw her bag into the trunk and came around to the passenger seat. "That doesn't mean I won't sleep well tonight, though."

The drive to the hotel was punctuated by donkey cart blockades and trucks overloaded with barely strapped-on wares. There was an expressway between the airport and the city, but Finley had elected to take the back way because she had used it before to avoid city traffic and because it would give Whitt a different view of Tangier—a city Finley remembered from years ago, when she and Max used to use this route to escape the city on weekends and head out into the countryside. *Max. I wonder where he is now.*

Back at the hotel, Finley stopped by the desk to let Sayeed know that Whitt had arrived and to ask for more towels. Raspy, angry words in Arabic spilled out from behind a carved screen, escalating to a controlled shout before dropping to a punctuated whisper. *Somebody's pissed.*

Whitt cleared her throat to get the attention of whoever was back there. She was greeted with silence. Strange. They hadn't heard anyone walk away, and no one had passed them, but whoever was back there wasn't there anymore. Or they were being really quiet.

"Good evening. I hope you had a pleasant flight." A voice echoed across the lobby. Finley and Whitt both turned in surprise to see Sayeed walking across the tiled expanse toward Whitt, arms open in welcome. *Where did he come from? And why is he being a lot nicer to Whitt than he was to me? Must be her Southern charm.*

Sayeed took the duffel from Whitt's hand and passed it to a porter that had materialized out of thin air. Moving behind the desk, he passed her a registration form and asked for her passport with a smile.

"Will you ladies be joining us for dinner, or are you going to go out? We have a list of restaurants nearby if you want to try the local cuisine," he continued, looking at Whitt warmly. Frustration flashed briefly across his face when she passed him the completed form and a certified copy of her passport.

"As I mentioned to your sister, we normally ask for the actual passport, which we hold here. But I understand that you are reluctant to relinquish your passports, so we will make do with this." He held the passport copy up like it had been soiled.

"I think we'll eat in tonight. My sister is a bit tired. If we could get some extra towels, though, please," Finley asked.

"Certainly," he replied, passing her the restaurant list anyway. "In case you change your mind."

Finley led the way to the room, pointing out features of the hotel as they moved through the courtyard and up the stairs. On each landing between the floors, there were traditional carved benches, chests, and armoires with brass studding. Whitt stopped to look at the intricacy of the woodworking and to admire some glass beads on a console table in the hall.

"The décor is exquisitely done," she observed. "Really lovely."

"Wait 'til you see the room," Finley interjected. "It is something else. And for this price!" she added as they stopped for her to pull out the key and open the room. Finley threw back the door and stood aside. Whitt stepped into the threshold, taking in the size and opulence of the room.

"This is *exceptionally* nice . . . Traditional design with a modern, minimalist flair. And the bathroom . . ." She headed across the room to the door she thought might be the bathroom and pushed back the door. There she stood until the porter's knock interrupted her.

"Okay, so who are the folks staying here? Are they sheiks and princes, and we just found a fluke in Expedia's pricing system?" Whitt asked, standing in the middle of the room after her bags had been delivered and the porter tipped.

"No, most of the rooms are taken by the crew of some movie they are shooting here in Tangier. I met some of them last night when I arrived. The heavy hitters, though, are apparently over at some chichi hotel somewhere else," Finley recounted. "The folks I met here are an odd bunch. Perfect for that murder game we used to play when we'd travel with Mama and Daddy. Remember, when we used to create backstories for the guests in the hotel and figure out who was the killer?"

Whitt laughed, flopping herself on the bed. "Yeah, it was like playing Clue in real life. Remember St. Lucia? That was the best. We had couples who were embezzling money and others who were bed hopping. And the story kept growing over the week we were there. It got to be embarrassing looking at those people over break-fast when we had created all sorts of sordid details about their lives at dinner the night before!" They started recalling some of the names they had made up for the various guests, then broke out laughing so hard that they were in tears.

"It is so good to see you," Whitt finally said to interrupt the hysterics. She got up and walked to the sitting area where Finley had claimed a chair. "Come give me a hug." She stood in front of Finley and waited while her sister wrapped her arms around her.

"Good to see you too, kid. I missed you," Finley whispered. "Now go take your shower so we can get some dinner before they close the kitchen. And don't use all the hot water."

Finley had expected most of the movie crew to be gone from the bar area and to have moved onto dinner, but many of the people she

34

had met the day before and a few new faces were crowded around tables that were laden with platters of mezze-type dishes.

There were bowls of spiced olives, marinated goat cheese, and mix of traditional dips—*zaalouk*, the Moroccan version of eggplant caviar; tapenade; a spicy, carrot-based hummus; and *chouchouka*, a tomato dish. Two of Whitt's favorites also adorned the table—*bastilla*, spiced meat stuffed in flaky pastry, and *briouat*, a Moroccan spring roll. Baskets of different breads and an array of domed condiment vessels, including one with Finley's preference, harissa, complemented the feast. Finley started to salivate.

As they neared the table, Peter got to his feet and walked over to meet them. "And who is this lovely lady?" he asked, fixing his mocha eyes on Whitt's clear green ones.

"This is my sister, Whitt. She just got in, so we came looking for libation and sustenance," Finley responded, giving Whitt a sideways glance and Peter a half smile. *He's going into full Casanova mode, but Whitt knows the drill.*

"Sustenance we can provide, and libation will soon come. Please join us. We decided on a tapas-style dinner tonight, mainly because we were too lazy to move to a proper table. There is far too much food," Peter remarked, already walking toward two people Finley hadn't met yet at another brightly tiled table and some cushioned chairs. "What are you drinking?"

While Peter ordered their glasses of local wine, Finley took Whitt over to the table and started introductions, noting the names and occupations of those that she had met. She didn't see Ross or Allan. She paused when she got to the members who were new to her. *The French contingent, I guess.*

"This is Julien," Stacey volunteered, nodding to a slightly rotund man with a Gallic profile. "He and Gavin do sound and sometimes effects." The man smiled slightly and went back to his drink. Whitt liked the sound of his name as she silently rolled it around in her mouth, but the name didn't match the man who struck her as "brown"—brown hair, brown eyes, brown clothes. She couldn't even begin to guess his age.

His compatriot, however, was another matter. He was disarmingly handsome—chiseled, angular features with deep-set blue eyes, a perfectly proportioned nose, and a sensuously curled bottom lip. Whitt was sure this was one of the actors in the movie, not a member of the crew.

"Hi, I'm Whitt," extending her hand first to Anna, and then to the handsome man beside her as she sat down in the chair Finley pointed to. Anna, the pretty set designer, if Whitt remembered correctly, leaned back in her chair, looking amused at the interaction. Whitt suspected that there was something between the two of them and that Anna had a lot of experience with women trying to hijack her guy. She decided to try to keep her facial expression—and her conversation—as neutral as possible, even though he was attractive.

"Thomas," he responded in heavily accented English so that the ending "s" was lifted with a breathy "ah." "I oversee preproduction." Whitt plied him with polite questions about what preproduction was, what he did precisely, what other movies he had worked on, and the like. He was easy to talk to but a little shy, and between the wine Peter had handed her and jetlag, she was feeling pretty mellow. Out of the corner of her eye, she watched Anna watching her talk to him. *She is a real viper, and the poor guy is clueless.*

Finley had sat down at the other end of the table and was talking to Stacey and Julien, even as she took in the dynamic being created by Whitt, Thomas, and Anna. *This is interesting. Does she even know she is poking the bear? Hope she knows what she is doing.* She knew that Whitt was probably playing the Murder Game, trying to get enough information to develop the backstory for Thomas and Anna in some larger, more complicated plot of murder and intrigue.

Finley wondered whether Whitt was going to make them Bonnie and Clyde–type drug lords or have them married and getting ready to file for divorce. Finley doubted that her conversation with any of the players at her end of the table would yield much fodder for their murder game, but she tried to keep the conversation going to learn as much as she could about Julien, who seemed the more interesting of the candidates for conversation near her.

The wind was coming off the water more strongly than it had the night before. She was glad she had brought a shawl with her and had encouraged Whitt to do the same. It was surprising how hot it could be during the day and how chilly the temperature became in the evening. Julien was asking Stacey about the availability in Tangier of something related to the movie, and she was prattling on about all the places she had found both in Tangier and further south to procure whatever the item was.

"Are you going to be filming in locations besides Tangier?" Finley asked, still thinking about the movie or the race or the Sahara as a premise for her article for *Traveler's Tales*. Her gut told her that if she probed long and hard enough, she might indeed un-earth a novel angle for her travel assignment.

It was rather fortuitous that she happened on the crew. This would be the type of story that other writers weren't likely to get. And if she could get interviews with the director and some of the more famous actors, she might have something that captured Dan and his other editors' attention.

"We are supposed to film here, in Agadir, and then along an off-road route Allan mapped out in the Sahara," Stacey explained. "We'll be camping in tents and RVs in godforsaken places out in the middle of nowhere. Frankly, I am a little scared. It could be dangerous."

Gavin rolled his eyes and got to his feet. "I'll be back. I'm going to get a jacket," he said. "It's getting chilly out here." He headed to the far set of stairs that led to his room. Finley turned back to her conversation with Stacey and Julien.

Stacey continued to fret. "Allan, the location manager, says that we'll all be safe. That there aren't any bandits or anyone who might try to rob us or take the equipment. Just to be sure, I've hired a security company to guard the equipment—and us—when we're out there in the middle of the Sahara."

She confided in a conspiratorial tone. "But what about the snakes and scorpions? Who's going to take care of those? And those are probably more deadly," she sputtered, her face getting red, and her eyes welling with tears. Taryn and Julien tried to calm her with feeble assurances.

In her mind, Finley was playing the Game, taking Stacey's worst-case scenario for disaster in the desert and amplifying it tenfold. She placed the group that was around the table in harrowing situations with dastardly villains and salacious schemes. She could have Stacey alone in the desert, everyone else having been lost or kidnapped one by one, like in Agatha Christie's *10 Little Indians*.

Or maybe one of the actors could end up dead, and one of the crew members could be arrested. *The options are endless. And silly.* Still, Finley wondered if Whitt was doing the same thing with her conversation partners at the other end of the table. She chortled to herself and came back to reality.

Stacey needed reassurance, not ridicule. Finley reached across and put her hand on Stacey's arm. The poor kid was shaking. She really was scared. "You can rest assured that all precautions to keep you safe . . ."

Finley only got midsentence before a high-pitched scream turned into a long, anguished moan. Others at the table turned, trying to figure out what the nerve-wracking sound was and where it came from. Another series of screams and moans jolted Peter and Finley to their feet and made them head for the stairs. Whitt wasn't far behind, the others moving more quickly now to uncover the source of the unnerving noise.

Peter's age didn't slow him down, as he raced down the stairs and rounded the corner, sprinting once he got to the hall on the second floor to reach Gavin first. He dropped to his knees near Gavin's prone figure. Gavin was crouched, almost in a fetal position, near the door of one of the rooms.

When Whitt and Finley reached him, they thought he was ill by the way he was rocking and moaning—perhaps a ruptured appendix. He clutched the jacket in his hand, thrusting his arm out from time to time. No words came, just a deep guttural sound that conveyed his anguish. Finally, he formed words. "Ross. Ross is dead," he said, thrusting his arm out again, but this time looking in the direction of the open atrium.

Finley stood, walked to the atrium railing, and looked down. Anna and Julien joined her at the rail. All three gasped as they took in the sight below. There, hanging like a rag doll from the massive brass chandelier, was Ross Malcolm. His neck was contorted in an unnatural position and a trickle of blood stained his cheek. His face revealed no fear or concern. He was beyond that. He was definitely dead.

WHITT STOOD IN THE LOBBY waiting for the Tangier Police to come. She had left Finley upstairs with Gavin and the rest of the crew while she ran down the back stairs to alert Sayeed. He had been in his office near the front desk and wondered what the commotion was about.

"What is all the noise upstairs? Is someone ill? Shall I call a doctor?" he demanded pointedly, upset that the calm of the atrium's inner sanctum had been disturbed.

When Sayeed saw Whitt running up to the desk, he assumed she had had an argument with Finley or a beau and had struck out, provoking this disorder. He had taken her arm to lead her to one of the divans in the courtyard. It was only after she explained the cause of the ruckus that he then saw the body suspended over the intricately grouted tile inlays.

He swallowed hard, a band of perspiration wetting his forehead. He looked at Whitt incredulously, "What happened? What is going on? Did you kill him?"

"No! Of course not!" Whitt recoiled in surprise and disgust. She then gave a brief account of what she knew. "Just call the police!" she spit back angrily.

In the meantime, waiters and porters had come from invisible portals that lined the lower level to see what the commotion was and stood transfixed by the horrific sight above them. They, like the group that was gathered on the second floor, couldn't figure out how the body had gotten there. Had it been a fall? But from where?

It couldn't have been placed there; its position on the chandelier was between floors. Suspending it there would require tethers and counter-balances that no one had seen anywhere near the atrium. In all the pandemonium, "the body" had become separated from "Ross Malcolm," the man and the victim.

It had taken only minutes for the police to arrive. A portly chief inspector from the Tangier Police had drawn up, followed by several police cars, sirens blaring. Sayeed must have told them it was serious when he called it in.

"*Bonsoir!* I am Chief Inspector Murad, Tangier Police. I am looking for Johannes Sayeed. We had a call about the death of a guest." He stated this all in Arabic before repeating himself in French-accented English.

Somewhere in his mid-forties, the chief inspector had a round face and unusually kind black eyes that turned down at the corners. It gave him a sad puppy look, a bit incongruous for the head of the local police. He had probably stomached a lot of teasing from his colleagues for his looks, but he must have overcome it. He was a chief inspector.

Sayeed stepped forward, leaving Whitt sitting on the divan. "I am Johannes Sayeed. I am the owner of this hotel. We have had an accident, it appears. A guest has fallen."

"Were you there when it happened?" the chief inspector inquired, his eyes pulling up a bit to form a squint that was accentuated by his pursed lips.

Sayeed took a step back. "No, I was downstairs in my office," he replied. "She was upstairs." It sounded as if he was insinuating that Whitt had committed the crime.

Whitt rose from the divan and offered the inspector her hand. "I am Whitt Blake. I am a guest here along with my sister," Whitt stated. "If you step over here, you can see the problem." She moved toward the center atrium, looking up.

The chief inspector followed her to the center courtyard and tilted his head upward. "*Mon dieu!*" he whispered, crossing himself as he stared at the body suspended from the chandelier. His eyes scanned the upper floors that opened out into the atrium and settled on the group of people clustered on the third level. "Who are they? What are they doing?"

Sayeed stood with his mouth open, not knowing what to say. Whitt responded instead.

"They're guests here. Members of a movie crew. They knew the man who died. One of their other friends found him. He's on the floor near that door." She pointed to the wooden door where she suspected Gavin was still cowering on the floor.

"If you want, I can show you up," she suggested, heading toward the stairs.

The chief inspector stopped her, asking instead who the crowd of people were that now filled a significant portion of the center courtyard. Sayeed recovered enough to answer. "They are hotel staff. I will send them back to work."

"One moment. Before you send them off, ask them to leave their names, what positions they hold and how to get in touch with them before they leave. My men will take their information. They may have seen something or be involved somehow. We will want to question them. If this is an accident," he hesitated, again looking up, "then we can clear this up pretty quickly. If not, I need to know where to find them."

The chief inspector signaled to one of the police officers and conferred with him briefly when he approached. The officer went back over to the waiting policemen. They moved toward the staff congregated in the courtyard, pads and pencils poised and ready. Sayeed called in Arabic to the waiters, porters, and other staff that populated the lobby and courtyard, explaining the chief inspector's request. The staff dutifully lined up along the far wall and waited while the police took down their information. Slowly, they started slipping into the wall portals, heading back to their sundry duties.

"We can head up now," the chief inspector indicated, moving toward the stairs but still eying the courtyard, the hidden portals, and the balustrades that lined the levels above him. When he reached the first level above the courtyard, he stopped and looked down and then up, seeming to position in his mind the chandelier, the distance between the floors, and the courtyard below. He then followed Whitt up the stairs to the next level. Sayeed slipped in step behind him.

When he reached the landing for the third level, the chief inspector stopped again. Looking down this time. He held that stance for several minutes, his head not moving, saying nothing. Whitt wondered what he was staring at, what was going through his mind.

"Over here," someone in the group called, breaking the chief inspector's concentration. He walked quickly down the hall, stopping at an angle almost directly in front of the body. He again looked down, moving closer to the rail to look at the dead man and at the railing in front of the body. He called one of the officers that had followed him up the stairs and inclined his head over something on the railing.

"So," he turned to the group still hovering around Gavin. "I am Chief Inspector Louis Murad. What seems to have happened?" He listened as various members of the crew offered their opinions, talking over each other and interrupting each other in turn.

"Who found the body?" he raised his voice slightly, enough to break through the din.

Gavin, who had risen from his huddled position on the floor to one more upright and was leaning against one of the doors, half raised his hand. "I found him," he mumbled. "I came down for a jacket. It was breezy on the terrace. That's when I saw him. When I was heading back to the roof," he said.

"Why were you heading to the roof?" the inspector asked, his brow furrowed.

"I was rejoining my colleagues. We were on the roof having drinks." He shrank back into himself, threatening to assume the fetal position again.

Stacey, recognizing his fear, patted him on the arm. "It's all right. You're going to be fine," she murmured quietly. Gavin, almost like a child, immediately calmed down and looked at the chief inspector.

"I didn't kill him," Gavin repeated firmly. "I didn't."

The chief inspector crouched down closer to the disoriented man. "Why do you say he was killed? It could have been an accident," he suggested softly.

Gavin remained on the floor but pulled himself up a little straighter against the door. "Hard to get to the chandelier from here without some help. It's the only way," he whispered. "The only way."

The chief inspector had to agree, but he wasn't ready to say that openly yet. He stood and surveyed the group. "I will need your names. I am assuming all of you are staying here." He searched the faces before him for confirmation." Please do not leave the hotel before you give this officer here your name and position." He turned to leave and paused, addressing the group over his shoulder. "And do not leave Tangier."

7

SLEEP DID NOT COME EASY to either Finley or Whitt that evening. Finley tossed and turned, finally drifting off at about three o'clock. When she awoke, Whitt was sitting at the desk, writing something in a long, yellow legal pad.

"Funny that I'm the lawyer, and I never use those things." Finley pointed to the yellow pad Whitt was still scribbling on, as Finley pulled herself into a sitting position.

"Did you sleep at all?" Finley asked.

"A few hours, but not well. Things kept running through my mind. Things I can't figure out."

Finley got up, grabbed her shawl, and came over to lounge on the sofa. "What're you thinking?" she asked. This was far more serious than the Murder Game they used to create from their imaginations. This was real—very real.

Whitt shifted in her chair to face Finley, holding the pad in her lap. "Well, let's see. How did the body get up there? That's the biggest question for me. I mean, he looked like his neck had been broken, and it hadn't been broken in the fall. That suggests murder to me—" Whitt surmised.

"But who's strong enough to both break the man's neck and toss him—not just over the railing—but out far enough to hit the chandelier?" Finley interrupted. "Not anyone that we know from here, I don't think."

"So, then maybe someone from outside the hotel came in. Maybe it was a robbery gone bad, and the robber silenced him before he could scream." Whitt was getting into this now, her eyes alternating between wide amazement at her theories and increased concentration as she dismantled the theories in her mind.

"But how would someone get in?" Finley added. "What about the timing? When could someone have killed him? And then, when could they have tossed him over without someone seeing them?"

Finley sighed dejectedly. "We have more questions than answers. We need more facts."

They both knew that the police would be back again later that day to question them further. Last night's interview with each of the guests seemed very preliminary. Each person was taken into a side room off the center courtyard and asked to tell their version of what happened.

Finley and Whitt recounted to each other what had transpired during each of their sessions. The questions in each instance had been uninspired, which suggested that the inspector had just been gathering information and would ask more probing questions today. Either that, or he was just ineffectual.

"Was there another inspector sitting in the back of the room when you were talked to?" Whitt had asked Finley last night. "Kind of tall, short dark hair. Think it had some grey. Rugged looking face, although it was hard to tell with the shadows."

"Yeah. Who was he?" Finley had tried to paint scenarios in her mind that explained his presence and had come up with little. "Maybe someone from another division in the police department?"

"Haven't a clue. This whole thing is confusing," Whitt had replied before they both attempted to sleep.

As the morning wore on, no more insight came to them. "Let's grab breakfast and see what information surfaces," Whitt suggested.

Finley nodded before heading off to the bathroom. "I get to go first this time," she mandated. Whitt tried to object, arguing that because she took longer, she should go in first, but Finley blocked the bathroom door.

"Not this morning, kiddo," Finley said, grabbing her clothes quickly from the closet. "I hate cold showers!"

Showered and dressed, the sisters headed up the stairs to the roof. A section of their hall on the second floor had been cordoned off with yellow police tape. Whitt wondered out loud whether there was a universal accord among policemen that only yellow tape would be used for crime scenes. Finley just shook her head. *Only you would think of something like that—and then go research it to find out!*

When they reached the restaurant, they saw a couple of people from the movie crew seated at a table along the wall in a bit of shade provided by the bougainvillea. The two women nodded, and then headed toward a smaller table overlooking the harbor.

"Come join us," Taryn called out. "It will get too hot over there. There's room." She stood to pull one of the tables out of the sun and into the additional shade of an umbrella.

Finley and Whitt moved to chairs on opposite corners of the table. Both knew that the unspoken goal was to find out as much as they could about Ross and who might have wanted to kill him. Accident theories had been dismissed in their minds, so conversation needed to be steered toward a murder hypothesis—which was sorely missing any factual basis besides the sense that an accident was impossible. Gavin had said as much. "It's the only way. The only way."

"Did you sleep well?" Stacey asked, circles etching dark shadows on her face. She was trying to smile, but tears kept welling up in her eyes and pooling over to slide down her cheeks.

"So sorry. I can't seem to control them anymore," she sputtered, her hand moving quickly to wipe away any evidence of her sadness. "He was such a brilliant man. So creative."

"Did you know him well?" Finley asked quietly. Perhaps they had worked together on previous movies or knew each other from London. *It is unlikely that they were lovers. But you never know. Stranger things . . .*

"No, not well, although we have worked together before. And then we've been working on this film for a few months. In the early stages of any film, tech and logistics work fairly closely." Stacey's voice tapered off and she sat staring.

"How did your conversations with the inspector go? You two were in there longer than the rest of us." Taryn asked, her eyes slowly moving back and forth across the table to the sisters.

Whitt decided to take the lead in this little exchange. "There wasn't much to it. A few basic questions about when we got here and how well we knew the deceased. How well we knew all of you, in fact." She turned slowly to lock eyes with the young Taryn.

Taryn paled and then the color returned to her face. "I didn't mean anything by it." She muttered under her breath. "They'll have another go at us today. I haven't the slightest idea what they're talking to us for. We have alibis! We were out here having drinks."

"What time did you guys come up for cocktails last night?" Finley asked, trying to reduce the intensity of the exchange between Whitt and Taryn. She looked at Allan, who had joined them and was digging into a plate of eggs and tomatoes.

"I wasn't up here yesterday. I got in late, so I missed all the brouhaha! Thomas said it was fairly gory." He looked up from his breakfast with the last few words. *There is something I don't like about this man. He definitely needs more therapy.* Finley opined.

As the waiters brought the rest of their breakfasts—various types of baked eggs, rolls, flatbreads, cheeses, and more coffee, Finley looked at the assembled group. What did she know about any of these people besides what they told her? What tensions among the group had there been that either she hadn't seen or that they had been able to mask? *There is a lot of backstabbing that can erupt when people are in close quarters over a few months.*

"I need coffee and lots of it before I can even begin to think of breakfast," Peter exclaimed, striding onto the terrace and grabbing a nearby chair. "I don't know about you, but I have had no sleep."

Despite his proclamation of no sleep, he looked none the worse for wear. His dark hair was glistening in the mid-morning sun, every hair perfectly in place. His clothes were immaculately pressed and coordinated. He didn't need a stylist. He was one.

"Have the police been back here yet? Do you think we should call the embassy in case one of us gets hauled away as a suspect? The thought is dreadful," Peter asked, his eyes searching the group for answers. "This is going to put production back awhile. If it is an accident, it won't cause a problem, but if it is more, this could be disastrous."

"I sent Thomas over to Villa de France to talk to Etienne about it." Allan failed to suppress his bemused surprise at Peter's agitation over the production schedule. "I don't know what they are going to say about it."

Finley observed Allan carefully. *And he looks like he doesn't really care. Strange.*

Whitt hadn't thought about needing to call the American Embassy, but with Peter's comment, she considered it a good idea. Just in case. Both she and Finley had registered with the embassy online before coming into the country, but this sort of incident warranted more direct contact with a consular officer. Being on the wrong side of the law in a foreign country would not be fun. She wondered whether the jails provided food here or whether it had to be brought in by family like in the Philippines and other places, she assumed. *I guess if you don't have family, you starve. Cheaper than hanging you.*

"Has anyone seen Gavin?" Although Peter made the question general, he focused his attention on Stacey.

She looked up from her flatbread and responded with a slight edge to her voice, "I believe he is still resting."

"Curious," was all Whitt heard from Peter before he hungrily attacked the food on his plate.

They were still eating when Julien slunk to the table, grabbed a cup for coffee, and angrily waved the waiters away. He sat looking pale—an unhealthy-looking beige against the brown of his hair and clothes, which appeared to be what he had slept in, given their rumpled state.

"How can you eat anything?" he grumbled. "A man died, and you act like nothing has happened."

At his outburst, Stacey broke into wails, upset her chair, and ran out of the room and down the stairs. Whitt and others at the table stared after her for a few seconds before Finley rose and followed her out. Julien pushed himself back and moved silently to another table, away from the rest of the crew. Taryn shot a quizzical glance at Allan before Peter started up again.

"What the hell was that all about? Such theatrics!" Peter exclaimed, wiping his mouth, and reaching for more coffee. "How did everyone's interview go last evening? I don't know how they can suspect any of us. We were all together up here."

Those around the table were quiet, staring at their plates or into space. Peter, seemingly unaware of the mood in the room, continued, "Mine was exceedingly dull. Someone died, and the inspector sat asking me how we all met and other inane questions. I did have to tell him about the terrible row that Julien and Ross were having yesterday morning." He shot a look at Julien, who was sitting apart but still within hearing distance.

"Sorry, old man," he said.

Julien appeared to be ready to jump from his chair and sock Peter, so great was his seething anger. Instead, he sunk deeper into his seat and glowered at the older man. He took a sip of coffee, and then got up abruptly and left. Again, the terrace was silent.

Finley found Stacey on the landing between the third and fourth levels. She had curled herself into a ball, feet tucked under her and head on the cushions of an ornately carved wooden sofa. Her eyes were open and red-rimmed from crying, but the sobbing had stopped. Finley moved to occupy the other half of the sofa.

"You okay?" Finley asked softly. "It's been a harrowing couple of days, eh?"

Stacey looked up and smiled slightly. She knew Finley was only trying to make her feel better. She wanted to talk, and she needed to talk, but somehow the words echoed inside her head, refusing to come out.

"This sucks!" she finally blurted, half laughing, then trying to stop herself before the laughter gave way to hysteria. "Ross was a real sod sometimes, but he didn't deserve to die that way." she continued. "Julien and Ross were mates. An odd couple."

Her expression changed and grew serious. "Oh, not romantically! Just good friends. They were so different, but they liked a lot of the same things. They were always debating something. Seemed like it was arguing for the sake of arguing at times. But it was good-natured for the most part."

"Did something change?" Finley ventured, trying to probe their relationship further.

"I don't want to speculate. The man is dead. His friend is hurting. Throwing out ideas is just going to jumble things." Stacey suddenly pulled herself off the sofa. She walked resolutely to the stairs. "I'm going to go check on Gavin. He still hasn't recovered."

"Let me know if there is anything I can do," Finley called after her, but Stacey had already descended the landing and was heading toward Gavin's door.

Finley began to mount the stairs to the rooftop but stopped midstride and started down the stairs instead. She was drawn to the railing that the inspector had examined. What was there that had so intrigued him? She kept her eyes on the railing, following it along from the stairs to just outside Gavin's door, where the inspector had stopped. On the face of it, there was nothing. She went back and traced her hand over the same area. When she got to the spot, she stopped again. Her hand felt a small indentation, a little nick. She dropped to her knees and looked under the rail.

"Find something?" She jerked up to find the inspector smiling at her, his eyes locked on the barely visible nick on the underside of the rail.

8

THE INSPECTOR ADVANCED TOWARD HER slightly, and then stopped and looked down at where the body of Ross Malcom had hanged. "I guess I will need to extend the tape to include this area. It will make it difficult for Mr. Jenson to get in and out of his door. Perhaps they can move him to another room." the inspector pondered.

"I'm sure he won't mind," Finley interjected, walking toward him and the stairs to the terrace.

"*Bien sur.* Could you ask Mr. Martin to join me downstairs in the interview room?" the inspector asked.

"I don't think he's here. Allan—Mr. Berger—mentioned that Thomas had gone over to the other hotel. The Villa de France. To let the producer and those guys know about what happened." Finley answered. *What the heck did happen?*

The chief inspector frowned. "Then send me Berger!" he barked.

Finley snickered slightly. "Yes, sir!" Then she turned on her heel and left.

Allan was still sitting on the terrace when she returned upstairs. Anna had joined the group and was sipping mint tea and eating from a large bowl of strawberries.

"Allan, the inspector is downstairs and wants to see you," Finley announced. Everyone stiffened.

"So, the interrogation begins!" Peter said, much too jovially.

Allan lowered his eyes, cutting Peter a glance, but said nothing. "Which inspector? The little round one or the tall one?" he asked.

"Yes, what's with the other inspector? Who is he? Why is he in there? He says nothing but just sits there, listening. Most disconcerting." Anna bit into another berry. "Unnerving, really."

"Chief Inspector Murad. The shorter one," Finley clarified, taking a seat close to Whitt this time. The other open seat was next to Peter, and frankly, she wasn't in the mood to deal with him just then.

Allan stood, taking one last gulp of coffee as if to fortify himself, and headed down the stairs. Finley looked at Whitt and signaled their exit.

"I think we're going to take Peter's suggestion and contact the Embassy," Finley shared, as she and Whitt headed toward the stairs. "Perhaps we'll see you at lunch."

Once in their room, Finley and Whitt kicked off their sandals and sprawled out on the bed, trying to make sense of the morning's events. Whitt turned on her back and watched a small spider scurry across the vaulted ceiling. Her fear of spiders would normally have sent her screaming for Finley to kill it, but the murder and the bizarre behavior of their fellow guests had so confused her that by the time she focused on what it was, the little spider had scuttled off to safety.

"What's going on? This is the biggest mess I have seen in a long time," Whitt exclaimed. "I think everyone has a motive—except us, of course. A few have means, and even fewer, opportunity."

She turned over again and rested her chin on her palms. "Let's think this through—" But before she could finish, someone rapped on the door.

Finley got up and went to the door. "Yes?" She said through the door. The muffled voice sounded like one of the porters. She cracked the door slightly. "Yes?" she repeated.

The porter responded politely, "Ma'am, the inspectors would like to see the ladies in the library now, please."

"Thank you." Finley closed the door on the waiting porter. She wasn't about to tip someone for summoning her to an interrogation, she thought testily, and then reconsidered. *The porter is just a kid doing his job.* She would slip him a tip when she got downstairs.

"We've been summoned." She turned back to face Whitt, "Who do you think they want to see first? I'll bet you dinner that it'll be me." Finley chewed her lower lip. "The inspector is going to want to know what I was doing snooping around the crime scene." She smiled to herself. *Frankly, I don't know myself.*

"What were you looking for?" Whitt sat up, looking bewildered at what prompted her sister to go to that side of the second floor. "I'm sure the inspector will not be pleased."

"I can't really tell you," Finley responded with slight frown on her face. "Something just didn't seem right. I can't explain it . . . but I guess I'll have to." She put on her sandals and ran her fingers through her short pixie cut. She pulled a tube of lipstick out of her bag and put some on before dropping it back in her purse.

"Getting pretty for the inspector, are we?" Whitt teased, pulling her long tresses off her neck, twisting her hair into a bun, and skewering it with a chopstick. "Let's get this over with."

Whitt and Finley met one of the officers at the bottom of the stairs and followed him through the archway that led to the side room that the porter called the library. At the officer's insistence, they stopped just outside the door.

"I didn't hurt him! I wouldn't hurt him!" a male voice inside screamed, alternating between French and English. "He was my friend. We had a philosophical disagreement. A difference of opinion."

Someone inside uttered something that neither of the women could hear. "So, I disagreed with him. Yes. I called him some horrible things. Told him that anyone that cruel should cease to exist. But those were just words," continued the male voice stridently. "People say things they don't mean all the time. It doesn't mean they are murderers." The voice insisted, "They were just words!"

Another voice, still garbled so that conversation was unintelligible, must have given the male voice the equivalent of a dismissal because, in the next moment, the door flew open and Julien stomped out, red in the face, looking sullen and angry. The officer stepped up to close the door, but as he was doing so, the other voice in the room made an apparent request, and the officer turned to ask Finley to enter. Finley arched an eyebrow to Whitt with an "I told you so" glance and stepped into the room.

She hadn't paid much attention to the library last night. Her mind was cluttered with too many other things. But today, in the filtered sunlight, she was struck by what a beautiful room it was. More a sitting room or lounge than a library, per se. The high ceilings were decorated with mosaic-like trompe l'oeil, and the walls were swathed in rich taupe-colored silk. It was a small room that housed several walls of books and a few tables spread with international and local newspapers. At the far end of the room, the rotund chief inspector and his tall sidekick had stationed themselves at a table. The chief inspector sat at the table, while the other inspector sat behind him.

The light was better today than it had been last night, so Finley could get a good look at the man. He was tall, almost gangly, so much so that he had to fold himself into the small chair in which he sat. He wasn't in uniform, like the chief inspector, but rather khaki pants, a white linen shirt and a coffee-colored linen jacket on which he had rolled back the sleeves to reveal muscled forearms. *This is not a man I would like to meet in a dark alley.*

His face was ruggedly handsome, with a strong nose that looked like it might have been broken once or twice, a broad forehead, and a wide mouth that turned down slightly at the ends, almost matching the chief inspector's eyes. What was most arresting, however, were his eyes—those of a hawk, a predator who watched your every move. They looked to be a dark slate grey, hooded by brows that made him seem to be frowning even when he wasn't.

"Good day, Miss Blake," the chief inspector welcomed." You are Miss Finley Blake, correct?" He referred to some papers on the table.

"Yes, sir. That is correct," Finley responded, taking the seat that the chief inspector indicated.

"Very well. So last night you were one of the first to get to the victim. What made you respond so quickly to the summons?"

"There was a scream and a moan that continued, which suggested that someone might be hurt," Finley recounted. "So, we all went down, I believe. Peter and I just got to Gavin first."

"Did you see the body immediately?"

"No, I didn't see it at all until Gavin kept pointing to the atrium, and then he said that Ross was dead. So, a few of us—I think it was Anna and Julien or . . . I can't really remember—we looked over the railing and saw the body." Finley paused before adding that she knew he was dead because of the position of his neck.

"Have you seen dead people before? Are you a doctor?" the chief inspector asked, shuffling through his papers to see whether he had missed that fact. The other inspector leaned forward, his brows drawn together, his eyes piercing.

"Yes, but generally they've been in coffins. No, I'm not a doctor, but I've seen people who have died. At wakes and funerals." Finley paused and smiled, "And I've watched enough detective and medical shows—and have enough common sense—to know that your head isn't supposed to sit on your neck like that." The other inspector's lip quirked upward, his brows relaxing a bit. *He is very nice looking when he smiles.*

The chief inspector chuckled. "So, what did you do after that?"

"I stayed with Gavin and the others, and my sister went downstairs to get Mr. Sayeed to call the police."

The other inspector spoke for the first time. "*Bonjour.* I am Inspector Evans." He paused as if unsure whether to say more. "Do you know Sayeed?"

"Not personally. Only that he owns this guesthouse. He runs the place," Finley responded.

"How did you find out about this hotel?" Evans continued his line of questioning.

"It was recommended by my boss and one of the staff writers at the magazine I work for." In answering, Finley remembered that she still had an assignment to complete and an article to write. She needed to get out of this hotel today and start developing some material for her story.

"Do you think Sayeed knew Mr. Malcom—the victim—before he came to the hotel?" Evans asked. His voice was a rich baritone. She still couldn't place his accent.

"I don't know." Finley thought for a minute, trying to see if she could recall any indication that suggested prior acquaintance between the two. "I don't think so."

The chief inspector looked back at Evans to see if he had any further questions. Evans shook his head.

"Well, thank you, mademoiselle." The chief inspector knew full well that Finley was past the age of a Miss but offered her the courtesy, nonetheless. "Would you please ask your sister to come in?"

Finley exited and signaled Whitt to enter. "I'll see you upstairs," she whispered as she passed Whitt in the doorway. "Good luck."

Whitt took in the decor of the library and made a mental note of the excellent quality of the materials and the designer's taste. *This is a room I would like in my house.* She raised her eyes and took in the ceiling artwork. So enthralled was she that she almost tripped over a tufted footstool in front of one of the reading chairs. She recovered and stood by a straight-backed chair in front of the chief inspector's table.

"Hello, Miss Blake. Please sit." The inspector nodded toward the open chair. "You are Miss Whitney Blake, are you not?"

"No, I am not Whitney Blake," Whitt responded, slightly annoyed. The chief inspector looked confused, rifling through his papers for some answer. The other inspector sat looking intently at Whitt. "My first name is not Whitney. I am S. *Whittaker* Blake. Whitt is my nickname."

The chief inspector made note of the correction and smiled, "My apologies, Miss Blake. So, you told me yesterday that after finding the body, you went downstairs to get someone to call the police. Who were you seeking?"

"Anyone who could help. I was looking for Mr. Sayeed, but at that point, if I hadn't seen him, I would've gotten the porters or someone else to call them."

"And where did you find him?" the chief inspector continued.

"In the little anteroom or office near the front desk. He came out immediately. I think he thought I was being a hysterical woman because I was so insistent that he call the police," Whitt replied.

The other inspector broke in. "My name is Inspector Evans. Sayeed didn't want to call the police?" he asked.

"He seemed a little reluctant. Like I was asking for something that he could take care of. He took me over to the divan to calm me down, but when I pointed out the body to him, he immediately made the call."

"Did you know Sayeed before you came to the hotel?" Evans continued.

"No, I've never met him in my life," Whitt responded quickly. She hunched her shoulders up like knowing Sayeed would be the most repellent thing in the world to her.

Evans gave her a crooked half smile. "Why are you in Tangier, Miss Blake?"

Whitt took him in before answering. She confirmed her earlier assessment that there was something attractive about the man, but he wasn't her type. Too self-possessed by half. "I'm just visiting," she said, "while my sister works on her travel article. I live overseas, so I don't get to see her often."

Evans sat forward at the last information. "Where do you live?" he asked. He waited for her response with a slight scowl on his face.

"Manila. But I travel a lot for work as well," Whitt volunteered.

Evans sat back and nodded for the chief inspector to proceed. "Had you met any of the other guests before coming to Morocco?" the chief inspector asked.

"Besides my sister, no." Whitt looked satisfied with herself.

"And you did not know the victim?"

"No. I never heard of him," Whitt responded. She was starting to get bored. She had no information, didn't know these people, and couldn't help them with their investigation—unless they gave her information. The best way to get information was to ask. *Sometimes you get lucky.* "Do you think he was killed by someone he knew, or was it a robber from outside?"

Her ploy worked. The chief inspector volunteered that it was not an accident based on the preliminary coroner's report, there had been no robbery, and he didn't know whether it was a stranger or someone the victim knew but suspected it was the latter since the place is pretty well secured and strangers who are not guests stand out. He looked up and smiled. Whitt, knowing when she was ahead, smiled back.

"You may go. Please do not leave Tangier without letting us know." The chief inspector went back to his files. Evans simply nodded. Whitt opened the door and left. Outside, waiting his turn was Thomas, looking none too happy with apparently being hauled back for another police interview.

"Haven't seen you today. How's it going?" Whitt stood to the side to allow one of the policemen to enter the library. He closed the door quietly.

"It would be going much better if they would get on with their investigation and let me work. This is an unfortunate situation that does not require my involvement. Yet, the inspector thinks it is necessary for me to stop my work and return," he complained.

"This is a murder investigation, so he has to be thorough," Whitt offered.

"But—" Thomas was interrupted by the door opening, and the police officer asking him to step inside.

9

WHEN WHITT REACHED HER ROOM, Finley had already changed into a cornflower blue sundress with cap sleeves and a fitted bodice, and tan espadrilles. "Put on your walking shoes, we're springing this joint and gathering some good info for my article." She pulled out her work camera, a tripod, and a bag with lenses and dropped those and three folding shopping bags into her satchel. "You never know what we might find in the souk."

Within the hour, Whitt and Finley were out the door. They had decided on a path through the sprawling old city based on what they wanted to buy the most. If they had time, they would come back to other shops not marked priority and move down the shopping list. Today they would focus on the highest priority items, which were mainly things for Mama and Daddy and then gifts for Mooney and Charlie, Whitt's best friend in Manila. But first, they needed coffee.

They headed out of the hotel and up the hill toward the Bab Kasbah, one of the many ancient stone arches that surrounded the old part of the city. Built during Tangier's medieval period, the gates had protected the labyrinth of alleyways that housed residents and shops that had plied trade through the times of the Romans to modern day. The bright white walls of the medina had survived the Phoenicians, the Romans, the Greeks, the Vandals, the Portuguese, the Spanish, the Brits, and the French.

Sometime during this rich history, Morocco refined the art of both tea and coffee. While mint tea was what was customarily drunk, Finley knew that Moroccans could also brew one hell of a cup of Turkish coffee. It had been one of the things she and Max had always looked for wherever they went—a café that served good coffee. They had found Cafe Baba by chance, discovering only later that it had been the haven of such greats as the Rolling Stones and Jack Kerouac, who visited the café to drink coffee or mint tea and smoke kief, a drug that has since been banned.

Finley and Whitt climbed the steep stairs to the café entrance and ordered their coffee. What they really wanted was a to-go cup so they could keep walking while they talked, but that was clearly a foreign concept here. So, the two sat at a small table that gave glimpses of the sea, heads together, trying to review what they knew. First, they knew that it was not an accident, but a murder. They also knew that Julien and Ross had had a falling out over something. While Julien claimed it was a philosophical difference, Peter suggested at breakfast that it had been a knock-down, drag-out fight between the two of them, indicating that it wasn't a minor difference.

Beyond that, they could only speculate. A natural suspect high on the list would be Gavin. He had been away from the terrace for a while, and he had found the body. But Gavin's slight frame and his pitiful reaction to Ross' death made his involvement unlikely. His terror was too real to be faked.

Sayeed might also have some role in this. His reluctance to call the police, and his dancing around while the police were there said that there was something he didn't want the little round inspector to know. What that was, neither Whitt nor Finley could figure out. Thomas's escape to the Villa de France, and his anger over being brought back for questioning seemed a little extreme, making him a new addition to the list. Maybe he really was busy, but still, his reaction had been a little over the top.

Then, there were all the other members of the crew. Any one of them could have had some past dealings with Ross that led to his death. Finley and Whitt just didn't have any facts that pointed their way. And there was the real possibility that someone from outside the guesthouse had come in to rob guests while they were upstairs and had gotten caught.

The timing for this sort of escapade would have required insider knowledge of when the various guests went to the terrace and how long they generally stayed. Although security was tight, with all the little portals opening and closing, it might have been possible for someone to come in unnoticed—maybe in one of the *djellabas* that the porters and waiters wore—and slip out through the secret passages. They needed to find out where those passages led.

First, however, they needed to finish their touring, and shopping, and Finley needed to settle on an angle for her article. Reenergized by the strong coffee, they trudged up the hill through the arched stone gateway of the Kasbah and took in the majestic view of the entire city and the water.

Whitt had thankfully designed their route so that, after their tour of the Kasbah, they would be going downhill most of the way. *Easier to lug packages down than up.* And they were likely to have a lot of packages to carry. When Finley had called the embassy to let them know about Ross Malcolm's murder, the consular officer, a pleasant woman from Texas who has been in Tangier just over a year, told Finley of several shops in the medina that had unique high-quality items good for gifting.

Of course, Finley had scribbled them down and Whitt was determined to go through the whole list today. Her reasoning was that they could see what each shop had, get the priority items, and then come back tomorrow or at the end of their trip to pick up the larger things if they didn't see them in other cities that they were planning to visit. But besides Chefchaouen, they hadn't decided which other cities those would be. They were still debating between Casablanca and Marrakesh.

While Whitt shopped, Finley pulled out her camera and began to take candid shots of people—women sitting on the steps along the narrow streets, kids playing ball in the alleyways, and cats stretching out in the midday sun among the geraniums. She was trying to somehow capture the smells and the sensation of the crowded medina, using the play of light and angle to suggest the senses not conveyed in two dimensions.

"Do you like these?" Whitt's voice brought Finley's gaze up from behind the camera. She was holding up several silver bracelets, each hammered with a different intricate pattern—leaves and flowers and birds.

"They're lovely. So delicate. How much are they?"

"That depends." Whitt began a carefully paced negotiation that included picking up more articles to buy, putting all of them down, walking out of the shop, and pretending to cross the narrow street to another shop, whose owner was standing at the door hawking his wares.

Before Whitt had stepped off the curb, though, the woman with whom she had begun the negotiation capitulated and was starting to wrap up the items, throwing in a few more trinkets for good measure. So that it wasn't a total loss for the poor woman, Finley bought a couple pairs of slippers at close to full price."

"You're such a sap!" Whitt shook her head. "They expect you to bargain."

"I know," Finley countered, "but I just keep thinking that those couple of dollars meant a cup of coffee to me. To her, it's food money for her kids."

Whitt couldn't disagree, but she wasn't willing to forego the exhilaration she got from bargaining, so the two were soon off to another shop. By the time they reached the hotel some three hours later, they were laden with woven plastic shopping bags stuffed with brown paper-wrapped packages.

"That was a very productive day!" Whitt declared, pushing open the wooden entry door to the hotel with her bum. She paused briefly, then continued her bum push. A porter slipped out from behind the desk hurriedly to help her with the door and her packages.

"Did you see that?" she asked under breath.

Finley looked puzzled. "See what?" She looked over her shoulder as the heavy door closed. "What was I supposed to be looking at?"

Whitt continued walking until she was through the lobby and had reached the bottom step of the far stairs. "That man. In the tan suit." When she reached their room, she pulled Finley in quickly and shut the door. After a short while, she opened it a crack and peeked out.

"What are you doing? What are you looking at?" Finley was trying to peer over her sister's head to identify what Whitt was seeing that she wasn't.

Whitt closed the door quietly and then went over to the bed. "There was a man on the street. I saw him earlier but didn't pay any attention to him until I saw him in front of the hotel. I don't see him now; maybe we can slip out and head up to the bar. I just don't want him to see us when we open the door for delivery of the packages."

Finley nodded, stuffed her camera in the safe and grabbed her satchel. "Let's go then."

They slowly opened the door, determined that no one was in the courtyard or lobby, and headed quietly for the back stairs. When they reached the terrace, Stacey and Taryn met them halfway across the room, peppering them with excited questioning.

"Where have you been?" Stacey snapped unexpectedly. "We searched the whole city for you. You shouldn't have left us like that." She was near tears.

Taryn picked up the exclamation. "Do you have any idea what's been going on here? We've all been at sixes and sevens. It all makes no sense."

Finley looked at Taryn quizzically and then at Whitt to see if she had made any sense of the conversation. Peter was the one who finally gave them the whole picture.

"The police have been here much of the day, as you saw. All of us were questioned this morning and then some of us were taken back in for another round. It was not pleasant, but I have nothing to hide."

He continued, "In any case, they ran poor Gavin through the ringer, so much so that he took to his bed. And then they started on Thomas—why had he left the hotel? Who did he talk to? What was he covering up?"

"Thomas took a swing at one of the policemen," Anna looked disgusted as she said it. "Will he never learn? They've sequestered him. He's lucky he isn't in jail right now."

"Why were they going after Gavin?" Whitt asked. She and Finley had crossed him off their list. He didn't seem capable of breaking a man's neck and then carelessly tossing him over the balcony.

"He apparently has had some sort of military training where you can kill a man with one hand." Peter added excitedly. "Surprises come in odd packages, eh?" He raised an eyebrow in Finley's direction and nodded.

"Where was Allan during all of this? He's the one who sent Thomas off on that fool's errand," Finley retorted.

"He was with us during most of the morning. He didn't hear about this until Thomas created all the commotion downstairs when he was called for a second interview. Allan tried to talk to the inspector," Anna sighed. "I think that was why Thomas was only put in a separate room rather than carted off to jail. Allan's intervention."

"And what about Julien? Did he get a second round?" Whitt asked.

"He's getting a third and fourth one, it appears." Stacey murmured, tearing up again. "They arrested him."

FINLEY AND **W**HITT SAT IN stunned silence, Whitt crinkling her brow the way she did when news was too incredible to believe. She pursed her lips and her shoulders tensed. She turned to Finley, head tilted, and stared for minute before speaking.

"Arrested? Why?" Whitt asked, with emphasis on the last word. "Julien told them just because you have a tiff doesn't make you a murderer. Was there something else, some other evidence, that they used to bring him in?"

"Apparently there was something because the two inspectors left for an hour or so. We all thought it was over. And then they came back—for Julien," Peter reported.

"We were having a late lunch and they just came up here and took him," Taryn said. "Just like that. We called the embassy, but who knows what you're supposed to do." Her youthful personality suggested that she felt she should always have an answer for everything, but she was at a loss.

"So, what did the embassy say?" Whitt asked.

"Not much. Just to cooperate with the police and stay put. We did contact Etienne. The producer," Anna stated in her deep languid voice, now strained with emotion. "Now we wait."

"And drink," Peter added. "What are you drinking? I think the day's events call for something stronger than wine." Whitt ordered a gin and tonic, and Finley a bourbon neat.

The group sat in silence, nursing their drinks, deep in thoughts that led to no conclusions. Whitt looked up from her G & T to see Finley staring at her. She was going through everything they knew, and something was missing.

Finley adjusted herself in the deep cushions of the chair. "We need to start at the beginning. The pieces aren't fitting for me. How they got to Julien just doesn't make sense." She leaned forward to pull a pad of paper and a pen from her satchel. "This is going to bother me all night long. What do you know about Ross? And then we will start on Julien."

The others must have been feeling the same way because they immediately turned their attention to Finley and Whitt and started talking. "Ross has been with the production house awhile. Etienne has worked with him before. Ross was a technical genius," Stacey shared willingly. "The special effects in the last two *Harry Potter* movies? That was Ross. There weren't any big specials in this film, but some with the rally cars and all."

"He was a fairly friendly fellow. No wife that I know of, but I think he had a pretty serious girlfriend back in London," Anna added, stretching herself across two chairs, drink in hand. She looked like a modern-day Cleopatra with her bluntly cut, straight dark hair. But a saddened, less haughty monarch now. "Goodness, someone is going to have the tell the poor dear the terrible news."

Peter continued in his all-knowing way, his eyebrows raised and his hands punctuating every phrase. "He and Julien have been friends for as long as I have known them. They were as different as chalk and cheese, but they got along well. I don't know what the tiff was over. Julien isn't saying."

"Okay, what do you know about Julien?" Whitt asked. "How long has he been around?"

"The last five years, I would say," Peter replied. "This crew works with the studio quite a bit. Most of us are not on contract, but once you get in, they keep calling you back."

Anna and Stacey nodded. "I've done at least two, no three, other projects with him," Stacey remembered.

"Anything else on Julien? This seems rather thin for someone you have worked with for five years." Finley was testy. She was frustrated. *They are holding something back. Arresting Julien still makes no sense, and they know it.*

"He has a wife and a young son, as I recall," Stacey interjected. "Julien is kind of moody. Nice enough, but he pretty much keeps to himself. He's even moodier than Allan."

Finley furrowed her brow. Conversation with this crew was getting her nowhere. She and Whitt needed to shift from why to how. If they could figure that out, then the rest might fall into place. They needed to get into the passageways behind those portals. Tonight seemed as good a time as any.

Whitt must have read Finley's thoughts. She rose from her seat and picked up her purse. "We'd best be on our way. This has been a trying day for you all. Please let us know if there is anything we can do to help."

Finley nodded goodbye and followed her to the stairs. Silently, Whitt stuck her head over the rail, making sure the man she had seen earlier was not in sight. Assured of that, she and Finley made their way back to their room.

Once inside, Finley quickly made for the closet, stripping off her sundress and espadrilles as she went. She grabbed some jeans, a black T-shirt, and black sneakers.

"Where are you going?" Whitt asked. "And what's the hurry?" She was standing in the middle of the room, hands on her hips, pivoting as Finley scurried about the room.

"We need to check out what's behind these walls. All those little doors. They have something to do with this." Finley said over her shoulder from the bathroom. "Change into something dark and less conspicuous!"

Whitt shimmied out of her linen skirt and dropped her shirt on the bed. She pulled on a pair of black capri pants and a black boat-neck tunic from the chest of drawers.

"I swear, girl. You get dressed up for everything!" Finley always teased Whitt good-naturedly about the formality of her dress, even for casual occasions. Like reconnaissance. "Just pull your hair back. It's probably going to end up covered in cobwebs."

Whitt screwed up her face at the thought of spiders. She hated them and the thought of them in her hair. She would just have to wash it when they came back.

"Do you have a flashlight?" Finley held one out to her sister. "Take it, just in case. It's a pretty handy weapon too!"

They slipped out of the room and headed toward the back stairs. They had only seen the portals on the lower level, but that didn't mean there weren't entrances and inside stairs on the upper levels. Finley quietly tapped the dark-paneled walls as they walked down the stairs, listening for hollowness. Hearing nothing, she and Whitt continued to the courtyard level.

Whitt pointed to one of the portals she had remembered near the far stairs. She pushed gently on the wood panel and a small door popped open. The two women snuck inside. Given the narrowness of the passageway and low height of the ceiling, it was surprisingly well lit, with small lanterns hung at regular intervals. The passages seemed empty of waiters or porters, or maybe they hadn't reached the more active areas yet. Whitt tried to map out in her head where they were in relation to where they had entered. If they continued straight, they should be nearing the front desk, which sat a little to the left of the main front door.

They advanced slowly, stopping periodically to listen for sounds around them that might clue them in on where they were. As they reached the end of the first passageway, they heard voices, as expected, in front of them. This would be beside the front desk and near the little anteroom that Sayeed used as his office. Whitt tried to remember where the portal for this area was. She had seen one near one of the columns off the center courtyard, but not one nearer than that. She hesitated to head toward the front desk for fear of stumbling into Sayeed's office itself. This was supposed to be a stealth operation.

Instead, she turned left toward a connecting passageway that led down a few stairs before continuing straight. Finley followed close behind her, marking down the way on her small pad. Whitt figured that they were now under the center courtyard heading toward the reflecting pool that was outside the bank of tall French doors on the far wall, opposite the front desk.

Finley tugged on her arm and showed her the small-scale diagram that she had sketched out. Finley had drawn in the center courtyard, the reflecting pool, and all the portals she could remember. Without speaking, she pointed to one of the X's that signified a portal, asking silently if this is where Whitt thought they were. Whitt nodded and signaled that they should turn left, which would arguably take them toward the library.

They mounted a few steps and then headed left along a long straight passageway. At the end of this passage, they started to hear more footsteps and movement. A door opened suddenly behind them. They pressed themselves against the wall in the darkened area between the lanterns and waited. A young man, dressed in the white *djellaba* and long brown vest of a porter, turned down the passage, heading the other way. Whitt stepped into the light and continued a few steps to a T-junction. By her estimation, a left would take them back to where they started. A right would take them either along the bottom or the top of the library.

She turned right, listening to what sounded like the bustling chaos of the kitchen. Pots clanged, dishes clinked, cooks cursed loudly in French and Arabic. Finley tapped her shoulder and pointed to suggest that they take a left at the end of this short passage. By now, Finley was hot and sweaty. The passageways, while lit, offered no air circulation, and were covered in dust. Yet, Whitt, when she came into the light, looked cool and collected, with every hair in place. *How did she do it? Life just ain't fair.*

If their sense of direction and Finley's little diagram had served them right, the door directly in front of them should open to the alleyway that ran behind the guesthouse. If this door wasn't locked, it might be the way that the killers had gotten into the hotel. There had to have been more than one to get Ross, who was not a small man, over the railing and onto the chandelier. Whitt paused a moment before pushing the door open.

The noise of the city at night rose around them—almost deafening after the muted sounds of the passageways. As soon as they exited the hotel passage, the door clicked behind them. Finley turned quickly to check the handle. It was locked. "There goes that theory," she quipped.

"Not completely," Whitt whispered as they walked toward the street. "Someone could have opened it for them, or they could have slipped in when someone came out."

Finley was still silent, thinking up possible scenarios that offered even a modicum of plausibility. She was coming up empty, but Whitt was determined to get Finley to air her thoughts so that they could discuss and refine them. They were so engrossed in conversation that they didn't see the large man looming in front of them until they had almost bumped into him.

"*Bonsoir*, ladies." Inspector Evans said, looking back along the darkened alley. "Out for a late-night stroll?" He was in another linen jacket, this time a dark gray, with jeans. He had wrapped one of the local black-and-white-checkered scarves around his neck.

Finley looked at the dust in Whitt's hair and imagined the grime on her face and simply smiled. She wasn't going to try to lie her way out of this one.

"If you have been snooping around the hotel, I would advise against it." His voice was deeply resonant, almost echoing in Finley's chest. She could see his gray eyes reflecting the light from the guest-house such that that they looked almost translucent. "It is not safe to get involved in this. One man has been killed. I would hate for one of you to be the next victim."

Before either of them could respond, he nodded slightly and was gone.

"We're busted!" Whitt drawled. "Let's take his advice and put this whole business out of our minds."

"For the rest of the night," her sister countered. "I'm suddenly really hungry. Let's get cleaned up and go find dinner. Outside the hotel. I don't want to run into Anna and her posse tonight."

When the taxi pulled up in front of the restaurant at around nine o'clock, the women realized that they could have walked from the hotel. In fact, Finley did suggest it, but Whitt was tired after getting showered and dressed, and neither was sure whether the whole way to the restaurant was a safe walk. Sometimes there were pockets of trouble along an otherwise safe street. After Evans's warning, it wouldn't do to have to call the police again because they were robbed or assaulted.

The restaurant that Finley had chosen was small, only six or seven tables. There were no reservations, but on the off-season, as this was, she figured there wouldn't be much of a wait. If there was, they could grab a drink and sit at the small bar. She was looking forward to a good fish tagine or seafood paella. This place was noted for both.

As luck would have it, there was an open table near the front. Finley and Whitt took their seats and exhaled. "I didn't know how tired I was," Whitt breathed heavily. "All that shopping and then the news about Julien."

"And then getting caught by Evans." Finley gave a half laugh and turned to give the waiter their drink orders. There really was no need for a menu, but she looked anyway. The options were chalked on a board hanging above the worn wooden bar. While it all looked good, Finley decided to stick to one of the two choices she had considered earlier. She would decide at the last minute, most likely, based on what was calling her taste buds the most.

"Have you been here before?" Whitt asked. "What's good?"

"Everything." Finley responded. "The mezze is out of this world and the tagines are to die for. They are known for their seafood, but they have a few meat and vegetable dishes on the menu as well. And save room for a little dessert," she added. "We can share."

They decided on *bastilla* to start, because it was Whitt's favorite, and the fish tagine to share. Even though they were hungry, they knew that some tagines could easily feed four people. There was no cuisine minceur in Morocco. Determined not to broach the topic of the murder, the sisters focused on planning their trip to Chefchaouen the next day. They had been looking forward to wandering around the city dubbed the Blue Pearl. It was only a couple of hours away.

Whitt had read a bit about the pretty, blue-washed city in the Rif Mountains. It was originally a small fortress built to defend against Portuguese invasions. Tangier and Chefchaouen would be featured significantly in Finley's article for *Traveler's Tales*.

Still Finley needed another major city to include. She had considered Marrakesh, but so much had been written on it, she was inclined to focus on one of the other cities like Fes or Casablanca. She and Whitt debated the merits of those two cities while they dug into the steaming tagine.

"So, what's the deal with you and the guy in Tbilisi?" Finley smirked while she wiped her mouth and laid her napkin back in her lap. Whitt knew Finley was getting ready to get in her business. She had ordered a second bottle of wine.

"He has a name. It's David," Whitt acknowledged, almost whispering the name.

"And?" Finley asked.

"And I think I like him." Whitt replied wistfully. "He's smart. He has his own exporting business. Wines and gourmet foods. He's nice and has a good sense of humor. And a wonderful appreciation of the absurd." Finley waited.

On cue, Whitt continued, leaning forward in her chair. "He's also gorgeously handsome with the softest dark blond, almost gingery, hair. And these big, liquid blue eyes that have little lines around them."

She was smiling openly now, imitating the little lines by pointing around her eyes. Finley looked at her sister. *So, she has touched that pretty blond head.* Finley was glad for her. As much as Whitt said she liked being single, she needed someone in her life. Or, at least, Finley wanted her sister to have someone special in her life. She couldn't wait to meet this guy who had her sister beaming.

"When do I get to meet this guy?" Finley asked.

Whitt paused before saying, "I secretly wanted him to come here for a bit. But it's not realistic." She diverted her eyes so that Finley couldn't see how fervently she had hoped that he would come.

"Why don't you head to Georgia a day or so early and surprise him? We can head to Casablanca the day after tomorrow. You can catch the flight from there to Georgia and I can finish my story. I may take the train to Fes to see what's there before I head home." Finley had it all planned out.

"I want to spend time with you, too," Whitt mumbled. "I don't want to cut short what precious time we have together for some guy who may not be in the picture a month from now."

Finley grinned. *The way she's talking about this boy, he's going to be around far longer than a month.*

"We'll see," Whitt mused. "Where's the loo? If I'm going to drink more wine . . ." she trailed off as she got up in search of the bathrooms.

Finley sipped a bit more of the vibrant white that was in her glass and smiled slyly. *We are going to need that other bottle.*

"Fin!" Finley froze. No one called her that. Except Max.

Her back had been to the rest of the room, so she hadn't seen the other guests in the restaurant. She was almost afraid to turn around now for fear that it was someone else and the disappointment would show on her face.

When he came around to face her, she was not disappointed. His dark hair had a few flecks of gray, but besides that, it was the same Max. Tall, broad shouldered, and still perfectly sculpted. She was glad she was seated. She might have swooned otherwise, and she had never fainted in her life.

"Aliyaa said she thought it was you," he confirmed quietly. Aliyaa was the owner. She had been a friend to both Max and Finley. "What are you doing here? I thought you were still in New York."

Finley had to take another gulp of wine before she found her voice. "I'm still based in New York, but I left the firm and am doing some travel stories for a magazine."

"So, you're back to writing again," Max smiled. "I was wondering when you'd return to your true calling. What are you writing about this time?"

He spoke as if he had just seen her last week and was catching up on the latest gossip. Instead, it had been over three years, and the parting had not been pleasant. At least from her side.

"Look, I won't keep you," Max said as he stared at the other plate opposite Finley and the shared tagine. "I don't want to interrupt your evening but call me. I'd love to catch up." He pulled out one of his cards, scribbled something on the back and put it on the table near her.

"You look well," he murmured. "As beautiful as ever." He turned and walked back to his table.

Whitt returned just as Max was leaving. She stared at his back, straining to see whether he was with someone. "Was that Max?"

Finley was glad the other bottle had arrived. She poured more wine into Whitt's glass and then topped hers off, her jaw working back and forth as she poured. She noticed that her breath had quickened. She fought to slow it and gain control.

"Do you want to go?" Whitt asked. She didn't know what had been said between the two of them. She couldn't remember all the details of the breakup years ago, only that her sister had been devastated, cut to the quick by whatever happened. She was still healing.

Finley smiled, if somewhat unsurely. "No, we have a bottle of wine to finish, a trip to plan, and some dessert to sample."

She called the waiter over and ordered the glazed oranges with cinnamon and one of the sweet *briouat*, a pastry cigar stuffed with almond paste. She also bucked tradition and ordered two Turkish coffees—without sugar.

"What's he doing here? Did he just stay after . . ."? She left the end of the question hanging. She didn't know what words to use to describe what had happened.

"Don't know," Finley said as she touched the card that was still facedown on the table.

"So, are we agreed that we'll go to Chefchaouen tomorrow and then to Casablanca the day after?" Finley continued.

Her breathing had returned to normal by the time she saw Max and a woman leave the restaurant. He held the door for her and looked back, catching Finley's eye and smiling as the door closed.

THE DRIVE TO CHEFCHAOUEN WAS just what Finley and Whitt needed. The chief inspector did not care that the two women wanted to leave the city. He had his suspect, and his focus now was on building a case to convict him. Given that neither sister knew Julien before coming to Morocco and had had little contact with him since arriving in Tangier, they were of no interest to his investigation.

Whitt had said she wanted to drive this time. It reminded Finley of road trips their family would take when they headed from Washington, DC, to South Carolina for holidays. Now, as it had been back then, the car was packed like they were going for a month-long trek—water bottles, snacks, changes of clothes, walking shoes, towels, day packs and backpacks.

Whitt, assuming the role of Mama, wanted to be sure that they were properly dressed for all possible events—hikes, tours, cocktails, and dinner. How she thought they were going to change clothes in the car was beyond Finley's imagination. *Heaven help us if we have to go to dinner inappropriately attired. Mama would never forgive us. At least, according to Whitt.*

Once out of Tangier, the scenery changed from a white-and-blue hardscape to a soft green landscape. The highway shortened the one-hundred-kilometer trip to less than two hours. But the sisters didn't rush, stopping for Finley to take shots of the changing topography, goats in the fields, and people in the towns as they passed through. Finley insisted that they stop for pictures of a lake near Tetouan that sparkled a clear aquamarine against the green foothills of the Rif Mountains.

By the time they got to Chefchaouen, they were both ready for more coffee and some food. They had had a quick breakfast in their room before making their way downstairs in the Tangier hotel. Sayeed had met them in the lobby, curious about the excursion.

"Why don't you take one of our cars and a driver?" he had frowned at Finley, seemingly sure that this was her idea. *I don't know why that man dislikes me, but he does.*

"Kind of you to offer, but we actually like driving and we prefer having control over our itinerary," Whitt had told him. "We might stay over. We haven't decided yet." Sayeed didn't say anything more, but it was obvious he was displeased with their decision.

Now, after over two hours in a car, they wanted to stretch, get some food, and see the sights of Chefchaouen. Looking at the steep cobbled street, Finley changed into walking shoes immediately. She had packed her backpack with her camera equipment and whatever else she thought she would need. A change of dress wasn't one of them. She had on a khaki linen dress that she could wear to dinner, and had her shawl, which went with everything. She would stick her patent sandals in her pack, just in case Whitt decided to go upscale.

Whitt had worn a pair of black linen pants and a white-on-white embroidered cotton kurta that she had picked up in India along with a pair of black slides. She took off the slides, dropped them into her day pack, and then donned her walking shoes, a pair of black MBT slip-ons. She then grabbed two patterned nylon fold-up bags and dropped them in as well. *Never know when you're gonna see something you can't live without!*

"Where'd you get those?" Finley asked, pointing to the nylon bags.

"From the Museum of Islamic Art gift store in the Doha airport. You like them?" Whitt replied. "I can get you some the next time I go through."

Finley nodded, pulling her backpack over one shoulder so she could always keep an eye on it. Whitt converted her backpack into a tote bag, threw it over her shoulder, and locked the car door.

The trek from the parking lot was short, but steep. Whitt thought back to a trip to San Gimignano that she had taken with her sister a few years ago. Soon after Finley came back from Tangier. Right after her breakup with Max. They had walked all over Italy as if they could walk away Finley's troubles. *Hopefully, this encounter with Max won't end up the same. She deserves better than heartache.*

"Where to?" Finley was standing in front of her, looking eager. "You're the tour guide today. I just want to get photos of people mostly, as well as some shots of the blue architecture."

Again, Whitt had done her homework. "Chefchaouen, which means 'horns' in Berber, was a fifteenth-century walled city thought to have been founded by the Moors and the Jews fleeing Spanish persecution. There is some speculation about the blues in which the houses are painted."

She paused and looked at the nearby houses. "One theory is that the Jews brought the tradition with them because the color was supposed to mirror the sky and remind them of God. I guess after fleeing the Inquisition and reaching the safety of this mountain town, that wouldn't be too far of a stretch."

She continued. "I figured we could wander around town a bit, get some lunch, do some shopping—they have nice leathers, I'm told. And I think there's an organic cosmetics shop that has great argan oil products. We'll save the Spanish Mosque for last in case we're running low on energy."

She paused, looking over at Finley to see if she approved of the itinerary. Finley was easy. All she wanted now was some coffee and then food. She hadn't decided whether she wanted to grab a *merguez* from one of the stalls or sit down for a proper midday meal. Her brain was too muddled to think clearly without more coffee.

"Let's find coffee first and then decide."

"Fine with me." Whitt led the way up a steep winding alley, heading as best she could tell toward the center of town. Off the plaza, there should be several cafés they could choose from if they didn't find one along the way before that.

From time to time, as they wove around tourists and shoppers and merchants on the narrow street, Whitt would stop at a stall and inspect the woven raffia handbags or leather goods hung on bright blue shutters. Finley often took advantage of the pause to pull her camera out and click a series of pictures of kids sticking their heads out from the bright blue doorways or kittens cuddled in baskets on the turquoise half walls that separated many of the houses. The colors, sounds, and smells were intoxicating, and Finley felt transported back in time.

After wandering for a half hour or so, Whitt pointed to a small platform carved into the incline on which there was a café with outside tables and chairs. Finley plopped down at one to claim it while Whitt went in and ordered their coffees.

"I also ordered some pastries," Whitt told her when she returned. "That should fuel us for a while so we can do a bit more exploring before lunch."

Finley nodded with her camera poised for more shots of the colorful streets. She put her camera away when the waiter brought their coffees and food.

"I was so busy taking pictures, I didn't see what you bought." Finley looked up.

"I got a leather bag for Mama and a portfolio for Daddy." Whitt replied. "The one you got him in Argentina is on its last leg."

Finley chuckled, a mouthful of croissant muffling her reply. "It should be. That thing is almost eight years old."

Finley had gotten the cognac-colored portfolio on her first business trip overseas. Her Daddy had been so proud of her—law school finished and out into the big world. Now, Whitt was replacing it when she was just about the same age Finley had been. Daddy would be proud again.

Whitt was studying the map, trying to figure out which way they should go next. When she looked up, she gasped and diverted her eyes. Finley, staring into space and daydreaming as she often did, frowned. "What is it?" she asked.

"Directly in front of me, a bit to the left, around eleven o'clock. It's the man from the hotel," Whitt whispered. "He followed us here."

"Are you sure he isn't just another tourist, and we just happen to be in the same places?" Finley asked.

"No. He's spying on us. He's following us." Whitt had blanched. She was scared. Finley didn't want to turn to look, so she rose from the table and headed into the café. "Stay here. You'll be okay."

Finley entered the crowded interior, pointed to more pastries, and turned to look out the window while the woman behind the counter wrapped up her purchase. The man was in the same tan suit that Whitt had described. *Did he not change clothes, or are all his suits tan?*

He was relatively young, probably in his late twenties, with dark curly hair. If he had been in a *djellaba* or jeans, he would have melted into the multitude of men wandering up and down the busy street. His suit set him apart. Why was he tailing them, and what would his reaction be if they confronted him? Finley couldn't see whether he was armed. The best option seemed to be to keep him in sight at all times and to stay together.

Finley took her pastries and went outside. As she approached Whitt at the table, she whispered, "We're going to tour just the way we planned. We'll just keep an eye on him. And stick together."

They headed up the street and entered the main square, the Place Outa el Hammam. In the center sat a red-walled Kasbah. Whitt relayed that it was dated from the late fifteenth century or early sixteenth century. Built by the city's founder, Moulay Ali Ben Moussa Ben Rached El Alami, it was part of the defense for the new settlement against the Portuguese and Spanish. Flanked with eleven towers, the kasbah had served as both a permanent military encampment and a seignorial residence, and now it housed the museum.

Even scared, Whitt was a wealth of information, spouting facts and dates from her guidebook. As they wandered around the square, shopkeepers called them into their stalls, promising, with a wink, special items that "weren't offered to just anyone." The sisters snickered and kept walking.

In one corner of the square, street musicians had set up a stage with a flatweave rug and some instrument stands. A crowd had gathered to listen to the music, clapping and swaying to the beat. Small children danced and sang along. The man in the tan suit had climbed the hill to the square and was worming his way through the crowd. He made no attempt to approach them. He just observed.

Whitt and Finley continued their shopping, aware but not necessarily wary of the man. After exhausting all the shops and stalls along the main street, they dropped into a café with outside seating. They asked for a seat against the wall with a clear view of the square. While they both wanted a stiff drink, they decided against it, opting for tea instead. They wanted to be mentally sharp.

Whitt and Finley watched the waiter pour tall arcs of steaming hot tea from a silver pot into crystal glasses and then retreat. When their kebab sandwiches came, they tucked into them, glad for the comfort of the food.

"So, did you decide what you're going to do about David?" Finley asked, chewing hungrily. She looked up from eating to eye her sister.

"What do you mean?" Whitt looked puzzled." If you're talking about heading back early, no, I haven't decided."

Finley waited. Whitt would talk through her logic, if given time. She always did.

"I mean, I want to see him, but I don't want to make him the reason that I'm going to Georgia early."

"Why?"

"Why what?" Whitt asked, a bit testily. "Why don't I want him to be the reason? Don't be daft." Finley smiled, taking another bite of kebab, and waited again.

"Okay, am I that transparent?" Whitt asked. "I should just go, shouldn't I?" Finley was silent. "Maybe just a day early. That won't look too obvious, will it?" Finley snickered, wiped her hands, and rested her napkin on her lap. She liked eating with her hands, but it sure was messy.

"And what about you, Miss pot-calling-the-kettle-black? What are you going to do about Max?" Whitt's voice had softened when she asked the last question.

"Can't say that I know." Finley responded matter-of-factly. "I'll probably call him for a drink." *It would be rude not to. I've made it to the other side of hurt. This will prove it. If only to myself.*

Whitt sat quietly for a moment. Then she suggested, "We probably should get going if we're going to the mosque."

They paid and then headed up the path behind the square that led to the Spanish Mosque. Sitting high on a hill about two kilometers from the main square, the Spanish Mosque had been constructed during Spanish control in the 1920s and offered the best vantage point of the town. Finley snapped shot after shot of the vista as well as the mosque. Although never really used as a mosque, the whitewashed structure had a haunting beauty about it. *Glad it is being saved from complete collapse with this recent renovation.*

The trip to the mosque had taken less time than they thought, and before seven o'clock, Finley and Whitt were back on the road to Tangier. Neither of them had seen the man in the tan suit again. Both desperately wanted a drink, but neither wanted to drink alone while the other was designated driver. They would head to the bar once they put the car away. The kebabs had been substantial, so dinner would probably be an afterthought—after a drink.

Whitt pulled the car into the narrow garage behind the hotel herself rather than bother the valet. She and Finley gathered their packages from the back seat and headed through the dimly lit doorway. They mounted the back stairs, passing the third level and landing on the fourth-level roof terrace with the determination of Sherman on his way to Atlanta. Peter was the only one from the crew at the bar.

"I know what you ladies have been up to," he said, spying their packages. "We wondered where you'd slipped off to."

Finley and Whitt slumped into the deep chairs, signaled the waiter, and ordered two glasses of local wine.

"Can we get you anything else?" Finley asked Peter looking at his half-filled glass.

"I'll have another," he nodded to the bartender. "This one will be gone soon."

"Anything interesting happen here today?" Whitt asked. She was sure if there was any drama to be told, Peter would know about it.

"No, nothing." Peter replied. "Etienne—you know, the producer—he was over to talk to all of us. Production will only be delayed a few days while they try to find a local grip and best boy." Whitt figured those were some terms for people like Julien who handled sound, but she wasn't interested enough to ask.

"Where is everybody?" Finley asked.

"Most went over to the other hotel to have lunch and swim. Gavin stayed in his room. Stacey couldn't get him to go over," he said. "But Stacey wanted to go." He was taking long pulls on his drink and traded his glass out as soon as the new drink came. Finley looked at Whitt, eyebrow raised.

"You decided not to go over?" Whitt asked.

Peter looked up. "I'm not sure I would have been welcome," he muttered glumly.

"What happened?" Finley asked. Something happened today. Something Peter didn't want to talk about.

"They let me go." Peter spoke quietly after a long pause, "Said I was drinking too much again. Etienne told me he could smell it on my breath this morning. So they let me go."

Finley and Whitt turned to face him. "We're so sorry. Will you be okay?" They wanted to be helpful, but neither was sure that she should lend him money to get home. In his current state, the money would never be seen again.

"Yes, I'll be fine. I booked a flight to London for early tomorrow." He shrugged. "No point in sticking around."

They all sat quietly, sipping their drinks. Finley and Whitt didn't know what else to say. After a while, Peter emptied his drink and stood up. "It has been a pleasure, ladies. I'm going to get some dinner. I would invite you, but I don't think I would be good company."

Finley stood to shake his hand. "If we don't see you tomorrow, travel safely. And good luck."

Whitt pushed her chair back and leaned over to give Peter a kiss on both cheeks. "I'm so sorry. You take care of yourself." With that, Peter turned and left.

Whitt signaled the waiter. She was switching from sauvignon blanc to a bourbon neat. Finley raised a finger to indicate she would have the same. It had been an interesting day. She wondered what new news the inspectors would have.

When their bourbons arrived, Finley leaned back, staring at the stars still visible in the city lights. "We have gone a whole day without talking about the murder," she noted. "Maybe now we can focus on my story. Casablanca or Fes?"

Whitt smiled. "I say Casablanca."

"Then, here's looking at you, kid." Finley mimicked. "When we finish these, let's go book a riad in Casablanca." She raised her glass and took another sip. The golden liquid burned as she drank. *They can take all this intrigue and shove it.*

FINLEY AND WHITT FINISHED THEIR drinks and the double order of
briouats, stuffed with meat and spices, that they had ordered
after Peter had left. Both sisters were ready to be done with
the movie crew and all the twists and turns in this murder
mess. Finley had decided that, whether it offered a unique angle or
not, a story on the movie being made in Morocco was not in the
cards. She would work with the pictures she had taken in Tangier
and Chefchaouen plus whatever travel insights she might get in
Casablanca and Fes into something interesting. Without the drama
of the movie crew.

Heading back to their room, they were struck by the eerie
silence in the hall. Maybe everyone had decided to take dinner at
the Villa de la France. Finley had almost unlocked the door when
she heard movement in their room. She stopped, key suspended
in midair and waited, listening closely to see if she heard it again.
She did—the opening of drawers. Whitt saw Finley pause and
waited for some indication of the cause. When Finley turned, Whitt

backed into the stairwell. "Someone is in the room. Do you still have the keys to the car?" Whitt nodded.

Finley quickly led the way down the stairs, stopping at the closest landing to open the large carved armoire and deposit their purses and the bags laden with purchases. "Grab your passport and some money and put the rest in here," she urged. "Hurry!" She thought she could hear some movement in the hall somewhere above.

Finley grabbed her passport, some cash, and her phone, shoving the passport and money in her bra and the phone in her dress pocket. She was glad she was still in her walking shoes, but wished she had on jeans or something that didn't restrict her movement. She quietly closed the armoire door, putting the key securely under the flap of her shoe. Whitt was already halfway down the back stairs, almost to the arch heading into the garage when she saw a man speaking hurriedly on his phone and saw a head pop over the railing.

Whitt hugged the wall, pushing hard against the panel nearest the stairs. She pulled Finley into the portal, closing the door behind them, and ran.

There was no map this time, and no time for them to orient themselves in the dim passageway. They had entered a different portal from the one they had used before, that much they knew, but they couldn't remember how far off the original starting point they actually were.

Whitt had led before. This time, she led again. Finley stayed close, listening hard for any indication of what was on the other side of the wall. If they could exit into the alley as they had before, assuming that the exit wasn't barred, they could enter the garage, get the car, and head somewhere safe. Wherever that was.

When they reached a T-junction, Whitt turned left and ran down the straight passageway. As she neared the end, she heard voices speaking loudly in Arabic. Both sisters stopped and waited in the shadows between the lanterns. No sound behind them and only voices ahead. "It's the office," Finley mouthed, nodding ahead. "I think we turn left. If we see the stairs, we're okay."

Whitt nodded and stepped out into the dim light. She waited until the voices started again before making a left and dashing down the stairs. Finley kept close. The last thing they needed was to be separated. They took another left at the next intersection. They should be near the reflecting pool and hear the kitchen noise straight ahead. The clatter from the kitchen sounded as if on cue. *Now a quick right, then a left, and out the door.*

The door loomed ahead. When they got into the alley, they would be exposed for a few feet before they could duck back into the garage. If they stayed close to the wall, they might be able to blend into the shadows. Whitt waited until Finley was right behind her. She paused again before slowly opening the door. She saw no one in the alley. She flung open the door and turned to run. As she moved into the alley, a hand reached out and grabbed her from behind. "Run!" was all she could say before a large hand covered her mouth.

Finley was halfway through the doorway when she heard the scuffle and her sister cry out. She turned to see Whitt being picked up and carried by a large man in jeans and a linen jacket. *Inspector Evans?* At that moment she heard a sound behind her. Out of the corner of her eye, she saw a familiar face before a cloth covered her nose, and the world went black.

Whitt lay blindfolded and bound in the bed of some sort of vehicle. She couldn't decide if it was a van or a truck. Whatever it was, it had terrible suspension. She was as banged up from bumping along the god-awful road as she had been when she had tried to fight the person whose hand covered her mouth. *I hope Finley got away. If not, she would be here with me. Why would they separate us? God, please let her be okay.*

Her mind raced. Better to focus on what she could hear and smell than speculate on what she could never know. The vehicle appeared to be off-road, given the bumpiness of the trip. She didn't think she had been in the vehicle more than thirty minutes or so. She had started to lose track of time, but the initial trip had been smooth on a road. Only the last five minutes were on a dirt track. Were there parts of the city that had dirt roads, or were they outside Tangier? She really couldn't tell, and even if she could, she didn't know the area well enough to even begin to orient herself. She relaxed her body against the ruts in the road. *I need to conserve energy. I don't know what is going to happen.*

When Finley came to, her head hurt like the dickens. She felt sick to her stomach, and the room was spinning. *Damn, I hope they didn't use ether. It makes me sick as a dog.* She appeared to be locked in the room of a small house. She could smell food cooking somewhere near—onions and spices. *I hope they don't give me anything to eat. It isn't going to stay down.*

Her hands and feet were bound, but she wasn't blindfolded. She was glad for that. She hated the dark, and while the room was unlit, she could see the moon through a narrow break in the shutters. She pulled herself into a sitting position as best as she could and scooted back to lean on the wall. *I hope there are no spiders. That is all I need. Whitt would be having a fit at just the thought of spiders. Whitt. Where is she?*

She slowed her breath and listened for any sign of movement. From beneath her, she could feel heavy footsteps and hear muffled voices. She needed to get these ropes off her hands and feet so she could move around. She began to work the ropes back and forth, gritting her teeth as the thick coils bit into the skin on her wrists. She paused when she heard a door downstairs close. She waited. Nothing. The only thing she heard appeared to come from outside.

As her eyes adjusted to the dark, she looked around the room to see if there was anything she could use to free her hands. She saw nothing. The room was empty. *Then twist away.* She returned to twisting the ropes back and forth, stretching her hands apart as she worked. After some time, the ropes loosened enough for her to slip one hand out, and then the other. *Thank goodness whoever tied these wasn't a Boy Scout.* Her wrists were raw and bleeding in places, but there wasn't time to care. She quickly untied the ropes around her feet and quietly pulled herself to stand. She had been sitting for a long time and her feet were unsure under her. She leaned on the wall and listened again. Still nothing. *They aren't going to stay away forever. Now may be your only chance.*

Finley used the wall to steady herself and moved quietly toward the door. She reached for the handle and rattled it. It was locked. But the key was still in the door. She pulled several dinar bills from her bra and rolled them into a tight funnel. She then slid her passport through the gap under the door. She waited, listening for any sound of her captors returning. Still nothing. She quickly stuck the rolled bills into the keyhole and pushed hard. Nothing. She retightened the coil and tried again. This time the key fell onto the passport and she slid it back under the door.

Finley opened the door slowly. *Lord, don't let there be a guard outside that I have to go through. I don't have energy for that.* There was no one. She quietly started down the stairs, careful of squeaky steps and the shaky railing. There was no one to hear it. The house was empty. There were two low doors on either side of the room. She stood, trying to remember the orientation of the room upstairs and from which side of the house the sound of the closing door had come. *I think I need to head the other way.*

She inched open the door on the far side of the room. It appeared to lead into a narrow street. She saw no one. Once outside, she closed the door quietly, and using the wall of the house as cover, moved to the end of the alleyway. She guessed she was still in town from the noise of the traffic, but clearly off the beaten track. She needed to find her way back to a major thoroughfare without alerting her captors. She needed to stay hidden until she could find a taxi or bus to take her home. *Home where? To the hotel? To the police?*

She started. The police? Could she trust them? That had looked like Inspector Evans who was carrying away her sister. And the other person she had seen before she blacked out, she also remembered as being with the police. She needed to sneak back into the hotel to get a few things to hold her over until she figured out what to do. Maybe the embassy could help. She walked along the side of the road, slipping between the narrow houses whenever a car passed by.

After thirty or so minutes of walking, she reached a main road and spotted a taxi. She flagged him down and gave him the name of a hotel several streets over from the Sultan. She must have looked like quite a sight, hair on end, dirty and bleeding, but the driver either didn't see or didn't care. *Mama was right, comportment is everything.*

Finley heard the call to prayer as she approached the Hotel Sultan. She checked her watch. 3:50 a.m. She had always been comforted by the sound of the *muezzin*, his voice breaking the silence of the morning. Today, it suggested normalcy, some routine that structured the chaos. She stayed in the shadows and entered through the garage, sliding between the barrels that blocked the entrance. She stepped quietly through the service door, propped open by early arriving staff. *God loves me.* She prayed that she would enter the room and find Whitt sitting on the bed, wondering where the hell she had been all night.

When she reached the landing, their handbags and shopping bags were still in the armoire. She retrieved her room key from her backpack and peeked around the corner. No one was about. She hurried down the hall and slipped into the room. Afraid the running water of a shower might alert the staff, she settled for washing her face in a basin of silently dribbling water. She pulled on jeans and a T-shirt, and threw a couple of changes of underwear, some sweats, and another T-shirt into her backpack. By now, she heard activity in the hall. Porters moving up and down the corridor in preparation for guests awakening.

Someone stopped in front of her door. She froze. A sheet of paper slid under the door and the person moved on. She waited for a minute or two and then quietly bent to pick it up. It was addressed to her. *"This is Whitt's friend, David. Arriving at 3:00 p.m. today (Tuesday) on Emirates from Dubai. Surprise for Whitt. David."*

Finley smiled ruefully at the message. *Won't he be surprised when he finds out she isn't here.* Finley started to tear up. *That will do you no good. Get a grip, girl.*

Finley went into the bathroom, closed the door, and dialed the number he had given in the message. The number rang a few times. *I hope he isn't on a plane. This isn't something you leave in a text.*

"Hello," a voice answered.

"David? This is Finley," she whispered. She hurried on. "Look, I only have a couple minutes to talk. I'm not trying to be rude, but I need you to listen first.

"We've been kidnapped. I don't know by whom," she continued in a hushed voice. "Whitt and I were separated. I don't know where she is." Her voice broke and she struggled for control. "Are you in Dubai yet? When will you get here?"

There was silence on the other end of the phone—a silence so long that Finley thought she had lost the connection. "I should be there in ten hours. I am in Dubai, and my flight leaves in another hour," he responded.

She could hear him gulp. "Where are you? Are you hurt?" he paused. "Is she? Did you go to the police?"

"I'm at the hotel. I escaped. I can't stay here. I thought she might've come back here, but she didn't. I'm going to write her a note and then leave." She continued, "I don't know if I can trust the police. When I figure out a place that's safe, I'll text you and let you know."

"Where will you go?" he asked.

"I don't know," she mumbled. "I'll think of something." She knew she didn't sound sane. She didn't know for sure that she was. "I've got to go." She ended the call and stuck her cell in her jeans pocket. She wrote Whitt a short note, and stuffed David's message in her pack.

Finley knew she couldn't risk getting caught by the staff or Sayeed using the stairs and was wary of trying the secret passage again given recent history. She couldn't trust anyone. She opened the French doors and stepped onto the small balcony. The street was some ways down, too far to try to climb, but the bathroom balcony was beside a set of outdoor stairs that led down to the street. If she could get across to the other balcony, she would be home free. *Why couldn't the bathroom have doors or a window too? Oh well.*

Finley flung her backpack over to the bathroom balcony. It hadn't been a hard throw. She needed to be sure the bag cleared the gap, but she also didn't want to damage her camera equipment. She climbed up onto the bedroom balcony. *This is crazy.* She stood on the wide edge and tried to mentally measure the size of the gap between the two balconies. It seemed to be less than a meter. *Don't try to gauge it, idiot. Just jump.* With the last two words, she launched herself off the ledge and landed on the edge of the bathroom balcony. She leaned forward to adjust her balance, stepped off the ledge onto the balcony, and grabbed her backpack. She sighed in relief.

At the foot of the stairs, she hung back, looking both ways to see if there was anyone on the street that gave her concern. Seeing no one, she walked quickly to the corner and hailed a taxi. She pulled a card from her pack and handed it to the driver. She looked back as they turned the corner. Leaning against a house opposite the hotel was the man in the tan suit. She prayed he hadn't seen her or at least wouldn't follow her.

The address on the card was only ten minutes from the hotel. She paid the taxi and walked slowly to the door. She hoped this wasn't a mistake. She knocked softly, and when there was no answer, she knocked again, harder. The door opened right as the voice behind it asked, "Who is it?" Max stood in torn grey sweats and an LSE T-shirt, a towel drying his still wet dark curls.

"Fin?" His mouth dropped open, his eyes questioning, as if trying to confirm what he was seeing.

"I'm sorry I didn't call first, but I didn't know where else to go," Finley said softly, her chin almost to her chest and eyes lowered. She was two seconds away from tears.

Max stepped back and pulled her inside. "What's happened? Are you all right? Where's Whitt?" He still held her arm, his eyes checking her body looking for injuries.

"I'm okay, but I don't know where Whitt is." Before she could get the words out, she had collapsed in his arms, sobs racking her body so hard that she couldn't speak.

Max stroked her hair and held her. "It's all right. It's all going to be all right."

FINLEY HAD IMAGINED RUNNING INTO Max again under several different scenarios, but none of them include a snotty blubber fest. She was embarrassed, but even more, she was exhausted, mentally and physically. And she was scared.

"I'm so sorry." She stepped back, took a breath, and wiped at her tears with the back of her hand. "I shouldn't have bothered you."

"Yes, you should have," Max countered. He continued in a soft voice. "And you're never bothering me. Let me make you some coffee, and then you tell me the whole story." He led her into the living room and pointed to the couch.

Finley held out her wrists, like a child showing a parent a serious boo-boo that they seemed to have overlooked. "May I have a Band-Aid, please?" she asked.

"Good God, Fin! Who did that to you?" he said angrily. He left the room and came back with a small first aid kit. "Come here." He drew her over to the dining table, laid out a towel, and started cleaning and wrapping her bloody wrists." Fin, what happened?" His voice was measured, his brow furrowed.

Finley told him about the noise in their hotel room and their attempt to escape. She recounted seeing Whitt being taken away, the brief glimpse of someone familiar, the house in the outskirts of town, and how her wrists had been injured. She explained her call to David, her balcony adventure, and the man in the tan suit. She also gave him background on the murder and the arrest and all the things that didn't make sense. When she finished, Max sat holding her hands and staring at her in disbelief.

"Let me get you that coffee. Are you sure you don't need a doctor?" He didn't let go of her hands. She savored his warmth. "What time does Whitt's friend get in? I'll go pick him up and bring him here."

He moved to the kitchen and started making coffee, his eyes darting between the coffee pot and Finley's face. "Are you sure you're okay?" he asked. Finley nodded again, stifling a yawn with the back of one of her bandaged hands.

Max turned on the coffee maker and came back into the living room. "I'll make up a guest room for you. You must be exhausted." He started toward the hall. "Have you eaten anything today?"

Finley sat on the edge of the couch. She couldn't remember what day it was or when she had eaten last. She stared at her hands, frowning slightly, "I can rest here, if that's okay. I don't want to put you out. I just need a little rest before I go find Whitt."

"Fin, you're not putting me out." He came back to stand in front of her. "You're in shock. You need some food and rest."

Max went to the hall closet and pulled out a pillow, some sheets, and a light blanket. "I'll make you some soup, and then you can lie down here."

"I'll go back to the hotel after you eat to see if Whitt's returned, and then I'll go get Whitt's friend. You stay here and sleep." He made up the couch and headed to the kitchen. Finley had already leaned her head on her backpack. By the time he turned around again, she had drifted off.

"Poor baby." He gently moved the pack and stuck the pillow under her head. He then pulled off her shoes and repositioned her on the couch before covering her with the blanket, tucking the edge around her. He stood looking at her and smiled.

When he came back down from getting dressed, she was still asleep. He opened her backpack, scrounging around to find David's message. It was folded in one of the side pockets. He took a picture of it and then shoved it back in her backpack. There was more than enough time to check the hotel before heading to the airport.

The young porter at the front desk of the Hotel Sultan had rung up to the room and, getting no answer, had offered to take a message. Max had written a short note that revealed nothing but his cell number. As he was stuffing it into an envelope, Sayeed came out of the office. "Are you being helped?" The porter explained that the gentleman was leaving a message for Whitt. Sayeed's eyes grew large.

"I haven't seen them this morning," Sayeed stated brusquely. "I didn't realize they had friends in the city."

Max smirked and calmly passed the envelope and a tip to the porter. "Please see that this is put under her door. Thanks." He nodded at Sayeed and left.

Outside, he stood pretending to check his watch. He scanned the narrow street, and seeing no one, headed to the corner, entered a small café, and sat down. From the window he had a good view of the front of the hotel and partial view of the alley. He ordered a coffee and a Moroccan pastry and waited. He hoped that he might see Whitt and bring her back with him.

He remembered her from a few years back. Tall, pretty, and hair a lot longer than Finley wore hers now. He would recognize Whitt, he was sure. His mind drifted and soon it was Finley's long hair, not Whitt's that he recalled. Back then, it had been almost to her waist. She had worn it in a bun or high ponytail most of the time but when she was home, she would let it down. It was such beautiful, heavy hair with a luster that gleamed a burnished bronze in the sunlight. Such beautiful hair. *Why had she cut it?*

After an hour, Max paid the check and left. He caught a cab back to the house. Finley was still curled up on the couch asleep. The pillow was wet with tears. A few clung to her cheek. She had cried herself to sleep. Worried about Whitt. *We'll find her. I promise.* He grabbed the car keys from the basket in the hall and headed out to the alley to get the car. He would be early, but he didn't want Finley to wake up and insist on going with him to the airport. She needed to rest if she was going to be of any help in trying to track her sister.

Max parked the car in the small short-term lot in front of the airport and headed in. Since the two men didn't know exactly what the other looked like, it was better to stand in plain view. Max had sent David a text letting him know that he was there to pick him up. He didn't say anything about Whitt or Finley. That was a better conversation for the ride into the city. Surprisingly, the flight was early. Customs was a rather routine affair and would take no time at all, especially during the off-season.

David recognized Max easily. He was clearly one of the taller men in the airport. Actually, the two of them were the tallest men in the airport. Max threw up his hand to be sure David saw him.

"David?" Max asked. "Hope you had a good flight—under the circumstances."

David smiled sadly. "Still no word?" He shook hands and walked with Max out to the car. He threw his bag on the back seat and hopped in beside Max.

"Nope. Finley's pretty torn up about it," Max said as he turned onto the highway. Any other time he might have taken the scenic route. Today, though, he wanted to get back to the house and figure out how to find Whitt. They could sightsee when this was all over.

"Has Finley contacted the police yet? She said that she wasn't sure who she could trust." David paused. "I'm glad she found you. She sounded so lost."

"Yeah, she still isn't sure about the police. She thinks she saw one police officer when they were taken and then she thinks another one carried Whitt away. She doesn't know what's going on," Max said. "She's afraid it's connected to the murder at the hotel."

David turned in his seat to face Max. "What murder? Finley didn't say anything about a murder." Max filled him in as best he could on what had happened to Ross Malcolm and that a suspect had been arrested. David sat listening, his eyes closed tightly.

"But I don't think Finley—or Whitt, for that matter—believes that the person arrested did it," Max conveyed. "Finley keeps talking about the pieces not fitting. She's asleep now. Maybe she'll make more sense when she gotten some rest."

Finley was awake and sipping coffee when Max and David got back. Finley stood to greet Whitt's friend. She smiled, taking him in as she approached. He was taller than she had imagined, almost as tall as Max, with an athletic build. His hair was more ginger than blond, but Whitt described his eyes well—pools of liquid blue—and his smile was inviting. So much so that instead of shaking his hand, Finley wrapped her arms around his neck and kissed his cheek, her eyes brimming with tears.

"Not the most pleasant welcome, but it'll get better," she stated stoically. "I know it'll get better soon. We'll find her."

Max put David's bag at the bottom of the stairs and invited him into the living room. Finley had folded up the sheets and blanket and stacked them with the pillow on the arm of one the easy chairs. She sat back down, nursing her coffee and staring straight ahead.

"Can I offer you coffee, tea—a drink? Have you eaten?" Max looked at David and then over at Finley. "I can't get this one to eat anything. You hungry yet?" She shook her head.

"I had something on the plane. But coffee would be nice." David sat down beside Finley. "What did you decide about the police?"

Finley looked over at him. "I haven't called them because I think at least some of them are involved. I don't know what's going on, but it has something to do with the hotel." She continued, "One person has been killed. We were kidnapped and one of us is still missing. I tried to call the embassy, but it's some holiday, and no one is there until tomorrow.

"We are going to have to find her ourselves."

Whitt felt the van move back onto a smoother road surface. She still couldn't tell where she was. She thought she could smell the sea, but it smelled more like sewage than surf. The bumping stopped so that she could stretch her body a bit. Her side ached from the constant pummeling of the rutted-out road. They must have hit every pothole there was. She had tried at some point to flip herself over to her other side but had ended up facedown, never quite able to make the full rotation, so she had rolled back over to her original position. She knew her side was purpled with bruises and her head hurt from hitting the metal floor several times. *They could have at least put a rug down.*

After what seemed like a lifetime, the vehicle slowed and then stopped. They had stopped several times before. Once for what felt like days. But each time, they had continued after talking to someone on the phone. Whitt prayed that her captors hadn't decided this time to drive her out to the middle of nowhere and shoot her.

When the door opened, she held her breath. Two large, rough hands grabbed her feet and pulled her to the edge of the flatbed. Another set of hands grabbed her shoulders. She smelled the strong saltiness of the ocean. *They are going to toss me into the sea. I am going to drown!* The thought terrified her, and she started to struggle against the two men carrying her. She could hear them cursing in Arabic as she kicked out and screamed under the gag in her mouth.

Before long they dropped her into what felt like a pile of grass and reeds. She heard feet running away and then truck doors opening and slamming. A truck engine started, and tires squealed. Before long, she was left with silence. *They have left me out here to die. The bastards were too cowardly to kill me. Thank God.* She listened closely. Under the drone of some sort of flying insects, she could hear boat horns signaling in the night. She assumed it was still night. She had no idea of the time.

She began to pick at the twine they had used to tie her. She had tried to untie herself earlier, but the bumping had made concentrated effort impossible. Now at least she could focus on unraveling the loose ends of the string. She almost had it off. Once she got her hands free, she pulled off the blindfold and the nasty rag that had been stuffed in her mouth, spitting several times to clear the foul taste.

She sat up and began to untie the thicker ropes that bound her feet. She could see that it was day, but she hadn't checked her watch. She wanted to get unbound first. She was soon able to slip one foot and then the other out of the ropes. She carefully raised herself to her knees and waited until her balance stabilized. She slowly put one foot under her and then the other. Her legs were too weak to hold her, and she fell back into the reeds.

She checked her watch. It was just past noon. She was glad that it was daylight. Trying to find her way back to the hotel at night would be difficult. It appeared that she was near one of the harbors so if she kept the water to her right, she thought, she should be heading back toward Tangier.

She pulled herself to her feet again, first getting to her knees and then one foot after the other. She leaned over with her hands on her knees until she regained her balance and then stood up. She tentatively stepped out, careful to check herself before fully committing to taking a step. After a couple of minutes, she was able to walk at a slow pace toward the harbor. She took out the chopstick that was holding her hair and let it fall. She ran her hands through the tangled mass, coiled it up again and reinserted the chopstick to hold it tight. *I may smell like a water rat, but I can at least attempt some semblance of proper hygiene and not look like a wild woman.*

She walked for what seemed like hours until she reached a narrow frontage road that ran along the harbor. The traffic had increased, and after a time, she was able to hail a taxi. She asked the driver to let her off just outside the Kasbah gate. She knew the way down the hill and could spot, from that angle, any activity that might prove dangerous. She had planned her approach so that she could slip into the alley, through the garage and up to the room, hopefully without anyone seeing her. She hoped Finley would be waiting for her. God, she hoped Finley was there.

It was now almost four o'clock in the afternoon. *Goodness, I could use a drink. A long, hot bath. And a drink. Bourbon neat.* Whitt saw the hotel in sight. She came down the hill, staying close to the walls of the houses, checking every so often for movement around her. When she reached the café on the corner, she stopped. She was hungry. She couldn't remember when she had eaten last. She stepped into the door and ordered a coffee and a savory, sitting in the corner window where she could see both the alley and the front door of the hotel. She ate hungrily. Mama would be mortified. But Mama wasn't here.

When she finished, she paid and moved to the door. She looked up and down the street again. Seeing no one, she crossed the narrow road quickly and headed into the alleyway. She slipped into the garage and headed toward the archway, but before she could reach it, a hand pulled her into the shadows. She fought hard against the arm that tried to wrap around her waist until she spun around and saw that the arm belonged to Max. Behind him stood David. She was confused, frightened. Her legs gave way. Max caught her before she hit the cement floor of the garage.

Max and David had made good time coming back from the airport. They had gone straight to the house and unloaded David's bag. Finley had been up. She had given them more information on the kidnapping, the murder, and her suspicions.

Finley knew that Max had gone by the hotel before he picked up David and had waited hoping Whitt would show up, to no avail.

He wanted to go back and see if she had tried to sneak in the hotel. Finley had mentioned the note she had left letting Whitt know she was to come to MM's—Mad Max, their nickname for Max. She had given her his number but no address.

Max and David had decided to try again at the hotel, this time waiting in the alley. They knew she wouldn't try to come through the front door. More likely through the garage based on what Finley had mentioned. Finley would wait for her at Max's just in case they missed her. As they expected, they had been able to intercept her in the garage.

David scooped up Whitt's limp form from Max and carried her to the car. Max opened the door and helped David slide her into the back seat. David hopped in the back, lifting Whitt's head gingerly to rest against his chest. Max drove quickly out of the alleyway, through the back streets until he reached home. He pulled into the alley near his house, and hurriedly opened the garden door. He quickly returned to help David carry Whitt into the house.

When Finley saw her sister, she almost fainted herself. "What happened? Where did you find her?" she asked, worry etching her face.

"Is she hurt? What does she need?" She ran to get the pillow and put it on the couch so that Max could lay her down.

"She just fainted. I think she's okay." Max stepped aside so that David could kneel close to Whitt's head.

"I'll get her some brandy. That might bring her around." He went into the kitchen and pulled open the cabinet. He grabbed a snifter and then reached into a cupboard underneath to pull out a bottle of brandy. He held the snifter under Whitt's nose until she drew back and sat up. "Drink this."

Whitt hesitated and then looked around. Finley spoke up. "It's okay. You're at Max's. David came to surprise you. I came here after I got back to the hotel."

Finley could tell that Whitt was still processing everything, and that David and Max were pieces that seemed out of place. Whitt took the snifter from Max and took a sip. She still said nothing. David didn't try to talk to her. He just knelt beside her, looking at her with a lopsided grin.

"Where'd you come from?" she finally asked.

"Georgia. I was going to surprise you, but I guess the surprise was on me," David replied. He slid his arm under her shoulders and pulled her to him. Whitt nestled into his shoulder and stayed there.

Finley picked her cup up from the coffee table and moved into the kitchen. She was tired again. So tired. Max slipped behind her, took her cup, and placed it on the counter. He put his arm around her waist and let her rest her head on his broad chest. "She's home. She's okay. And you're okay, too," he murmured. She relaxed into his arms.

It was hard rapping on the door that broke her quiet. Max released her and headed into the hall. The door opened and Finley heard voices. She recognized the other voice besides Max and moved swiftly to stand beside her sister. *He isn't going to get her again.*

Max came into the living room, followed by Inspector Evans and the man in the tan suit. Finley looked for something with which to defend herself. Why wasn't Max reacting? He couldn't be in on it too, could he? She was confused again. Her head ached and she didn't know whether she was going to be able to control the fear.

"Misses Blake, are you both all right? We've been trying to follow you, but you got past us," Inspector Evans explained. "Have you been hurt?"

Finley heard but didn't understand. "You've been following us?" She finally articulated the question. Whitt sat staring at the man in the tan suit.

"Does he work with you?" Whitt asked, pointing with her snifter at the man who had now entered the room.

"Yes, he's one of my men. I told him to follow you, but then he lost you," Evans indicated. "And when he saw these men put you in the car, he called me, and we followed them here."

"Well, you both should be fired!" Whitt said languidly, her eyes closed. "You're like firefighters coming after the house has burned down. We don't need you now." She was clearly not amused. If she had had the energy to banish them from the house, she would have. *Mama would have.*

Evans looked puzzled. Finley tried to explain. "We were both abducted and had to make our way back by ourselves." Her voice was tired. "Clearly, your protection didn't help us much."

Evans noticed her wrists. "Who did that to you?" his voice was steely, his eyes angry.

"I injured them trying to get the ropes off," Finley explained quietly. "My sister probably has souvenirs of her adventure as well."

"Thank God they didn't kill you. Mr. Laur was not so lucky," he said, hoarsely.

Whitt opened her eyes and focused on Evans. "What do you mean? What happened to Julien?"

"Julien Laur was found stabbed to death this morning a few streets away from the hotel," Evans stated. "We had released him until the trial. It appears he was safer in jail."

FINLEY PULLED OUT A DINING chair and eased herself into it. She was shaking uncontrollably. She didn't know why. She hadn't known Julien well, but the fact that people kept dying scared her. She looked over at Whitt. She realized how lucky they had been. How close both may have been to dying.

"Do you have anyone in custody yet?" Finley closed her eyes and clasped her hands together to reduce the tremors. She wanted whoever was hurting people caught. Now. She wanted to hurt someone for hurting her sister, for hurting her, for hurting those that they knew.

"No one yet. We've moved up the timing of the raid we had planned for the hotel. That should be happening as we speak," Evans said.

"Raid on the hotel? Why?"

"If I may," Evans pointed at a chair. This was going to be a long story, seemingly. Max pulled up chairs for himself and the man in the tan suit and waited. "As you know, I'm Inspector Gareth Evans from Interpol. This is Taylor. He works with me."

"Interpol?" Whitt asked. She was fully alert now. She had swung her legs to the floor and patted the seat beside her for David. "Why is Interpol involved?"

Finley closed her eyes again. Her hands were still shaking. They had gotten mixed up in something bigger than just murder. *This is bad. God, we were lucky to get away with just bruises. It would have killed Mama—and Daddy—if anything had happened to either of us.* Tears slid down her cheeks. Max moved his chair closer and wrapped her hands in his.

"For the past nine months, we've been tracking the movements of Sayeed and a man we know only as Georg, a major player in the human trafficking market between Northern Africa and Europe," Evans related. Whitt sucked in a breath when trafficking was mentioned. She remembered the harbor where they had left her. Had they planned to sell her and then changed their minds? "We knew Sayeed was involved but didn't know how."

"We placed men inside the hotel as porters, waiters, and cooks so that we would have enough coverage throughout the hotel," Evans continued. "Early on, we confirmed that Sayeed was involved in passports and money laundering—the front and back ends of the business—but no actual transport. We wanted to get the traffickers, so we had to wait."

"We'd hoped to get a bit more time to flush out the kingpins, but with two murders, we can't wait any longer."

"So, what happens now?" Max asked, nodding at Finley and Whitt. "And are they safe?"

"When we finish the sweep this evening, they should be okay," Evans said. "We're bringing in everyone involved that we know of."

"Including some members of the local police who've proven to be less than reputable," he added as a look of disgust crossed his face. "We can hold them for forty-eight hours at least. We're hoping that those not in the net will try to pack up, and we can grab them too."

Finley had opened her eyes slowly. Her jaw was still clenched shut, but her breath and hands were now steady. She remembered the familiar face she had seen before she blacked out. It had been one of the chief inspector's sergeants. Was the chief inspector involved? She didn't want to know. "You think the traffickers killed Ross and Julien? But why? What did they see? What did Sayeed think we saw?"

"We don't know. That's what we're hoping to find out." Evans looked at Finley's jaw, and his voice softened. "But you should be safe now."

Evans listened to Whitt and Finley's description of their abduction, taking notes as they spoke. After a time, he stood. The man in the tan suit stood too.

"We'll send teams out to canvas locations that match these descriptions. We'll find them. Just to be certain, though," Evans smiled. "I'm going to leave Taylor outside. I'm sure he will bend over backward to redeem himself."

Max walked Evans and Taylor out and came back to stand in the doorway. Finley sat rigid in her chair, but Whitt had leaned her head on David's shoulder and was finishing the rest of her brandy. The sun had dropped, and he could hear the evening call to prayer at the nearby mosque. "Anybody hungry? I can cook, or we can order in."

"Let's order in, if it's convenient," David said. "These two have had enough excitement for today, I think." Whitt nodded, her head still resting on his arm.

"Fin, anything you want in particular?" Max asked, a look of concern in his face. "You haven't eaten in a couple of days." Finley shook her head.

"Nope, just some bread," she uttered. "That's all I think I can keep down. They gave me ether." Max and Whitt both frowned, knowing what anesthesia did to Finley.

"Whitt? David? Anything you're craving?" Max asked.

"Whatever you order is fine," David said. "And this one is on me. Your whole day has been disrupted. It's the least I can do." Max started to protest and then gave up.

By the time Max and David returned from the little restaurant around the corner with bags filled with mezze, *bastilla*, two different tagines, condiments, and bread, Whitt had cleaned the first layer of grime off herself and changed into the clean T-shirt and sweats that Finley had brought. Meanwhile, Finley had rummaged through the cabinets and found plates and glasses to set the table. "Do you have any wine?" Whitt asked Max as she entered the room looking slightly less distressed.

"Guess you don't know me that well. There's always wine." Max set the bags down and opened a narrow closet door. Inside, stacked in wooden cubes, were at least sixty bottles of wine—Moroccan, French, Italian, Hungarian, and even a Moldovan Fetească neagră. "Not a large selection, but you should find something you like."

Finley chuckled to herself. *Max's house without wine would be like Mama's without butter. A sorry state indeed.*

Over dinner, the four tried to make sense of what they had heard. *Glad we held onto our passports, or our faces might have shown up in Zagreb, Istanbul, or a number of cities worldwide,* Finley thought. *Evans's role with Interpol and the way he had interacted with the police fit, but that didn't explain why Sayeed, and whoever he worked for, would kill Ross and Julien. What had they seen that made them targets?*

"I know Interpol thinks the traffickers killed Ross and Julien, but something isn't tying together for me," Whitt twisted her mouth, her brows knitted. "It's not fitting with what we know. Maybe saying it out loud—"

"—and to people who weren't there," Finley added. "I agree—something is off."

Finley started recounting in some detail her first afternoon and evening at the riad—who was at the table when she went to the bar, where they sat, what they said, what people did. She had had breakfast the next morning in her room and made calls to the *Traveler's Tales* contacts, setting up interviews until she picked up Whitt at the airport. Was there someone on that list that had caused Sayeed concern? But how would he have known since she had used her cell phone with the local SIM card for that? Was the room bugged? Now she was starting to get paranoid.

After she and Whitt had arrived from the airport, they had gone up for a drink and a light dinner. Whitt described who she met, what they talked about at her end of the table, and whether there was anything of note before Gavin's scream and the rush out to the hall. Nothing seemed out of place. Besides the body hanging from the chandelier.

"Did anyone explain how the body got there?" David asked. "You said he was an average or above average size man. That isn't something you just chuck over the balcony."

Max added, "If he was pushed, he would have fallen straight down. Not that far out. And you said the edge of the light was pretty far from the railing."

"Do you think he could've been pushed hard enough to have arched out and gotten hung by accident?" Whitt asked.

"Even so, that doesn't point to who pushed him," Finley pointed out. "To end up like that, it would've had to have been a really hard shove. And he would've had to have been surprised, or he would've tried to catch himself."

"That leaves out the women," Whitt remarked. "None of them—including us, who don't have a motive—would be strong enough. And they were all on the terrace with us."

"So, what about the guys?" David asked. "Who were the brawniest?"

Whitt and Finley took turns throwing out names.

"Thomas."

"Allan."

"Gavin, now that we know he was special ops or whatever the Brits call it."

"Julien is out. He just didn't look strong enough to have killed Ross—and we know his death wasn't a suicide."

"And Peter's too old. He's in good shape, but that would be a stretch."

"So, we are back to someone from the outside killing him—one of Sayeed's goons."

"But why?"

Finley nibbled on a piece of flatbread and drank her tea. *Damn, I need a drink. But hurling is not polite.* "I say we leave it alone and go to Casablanca for a few days. We can leave tomorrow morning and get there by lunch time. Evans has this under control."

"That would get you out of the city," Max opined. "In case Sayeed or Georg decide to clean up any loose ends."

He grinned and waited for Finley's reaction. She turned to look at him with a pout. "You trying to get rid of us for good?"

"Never."

Finley returned his smile. *At least we can still be friends. I miss joking with him. It feels so . . . comfortable.* She got up and headed into the kitchen. "Anyone want tea . . . or coffee?" shooting a glance at Max.

"If you're going to make some coffee, I'll take some," Max said and leaned back in his chair to stretch his long legs. David and Whitt shook their heads. Whitt pointed to her wine glass.

"So, you guys up for a couple of days in Casablanca then?" Finley asked again after a while, bringing two mugs of steaming coffee back to the table. She pulled off a hunk of the cinnamon flatbread that Max had brought for dessert and put the rest of the buttery round on his plate. He bit into his piece of the sticky pastry matter-of-factly, like they were supposed to share.

"Yep, works for me," David replied.

Whitt pointed. "I'm with him."

Max looked up from his coffee to catch Finley's eye. "Unfortunately, I have to work. But I could meet you guys for dinner Thursday or Friday whenever you get back." He hoped she would say yes.

"Sure. That would work," Finley replied, trying to mask her disappointment. *Of course, he has to work. You have no right to his time. You can't go back. Whatever there was is gone.* "Can you give us a list of some good places to stay in Casablanca, and maybe some places off the beaten track that would make for a good article?"

Max grabbed some paper from the kitchen counter and started writing. By the time he finished, Finley had a list of at least three riads, a dozen restaurants, and a handful of picture-worthy spots to consider.

"Thanks," she said lightly. "If you guys have finished eating, we better get back to the hotel before it gets too late."

Max looked disappointed. "I thought you were staying here. I made up the beds."

"Sorry to put you out, but we'll be okay now at the hotel," Finley said and returned his gaze. "Whitt doesn't have any clothes. And we both could use a long bath. Besides, our car is over there."

"Then, at least leave David here in case there are no rooms at the Sultan," Max suggested.

Finley sniggered to herself. *Whitt would be happy about that. She and David would share the bed and I would get the couch.*

"Here, take the keys." He reached into his pocket and handed Finley the car keys. "I don't need the car tonight, and you each can drive one over tomorrow."

He paused. "I know you won't wreck it." His smile brought back the image of an accident almost five years ago when Finley had almost totaled her car avoiding a goat that had run into the road. Finley and Max laughed at the memory.

They seemed to enjoy that inside joke, Whitt thought as she watched the two of them. *Maybe? I hope.* "Well, if we are going, we'd better go now. I'm fading fast." She stifled a yawn.

Finley got up and grabbed her backpack. She leaned into David and kissed him on the cheek. "Nice to meet you, and thanks." She squeezed his shoulder. "We'll see you tomorrow about nine o'clock. Sleep well."

By the time she had moved toward Max, he was standing. He reached for her and pulled her to him. He gently kissed her forehead and looked down at her. "Sleep tight. I hope your tummy feels better soon."

She smiled and eased out of his arms. Whitt and David were locked in a thorough kiss, so Finley and Max went into the hall. "Thank you again for everything. I really don't know what I would've done . . ." her voice trailed off.

"No need for thanks. You're safe. That's all that matters." He took her hand and kissed the inside of her wrist, above the bandages. *The way he used to do.* She looked at the loose curls on his lowered head. She so wanted to touch them, but she held back. Instead, she leaned toward the door, signaling her exit. Whitt came around the corner, hair undone, grinning.

"Night," Whitt said, walking as if in a dream, and they were gone.

The Hotel Sultan was lit up like a Christmas tree. Even the alleyway was bright. Finley got out and moved the barrels blocking the entrance enough to allow her to squeeze the car into the garage and find a parking space. She and Whitt got out and used Finley's key to get into the hotel corridor. Neither of them wanted to run into the crew. They didn't want to talk about the murder of Ross or the murder of Julien or the arrest of Sayeed or the raid of the hotel or anything else. They wanted a bath and bed.

Whitt pushed the panel on the wall around the corner from the front desk. She and Finley slipped into the dimly lit passageway. They knew their way by now. There was no need to hurry. They walked the straightaway, then turned slightly to the right, and pushed open the portal. No one was in the hall. A porter could be seen moving quietly on the uppermost level, but besides that, there was no one. They made their way up the back stairs and along the hall to their room. Finley looked again for movement in the hallway. Nothing. She listened for any sound in the room. Nothing.

She opened the door, turned on the light, and checked the bathroom. She then pulled Whitt into the room and hugged her until she thought Whitt might go limp from lack of air. "I love you to bits, kid."

GOOD LORD, I WAS FILTHY. Whitt had had to let out the water and run a second bath. She had showered before she got in, thinking that the shower would knock off the hard dirt, but after ten minutes in her first bubble bath, the water had turned gray, and the big airy bubbles had deflated into a filmy foam on the water. The second bath had fewer bubbles and was starting to cool, but the water was still clear. *I'm clean, at last. I am glad Finley showered first. She'd kill me if I left her with a cold shower.*

Whitt rose from the lukewarm bath and wrapped herself in the large fluffy white bath towels that the porters brought in every morning. Bruises the size of small bats purpled her side and buttocks. Her shoulder had a raw red scrape that had started to scab already. Her other side looked pretty good. A few scrapes but no ugly bruises. She wondered how beat up Finley had gotten.

When she rewrapped Finley's wrists with the gauze that Max had given them, Finley had turned her head away from the rope burns that were still bloody in places. They must hurt like hell. It would take a while for those to completely heal. It would take even longer for both of them to heal emotionally, especially Finley. She must be all twisted up inside seeing Max, having to depend on him, and having him acting like there wasn't a boatload of history that had yet to be unloaded, much less unpacked.

Whitt had to acknowledge that she had a lot of nerve talking about what Finley wasn't facing up to. She had her own elephant in the room that was dancing a jig, begging to be recognized. It felt so easy to lean on David. He was so comfortable, so available, but then again, so was her favorite couch. That didn't mean they should be inseparable. Did she like him because he had been there, or because she really liked him? He did come to surprise her, though. Just like she had hoped he would. Was the kidnapping the reason for her dampened feelings, or was there something else?

Finley looked up from her book when Whitt walked back into the room. "You clean finally? I am so glad I took a shower first. I would've been pissed if I had had to wait for the water to warm up before I could get clean." She sounded like a nursery schoolteacher trying to teach her four-year-old charges about the importance of sharing. She was already resigned to failure.

"But you did get to go first. So, I didn't have to worry about using all the water," Whitt protested as she plopped down on her side of the bed and stuck her toes under the bedspread. "Besides, with your hair that short, you don't use that much water. I had to wash mine three times to get the weeds and grunge out. You didn't get thrown in the muck and reeds. God knows what else was in there."

She scrunched up her face and shuddered. Finley got a mental picture of all the possibilities and kept her mouth shut. Whitt had had the worst of the abduction experiences, by far. Frankly, Finley didn't want to think about it anymore.

"You and Tbilisi Boy seemed to fall right into it. He seems like a nice guy. Fine, to be sure."

Finley wasn't wasting any time getting into Whitt's business, and Whitt knew they were going to talk about it whether she wanted to or not. Finley would have made a great police interrogator. She had that ability to wait you out, with a face as neutral as flour paste, until you started spilling your guts with no way to put a cork in it.

After years of suffering through conversations that had started innocently enough, only to end with confessions of deep, deep secrets, Whitt just decided to give in at the beginning of these talks. It was less painful that way. Like a tooth fell out rather than gotten pulled.

"Yeah, I must've wished harder than I thought," Whitt said and paused, staring at the patterns made by the threads on the spread and tracing them with her finger.

"You sound disappointed."

"Not disappointed. Just confused."

Finley waited.

"I mean, I wanted him to come, and I had in mind all sort of ways I would greet him. What I'd say. And what would happen next . . . you know. And then, I see him, and I faint. I hate women who swoon," she said with a frown, disgust sitting on her curled lip.

Finley adjusted herself in the bed to turn to face Whitt. "I don't think any of this happened like we wanted it to. If we had had our way, we would've gone to the room. I'd have gotten David's note and had to keep a secret for twenty-four hours, which would've had me smirking and grinning all day. And you'd have been pissed because I wouldn't have spilled the beans."

"I really would have been in a foul mood when he arrived. I guess, given the choice, fainting wasn't so bad." Whitt gave a half smile and continued tracing the patterns without looking up. "What if, after all this, I really don't like him as much as I thought I did? How awkward would that be! We have mutual friends."

"You like him. You know you do." Finley stretched out further, resting her head on the double pillows stacked behind her and turned to look at what part of Whitt's face wasn't obscured by a mass of long, straight hair. "So, what's the deal? Why are you shying away from him?"

119

"I don't know," Whitt stopped tracing, her finger held midair, and sighed deeply. "Okay, I'm scared. What if I like him more than he likes me?" She paused again. Then laughter shook her so hard that she fell backward. "God, I sound like I am in middle school!"

"And what did I tell you then?"

"You play the hand all the way, even if you have to bluff."

"You don't fold because you're afraid you'll lose. You play because you think you might win." They said this in unison, laughing through tears that could tip any minute to hysteria. They both sat up after a while. Finley reached and grabbed tissues from the box on the night table and passed a couple to Whitt.

"And what about you?" Whitt's voice was gentle. She knew she had to ask even if it might cause Finley pain. *What's good for the goose is good for the gander.*

Finley knew it was coming. She had been waiting for Whitt to ask. She had been thinking about it herself. Being with Max had been, for lack of a better word, nice. It had been nice, even under the circumstances.

He had made her feel safe—and cared for. In a far different way than they had cared for each other before, but it was comforting to know that he still had her back. *Even after he stabbed you in the heart.* She was happy that she could make a joke of it. *Grow up, kid. At least, you still have a friend. Be glad for that.*

"We might be able to be good friends. I hope so. I think we are past the ugliness, even if we haven't talked about it. I hope we are." She sounded wistful, as if wishing it might indeed make it so.

"I don't think I realized how much I missed him," Finley said with a puzzled look as if this thought had just come to her. "You get used to someone not being there, and then when they're back, you realize there was a hole that you hadn't filled."

Whitt said nothing. Finley thought for a moment that she had fallen asleep. "He cares for you. Maybe we had it all wrong." Whitt's voice had a sadness to it that caught Finley unaware. Her chest seized. Her breath caught. She turned over and hugged her pillow.

"Some day, eh?" Max filled David's glass with an Argentine Malbec that he had brought back from his favorite wine shop in Chelsea last trip. There were times like today when he missed London. If he were home, he would have pulled out a whiskey rather than the wine. He needed something a little stronger. He suspected David did too.

"An understatement. Just glad they're okay."

Max nodded. "You known Whitt long?"

"No, actually only a few months."

Max waited.

"I know, but I thought it would be a fun to surprise her. Besides, I've never been to Morocco. The worst I thought would happen was that I'd travel to Tangier and find out she couldn't care less about me."

"I don't think that was ever likely. If, indeed, actions speak louder than words." Max had a sly smile on his face, remembering Whitt's hair and her expression when she walked out of the door tonight. She cared. His mind flashed back to another girl with long chocolate brown hair and green eyes. Only hers were a dark swamp water green with an intensity that pierced your soul, probing its depths for answers you weren't always ready to share. *Was that what had happened? She wanted answers that I wasn't ready to share. So, she left when she didn't hear what she needed to?* He had never really figured it out. She was there, and then she was gone.

"So, what about you and Finley? Seems like there's history." He hadn't heard anything from Whitt, but he could sense from the tone of Max's voice today that there was or had been more than a professional relationship between them.

Max didn't know how much to reveal. This was Whitt's boyfriend, potentially. He might even be part of Finley's family someday. He needed to tread carefully.

"We were close years ago. I ran into her a couple of days ago at a friend's restaurant. It was good to see her. Wish today's conversations had been under different conditions," he said and paused, his voice softening. "But I'm glad she trusted me enough to let me help her this morning."

David looked at him hard, sensing that there was more than what was being said—a lot more. Now might be a good time to head to bed. Both of them had gone quiet, staring into their wine as if answers to the unanswered might be found there. "I think I'm going to head up, if that's okay. It's been a long day, and I don't want to get left behind tomorrow."

"Sure, the bed is made up. I put your bag upstairs already. I think Fin said they would swing by around eighty thirty or nine o'clock. I think nine thirty or ten is more likely." He chuckled at the thought of Finley trying to get Whitt out of bed, dressed, and fed in time to get over there by 9:00 a.m. "I probably will go for a run around seven or so if you want to join me. No pressure, if you want to rest."

David nodded and headed toward the stairs. He would decide in the morning. Now he just wanted a shower and sleep. He hoped Whitt would finally get some rest. He wished he were there to hold her while she drifted off. She might play Miss Independent, but she had been scared—scared beyond belief.

Whitt and Finley were up at seven so that Whitt would have enough time in the bathroom to get ready. While Finley showered, Whitt ironed hard creases into her navy linen pants and blue-and-white striped French sailor's T-shirt. As she pulled on her white jeans and navy linen tunic, Finley smiled at the starched ensemble laid out on Whitt's bed. *She's been ironing since grade school. Glory be if a wrinkle should deface her royal crispness!*

Much to Finley's surprise, Whitt was dressed in less than an hour, and they were up on the terrace for breakfast a little after eight o'clock. Only Taryn and Anna were upstairs, sitting at a table in the shade. They motioned Whitt and Finley to come over.

"Please join us. Our numbers are few."

Whitt and Finley crossed the terrace and sat at the small, tiled table. "Where is everyone?" They ordered another pot of coffee and some croissants.

"They've all headed to Agadir. To scout. There isn't any need for us yet, so we decided to stay here in relative comfort for a few more days." Taryn took a sip of her coffee.

"There's no telling what sort of accommodations Stacey is going to subject us to once we get on the road," Anna added. "You heard about Peter, I assume." Finley and Whitt nodded.

"He left for London yesterday. I don't know what bits you were here for and what you missed," Taryn said. "Did you have a nice trip?"

Finley and Whitt traded glances. They didn't know where the crew thought they had gone, but they didn't want to talk anymore about the kidnapping or their conversation with Inspector Evans. From Anna and Taryrn's demeanor, it was also evident they hadn't heard about Julien's death. The sisters decided it was best to just play along.

"Yes, it was quite nice. We saw Peter the day that you all went over to the other hotel. We've been away a couple of days. Anything new happen besides that?" Whitt asked.

Anna and Taryn looked at each other in surprise. "You didn't hear about the raid? Sayeed and several of the people in the front office were carted away by the police on the same day that Peter left. They swooped in just like in the movies, except this was for real," Taryn exclaimed.

"Etienne couldn't have staged it better," Anna said as she stretched like a Siamese cat. "That lusciously tall inspector came toward the end to see that everything was all settled. We haven't seen him since. Pity."

"We still have no idea if some of the people who were arrested were responsible for Ross's death. We're completely in the dark, but that is fine with us," Taryn acknowledged. "As long as we aren't in any more danger."

16

DAVID WAS READY AND WAITING for Finley and Whitt when they arrived a quarter past nine. Finley pulled the car into the alley behind the garden and knocked on the side door. Max opened it and met her with a cup of black coffee that smelled of chocolate and roasted cinnamon. She had to smile. He knew her too well. Whitt had come through the front door and was in the hall talking to David in hushed tones. *I hope she gives him a chance. He took a big risk coming to surprise her. If that isn't evidence, what is?*

"Is he ready?" Finley asked, savoring the fragrant steam coming from her coffee.

"Yeah. We got in an early run. And we ate, so you probably don't need to stop until you get to Casablanca. Except for gas." He finished moving the breakfast dishes to the counter and pulled out his computer. "Wish I could go with you. Did you find a place to stay?"

She nodded. "The place on Rue Abda."

"Nice. You'll like it. It has a great view of the sea. And if I'm remembering the right one, really good croissants." He paused for effect. "And good coffee." Their eyes met, and she returned his smile.

"We'd better go. It's not as if they don't have three and a half hours to talk on the way down."

Max grabbed David's bag from the hall landing and shoved it at him with a smile. "Load up," he directed, and David obeyed. He and Whitt headed to the car, but Max hung back. Finley had just put her cup in the sink when he came up behind her and put his hands on her shoulders. She drew in a deep breath and held it.

"When you get back, can we talk?' He slowly turned her around to face him. She had always dreaded it whenever he said that. She hated "talks." They never ended well. But she just nodded. He kissed her forehead, and she slipped out of his grasp and headed to the door.

"See you in a few days. Don't work too hard." She didn't want him to come out, to see them off, to watch them leave. She just wanted to get away, so she closed the door with a quiet click.

They appeared to have missed the morning traffic and were soon on the highway toward Rabat, one of the four Imperial Cities and currently the country's laidback capital. Whitt had again charted the direction and planned the itinerary. They would stop in Rabat, and maybe neighboring Salé, for a quick driving tour and some picture taking before continuing to Casablanca where they would check in and then wander around looking for a good place for a late lunch. Finley still had Max's list, so they wouldn't be without any guidance. Then, depending on how tired they were, they would find some good shopping. *Of course.*

Finley had already planned on being tired to give Whitt and David a little time alone. She could go to the roof terrace that the guesthouse had shown online and shoot some pictures of the rooftops or street scenes. Or she could just sit in her room and work on her story. What she didn't want to do was think. Max had unnerved her with his request for a "talk." *Why can't we just leave things alone? What is there to talk about?*

Whitt was driving while David was supposed to be navigating. He didn't have much to do since the GPS was on, giving Whitt turn-by-turn directions. But he had the map out, and he was pointing out all the obscure towns and villages along the way—Khemis Sahel, Chewaffaae, Moulay Boussselham, Ouled Mesbah. Whitt was laughing at his pronunciation of the run-on Arabic names.

He had plugged his phone into the console and was blaring songs from his playlist. The man had some eclectic taste in music—from Coltrane to Guns N' Roses to Callas. *The boy is deeper than I thought. Interesting.*

The train would have saved them over an hour, but the trip would have been far less fun. After a while in the car, David started singing along to Sting's "Roxanne," and soon, Whitt joined in. She glanced back to see if Finley was singing and nudged her when she saw her older sister laughing at them rather than joining in. Finley finally gave up and added her alto to their slightly off-key tenors. Life felt good, especially when they had been so close to death. She thought of Julien and then Ross, before trying to push the image out of her mind.

Whitt skillfully negotiated the winding streets of Rabat, driving them past the major tourist sites—Challah, the Mausoleum of Mohammed V. When they got to Hassan Tower, however, Finley asked Whitt to find a place to park. She hopped out and ran across the plaza to catch the sun reflecting off the tower and the surrounding ruins.

There was very little to see, since the twelfth-century effort had been abandoned and all that remained were rows and rows of plain white columns contrasting with the ornate red sandstone face of the tower, which was actually the minaret shaft of an incomplete mosque. The dancing light, however, caught Finley's eye, and she spent ten minutes snapping shot after shot until Whitt started laying on the horn.

By the time they got back on the highway to Casablanca almost two hours later, Whitt had David carrying two large canvas bags with tsatskes that she had purchased while Finley was playing photographer in the Kasbah des Oudayas, marveling at the intricately carved sandstone around the walled city's massive doors and the blue-and-whitewashed walls of its interior.

For over an hour, they wandered the curved and narrow pathways, dropping into shopping galleries that were heaven to Whitt and architectural nirvana to Finley. David followed good-naturedly behind Whitt as she ducked in to shop after shop, picking up more things than she could ever use for housewares or gifts.

Her last stop was at a women's cooperative that wove Whitt's beloved textiles. She had to be physically pulled out of the shop to prevent her from purchasing more. When the Kasbah opened to reveal the sea, they stopped for mint tea on one of the terraces that circled the medina before heading back to the car.

"You know you're going to want to shop again in an hour once we get to Casablanca," Finley remarked snidely.

"I know," Whitt replied as she slid behind the wheel. "But you know me. If I can buy it, I will." David looked away, knowing he had no dog in this fight.

"Where are you going to put all this stuff? You haven't unpacked half of the things you brought back from your last trip. You just stuck them in storage."

Finley and Whitt had this conversation every time they took a trip together. Since coming back from Morocco the first time, Finley had packed away many of the table toppers that graced her previous Manhattan apartments, adopting a very sparing design style, adorning her space only with paintings.

Whitt, on the other hand, had acquired so many intriguing, and often rare, art objects that she would from time to time completely change out the décor in her house in Manila, replacing chests or wall hangings that she had tired of with new items pulled from storage.

"And more importantly, how are you going to get all of this back?" Finley continued. She was impressed when Whitt explained. Tbilisi Boy, Finley's new name for David, was going to use his baggage allowance for Whitt, and then arrange with Luka, Whitt's handler, to get the purchases packed and shipped to Manila. David was an exporter. He had the connections to get her items shipped at nominal cost. Finley shook her head and went back to studying some of the shots she had gotten.

The hotel in Casablanca was one that Max had recommended. Just off Rue Sour Jdid near the old medina, the guesthouse reflected traditional Moroccan architecture, but was less regal in style than the riad in Tangier. Tucked between larger apartment buildings and hotels, the Guesthouse Abda had eight well-appointed rooms and a small common area off the lobby. What it lacked downstairs, it made up for with a wraparound patio on the top floor that looked out to the Atlantic.

"I am looking forward to a stiff drink tonight," Whitt noted. "But right now, I want to go sightseeing. You want to rest or wander?" She turned to David, and then to Finley.

"Whatever. I'm with you." David had dropped all the packages in the closet in Whitt and Finley's room. He grabbed his suitcase from Finley, who had carried it up for him, and started for his room. "Thanks."

This boy is going to have a long row to hoe with Whitt, but he seems up for it. "I'm hungry, so I'll head out with you guys until we find food, and then I think I'm going to wander while you shop," Finley said.

They met downstairs after freshening up. Finley had repacked her backpack with a few extra lenses and some filters to help with the glare that bounced off the sand-colored buildings. She pulled out the list of places Max had suggested that she go to get some good shots for her story.

A story she still hadn't thought through yet. She had been sending Dan, her boss, cryptic messages about the trip, ones that left out murder and kidnapping. *I'll think of something. I have another week or so to find an angle and send something back. I've been here less than a week.* She stopped mid-thought. *Damn, a lot has happened.*

"What do you say we head into the medina and find something to eat? The guy at the desk says there are several places we can try."

David had a list written in messy script by the man Finley and Whitt had assumed was the owner. Finley put her list against it and checked off two places that were on both.

"As good a place to start as any."

They set off, soon leaving Rue Abda to walk along a wide boulevard that followed the seaside. Both Whitt and Finley had been drawn to water since they were children. The satisfied look on David's face marked him as a water baby too.

When they entered the towering arched gate that led into the old medina, it was like they had stepped back in time. Cobbled streets lined with workshops and stores and stalls stood in sharp contrast to the bustling metropolis outside the medina walls. Men sat at tables that blocked half of the narrow alleys, drinking fragrant mint tea or dark, thick coffee. No women in sight. Wide-eyed children, curious about the tall strangers, ducked out of slivers of passageways into the small shops that sold fruits and vegetables and other staples. The smells of mint and coffee and spices and ripe fruit made an intoxicating blend.

Whitt stopped in the middle of the street, taking in all the sights and sounds and smells. "I think I might die of sensory overload before we reach the restaurant." She picked up a few apricots at a nearby stall, sniffed them, and then held them out for Finley and David to smell. David leaned into the sweet fragrance of the fruit. His eyes closed, and a grin spread across his face.

"Smells like home." He took the fruit from Whitt's hands, added a few more to the pile, and put them on the counter. "Anything else you ladies want?" Finley and Whitt both shook their heads while he paid the young woman behind the register.

"Where's he from anyway?" Finley asked under her breath.

"California, but don't hold it against him." Whitt knew Finley's bias toward the East Coast. If Finley was going to spend five hours on a plane, she'd prefer heading east to London than west to San Francisco or Los Angeles. Whitt's opinion of California wasn't far off.

"May I have one of the apricots, please?" Whitt held out her hand when David joined them on the street. "Hunger has overtaken me."

David took out two pieces of fruit and handed her the bag. He passed one to Finley and polished the other on his shirt. Finley knew they were taking a risk by not peeling the fruit, but it seemed worth it. She pulled out some tissues, passed them around, and used a few to clean her apricot. When she bit into it, juice spilled from the deep orange yellow flesh and dribbled on her fingers.

"Maybe we should forget the restaurant and binge on these."

"That may be enough for you, but this doesn't even make up an appetizer for me," David laughed, wiping juice off his chin. "The lady said it was just up the street. And that it was well worth it. I think a family member must own it."

The contrasting darkness of the restaurant and the light coming off the street temporarily blinded them when they stepped into the narrow room. There was a garden in the back, which was where most of the tables were. A young man in his mid-twenties wearing a striped *djellaba* grabbed a menu from the counter and led them back to the tiled garden.

They settled into a brightly patterned table in the corner. They ordered a bottle of wine and some carrot dip and bread while they decided what they wanted for lunch.

"Are we having dinner tonight or just mezze?" Finley asked.

"I was thinking we would be kitschy tomorrow and head to Rick's Café, so tonight we can play it by ear," Whitt suggested.

David smiled. He was always hungry, so even if he ate heavily now, he would be ready to find food again later. Whitt seemed used to it. *He's a growing boy.* She was happy just to watch him eat while she nibbled on a salad. That's probably what she would do tonight.

By the time the wine came, they had decided to graze on a mix of mezze and a couscous. David stretched out his legs and sighed as he filled their glasses. "A pretty nice day. An enlightening tour of Rabat, thanks to hers truly. No police, no money launderers, no murderers." He put the bottle down and reached over to a small, potted orange tree. "Knock on wood."

"Yep. We can actually have a relaxing few days before we head back to work. When is your flight back to Tbilisi?" Whitt turned to David. "Maybe we can go out on the same flight."

While they talked flight times, Finley scanned the garden. It was pleasant space—small but well laid out to maximize the cross breeze that came through the wide wooden doors at each end. Pots of flowers mixed in with lemon and orange trees. Finley imagined that when the trees were in bloom the air would be thick with nectar.

Through the far door, she caught sight of someone she surmised might be a foreigner, based on the height and build, wearing a brown *djellaba*. *He must be an expat who's gone local. Those djellabas are probably quite comfortable. If I didn't know better, I would have thought that was a younger Peter.*

When they finished lunch, Finley grabbed her backpack and headed deeper into the medina. Whitt and David had decided to grab a cab to the Corniche where they could stroll—and Whitt could shop. They would do the Central Market and the Hassan II Mosque tomorrow. Today, Finley wanted to wander parts of the old city looking for more fodder for her article. Faces and places that would help her tell the story of Casablanca's captivating mix of old and new.

She wished she spoke Arabic. It would make navigating the web of alleyways in the old medina a lot easier. As it was, she listened for the laughter of children or women talking to customers in the shops to determine which way to turn. While she didn't feel unsafe, she didn't want to end up being stared down by a café full of men whose peace had been invaded by a strange Amazonian woman.

The lengthening shadows and subdued light told her that it would soon be dark in the narrow alleys of the medina, but the shadows also made for stunning pictures of doorways and silhouettes, fezzes and veils, and proud stances and bashful smiles.

Finley wasn't sure what she had captured. She just kept shooting, trying to remember the sounds that went with each image. The hush of voices, the clanging of pots, the rhythm of the music, the cries of babies that echoed off the walls of the old city.

She had collected a cadre of small boys who had agreed to help her make her way to one of the gates nearest the sea for a few coins. *Or at least that's what I think I agreed to.* As they made their way, she kept taking pictures, sometimes of the boys, to help keep them with her, sometimes of other things or people who were nearby.

After a while, she caught a glimpse of the sea. She paid the boys and started her trek toward the hotel. It was so much brighter outside the medina. The sea breeze felt good. The saltiness of the water was sharper than it had been in Tangier, but it was a clean smell that invigorated her.

The sun was still high in the sky, so when she got back to the hotel, she headed up to the roof to catch the sunset on the water. The view was mesmerizing—so much so that she didn't hear Whitt and David when they came up the stairs.

"How was the medina? Did you get the shots you wanted?" Whitt asked. She summoned the waiter. She wanted a gin and tonic. No—she needed a gin and tonic. This week had been trying, to say the least. First the murder, then the kidnapping. And now having to face up to the fact that she really liked David. That was just a bridge too far.

Whitt sat staring at the water and the slowly dipping sun. David sat looking at her. He didn't touch her, and yet he felt connected. She was one of the most confusing women he had ever met. She ran hot and cold, so he was never completely sure how she felt about him. But she hadn't sent him home, and she still laughed at his jokes, so he guessed all wasn't lost.

Finley put the camera in her pack and picked up her wine. She held her glass until the waiter put down their drinks. "Well, here's to a very pleasant day! And a spectacular sunset! Where'd you guys go? How was the Corniche?"

Whitt described their afternoon wandering along the water and her ventures into the shops in Anfa. She pulled out a silver ring that she had gotten from one of the artisans. "What do you think?"

Finley took the ring and turned it in her hand. It was well designed with filigreed leaves surrounding the band. She handed it back to her sister. "It's lovely. How did you find the shop? The design doesn't look to be traditional Berber."

"It was in one of the Luxe City Guide knock-offs that I had gotten before I arrived. They have some good finds." Whitt looked quite pleased with herself and blushed slightly. "David got it for me."

Finley looked up over the rim of her wine glass. First at Whitt, then at David. *Tbilisi Boy is getting bold. He's taking a lot of chances. I just hope Whitt doesn't run scared. She deserves something good.*

He shrugged and said, "She liked it. And it seems to be well made."

Finley said nothing. David gave a half smile and changed the subject.

"Are we going to eat in, or should we look for another restaurant for dinner tonight?"

"You guys can figure it out. I'm going to finish my wine and then take a long shower. I have to wake myself up and at least outline my article." She took a long pull of her wine and stood up. "Have fun. Goodnight."

When Finley woke up at three in the morning, she thought she had fallen asleep and missed Whitt. She looked over and saw that the other bed was empty. She made some coffee with the mini-coffee maker when she had gotten back to the room. Not the good Turkish stuff, but it still warmed her. Her article was progressing well—she had decided on her angle, laid out the factual skeleton, and detailed the gaps in her information that needed to be filled in with research or interviews. And then she had gone to bed. But no, she hadn't missed Whitt. She heard her when Whitt crept into the room at six o'clock. Finley smiled to herself and went back to sleep.

17

"**W**HERE ARE WE OFF TO** first? We still have the Central Market, the mosque, the rest of the old medina, and all the new medina to cover. They say the old medina has some unusual finds—great Berber silver—and tagines. I still want one of those!"

Whitt was on a roll in the morning. At breakfast, she and David had talked about the amazing meal they had had at La Squala, a Moroccan restaurant not far from the hotel. Every detail had been shared. But Whitt had said nothing about what happened after. *She's a big girl. And that is her business.*

"Why don't we start at the Central Market and make our way through the medina back to the hotel? Then you can drop your shopping bags before we head to the mosque." David had figured Whitt out and was learning how to minimize his shopping pain. "There is also a wine purveyor near the market I wanted to drop in on."

"Perfect. While you are in your meeting, Finley and I can wander the shops in the medina, and we'll meet you back at the restaurant we had lunch at yesterday."

Finley had grabbed a different camera to use today and was fiddling with the features while they talked. She didn't really care where they went. The city was visually rich enough that she could get a good shot almost anywhere. When she looked up, both David and Whitt were looking at her for agreement. She arched an eyebrow in question and nodded. "Fine with me."

Rather than eat up precious time winding their way through the medina or the narrow streets in the older part of the city, they followed Rue Sour Jhid to the Central Market. The weather was bright and clear, with a welcome breeze off the ocean. The Central Market was at a fever pitch this morning. The restaurant owners, who did their shopping in the wee hours of the morning, had been there already and gone, so it was housewives who had command of the market now, and they were proving to be fierce negotiators. The din was loud and punctuated by women in colorful djellabas arguing prices with fish mongers and fruit sellers.

Whitt, put off by the smell, had steered them clear of the cupola that housed the fish market and directed them to the rows of stalls with a patchwork of colored vegetables and fruit. Although only one hundred years old, the Central Market's Neo-Mauresque architectural style was reminiscent of what they had seen in the imperial city of Rabat.

When David peeled off for his meeting, Whitt and Finley wandered deeper into the market, passing flower stalls with exquisitely designed bouquets and spice stands with mounds of turmeric, cumin, and saffron; strings of vanilla beans, cloves, and nutmegs; and small jars of dried herbs.

Finley experimented with the light in the shadowed stalls, looking for patterned shafts of sunlight that broke through the shutters, latticework, and reed ceilings. Some shots she knew would never work but others had just enough light to yield something noteworthy. She didn't take time to decide. She just focused and shot, more from instinct than vision.

After buying some saffron and a few other spices, Whitt had had enough of the market and asked Finley to lead her back into the medina. Following alleyways that time had forced her to ignore the day before, Finley led her to the section of the medina in which flatweave rugs of every color and pattern gave way to another section with brassware followed by still another whose walls were lined with festive pottery platters and steepled tagines.

As was her habit, Whitt outlined a preferred plan of attack, which started with the flatweaves and the brassware before lunch and continued just after lunch with a swing through the pottery section, where she hoped to snag her long-desired tagine.

"Less chance of things getting broken before I even get them back to the hotel. Does that work for you?" Whitt asked. She knew that Finley would be indifferent as long as she could use her camera.

Max had said when he was making out the list of best places for Finley to shoot that it would be easy for her to spend a week in the medina without running out of subjects. Whitt had doubted him. Now she could see what he meant. *He knows her pretty well. I guess two years together gives you some fairly deep knowledge.*

"Sure," said Finley, who hadn't even pulled her face out from behind the camera. "As long as we don't lose track of time. Which is likely given that we have no adult supervision to keep us on track." She grinned at her sister. "You know we're going to be late! We can't help it."

"I'll set my phone alarm. Stop fretting." Whitt had pulled out her phone, even as she slipped into the first Berber rug stall. Some forty minutes and three rugs later, she emerged from the shop with several tightly rolled packages looped together with twine and finished off with a functioning rope handle.

The owners had invited the sisters for tea while Whitt was making her decision about the rugs. Finley had gotten some workable pictures of the pouring of the steaming liquid from high above a mother-of-pearl inlaid table. Whitt had marveled at the design and artistry of the tea service, which gave way to a conversation about the best places to acquire one. The owner, of course, had a recommendation, which would surely turn out to be a shop owned by his cousin on his mother's side twice removed.

Stepping into the street, Whitt checked the alarm. "Drat, we only have time to run and get the teapot before lunch. I'm going to have to miss the brass wares."

She was already pulling Finley along the alleyway that the rug merchant had pointed to, stopping in spite of herself to check the weight of some of the brass platters as she passed. While Whitt ran into the silver shop to pick out her teapot, Finley continued to capture pictures of the metal-studded doors, the multicolored ceramic door stoops, and the hand-painted street number tiles. The indigoes, ochres, terra cottas, greens, and purples festooned the street in bright hues—the vibrancy of which Finley struggled to catch.

"Let's go. Mission complete," Whitt chirped and passed the latest acquisition for Finley to hold. Finley stuck her camera back in her pack and reached for the package.

"Whoa. This is more than a little teapot. What did you buy?"

"A few things," Whitt turned and started up toward the restaurant. Finley just shook her head. *If I got the late gene, Whitt surely got Mama's shopping bug.*

As expected, David was waiting for them near the restaurant. He grabbed the rugs from Whitt and the wrapped package from Finley. When he felt the pull of the package containing the silver, he looked quizzically at Finley, and then turned to Whitt and sighed resignedly. "Shall we try another restaurant? There are few in this area that are supposed to be good."

Whitt sidled up beside him. "Sounds good to me. Let's try somewhere different. Are you sure those" she pointed to the packages, "aren't too heavy?" David just smiled and readjusted the packages.

David led the way to a restaurant that was tucked away beside a small public green area a few alleyways over. The restaurant's outdoor area bled into the public space, but no one seemed to mind. Children playing soccer skillfully maneuvered the ball past the tables, and patrons, who seemed to be locals, applauded their footwork. The waiter found them a table with a front-row seat and handed them a couple of menus.

"Now, remember, we have Rick's tonight. We have reservations at eight o'clock." Whitt was looking forward to getting dressed up and playing pretend. Rick's Café had replicated the décor—and some said the ambiance—of the café of the same name from the movie *Casablanca*. Who cared if it was a bit touristy? They were tourists!

Taking Whitt's cue, they settled on mezze—olives, *bastilla*, of course, *merguez* rolls, and harissa. The waiter brought fresh bread and marinated goat cheese with the wine.

"Goodness, I could eat like this for a lifetime." Whitt dipped the warm bread into the golden olive oil that surrounded the herbed cheese.

"Oh, yes!" Finley sighed. She was the sort of satisfied tired that came from a good day's work. While her sister shopped, she had started to put some meat on the story skeleton in her mind. The pictures would be triggers for recalling and describing in her article the things she had seen that were quintessentially Casablanca. She couldn't wait to review the scenes that she had shot when she got back to the hotel after dinner tonight.

She raised her glass, "To another great day!" She clinked glasses and sipped. "How was your meeting?"

David told them about his conversation with the wine broker while they ate. It looked like there might be some opportunity for the two of them to collaborate on bringing Moroccan wines, olives, and oils into the United States and Europe under David's brand. He was excited, and the feeling was contagious.

The soccer game was reaching a fever pitch. Finley grabbed her camera and started capturing the action. When the game was over, the restaurant patrons erupted into "bravos" and the owners laid out a table of bread, cheese, and water for the boys.

"When you were wandering yesterday, did you see tagines?" Whitt asked. "I don't want to leave Morocco without one, and I know when we get back to Tangier, we are going to have limited shopping time before I leave."

Finley indicated a few places on the way back to the hotel where she had seen shops selling pottery, including tagines. She dropped her camera into her bag, paid the bill, and stood up. David was still protesting her picking up the tab, but she smirked and pointed at the packages he had to carry.

"We always feed the Sherpas. You will have earned your meal by the time she's finished!"

After lunch, Whitt wandered the row of shops along the alleyway that sold what she considered higher quality pottery, and in the end, returned to a shop that had a wide range of colored and patterned tagines along the wall outside the shop.

While David stood with the packages, Finley took another stab at playing with light and shadows in the sliver of a street that fronted the shop. She had seen a little girl half hidden in a doorway, her face divided by the light of the street and the dark of the door. She turned on her auto-shutter to be sure to catch the shot.

Whitt was having a hard time making up her mind. She knew that David, while generally patient, wanted to see the Hassan II Mosque this afternoon, and they still had to drop the packages back at the hotel. She moved from one tagine to the other, opening the lids and looking at the color baked inside. She had narrowed it down to three—a patterned blue-and-white one, a multicolored flowered one, and a more traditional brown-and-ochre one.

As she lifted the lid to the brown tagine, something slithered from under the partially opened top. Whitt jump back and gasped. Finley and David, hearing Whitt, turned to see a dusty colored snake drop from the vessel and side wind down the cobbles. A man who had been standing in a nearby doorway grabbed a shovel and brought it down hard on the snake, severing its head from its body, which kept moving for several seconds after the deathblow.

Whitt seemed to leap the several feet that separated her from David, the tagine lid still in her hand. He wrapped his arms around her and let her bury her face in his chest. Finley stood frozen in front of the row of vessels. Her mind was a tangle of questions, but one thing she knew for sure was that this was no accident. On the cobbles in front of that tagine was a small hemp bag. That snake had been placed in that tagine on purpose—if not to kill, then to maim, one of them.

A woman from inside the shop came out to take David and Whitt inside. She brought tea and seemed to be expressing in Arabic both her horror and remorse for the incident. Finley stepped into the shop with the bag. She gently touched Whitt's shoulder. Whitt didn't move—she was in shock and still nonverbal. She sipped her tea without expression. Finley knew she needed to get her back to the hotel, but she also needed to preserve as much of the evidence as she could for the police.

Finley turned and headed back into the street. "Do you have a larger sack to put the dead snake in?" She asked the man who had killed the snake in French. He headed into his house, and after some time, came back with some burlap and a span of rope. The man used the shovel to put the snake into the burlap and tie it up.

"*Attention! C'est toujours dangereux!*" the man explained. Several men from the street had gathered around. They took a step back as the snake was lowered into the burlap.

"May I ask you some questions? No one will get in trouble. I'm just trying to understand how the snake got here. Could it have gotten in there by itself?" Some of the men laughed. Others just shook their heads.

"Did you see anyone put it in the tagine?" She held up the smaller hemp bag. They stared at her without responding. She knew this line of questioning wasn't going to work. Even if they had, they would be unlikely to say.

"Do you know what kind of snake this is?" One of the bystanders pointed to the spikes on the snake's head. "A horned desert viper. This was a desert snake. It might have come in on one of the transports from the east but . . ." He trailed off. Again, no one wanted to get in trouble, but he was implying that even it if had come on a transport, it didn't jump into the tagine by itself.

"Is it poisonous?" The men answered yes, almost in unison. It was a snake they feared, not because it would kill you, but it would make you very, very sick. Finley offered the man money to compensate him for the burlap—and for killing the snake—but he waved her off, handing her the sack. She thanked him and then headed inside again to check on Whitt. The tea seemed to have revived her. She and David were standing just inside the shop waiting for her.

"You ready?" Whitt asked, her voice strong again. Finley nodded. David picked up the packages and thanked the shop owner. Despite her trauma, Whitt had settled on the blue-and-white tagine and the woman had packed and wrapped the vessel for her, handing it to David to carry.

"What did you learn?" Whitt was striding purposefully toward the arch that led out to the boulevard and toward the hotel. When she was little and had fallen or gotten knocked down, her immediate response was a proud exit from the playground. She might have cried when she got home, but "they" would never see her crumple.

"Nothing much," Finley responded. "The snake wouldn't have killed you, but it would've made you sick. And it didn't get there by itself." She paused, showing them the small hemp bag. "While you had your tea, I called and left a message for Inspector Evans. This was no accident."

The trio marched through the lobby, packages in tow, and headed to Whitt and Finley's room. Finley gently laid the burlap in the corner, checking periodically to be sure that it hadn't suddenly come back to life. "We need a drink. Evans will call us back. We'll kill ourselves with anticipation waiting in here."

On the roof, they ordered their drinks. Not surprisingly, David was hungry again. By the time their drinks and food came, Evans had texted back. He was on his way. He just needed to know where to meet them. It was now a little before five o'clock. He had just gotten on the train and would get into Casablanca around 7:00 p.m.

"I'll go downstairs and get a room for him," Finley said. She stood and grabbed her wallet from her bag.

"While you do that, we can change the reservation from three to four," Whitt said. David and Finley looked at her, surprised. "I'm not letting some crazy ruin my holiday. I still want to go to Rick's."

When Finley returned to the terrace, Whitt was laughing at something David had said. She was reclined in her chair, half on him, half on the seat. Seeing Finley, she straightened up with a guilty smile on her face. "Is his room all settled?" she asked.

"Yep. I am going to head down and hop in the shower since we're still going to dinner. I'll wait for Evans downstairs. Why don't we meet in the lobby at a quarter to eight? The restaurant is just down the street." Finley grabbed her backpack and smiled at her sister. "Have fun."

Downstairs, Finley stripped down and headed into the bathroom. She still had bandages on one wrist. The other had healed enough so she could just put on Band-Aids. She had caught people on the street yesterday and today looking at them. She wondered what they thought. Trauma? Suicide? Accident? She knew kidnapped hadn't entered their mind.

The water felt good and helped clear her mind. Who the hell was after them now? She thought that when Interpol had rounded up Sayeed and shut down his operations, they were out of the woods. Evans had said they were tracking all known traffickers. Even if he couldn't arrest them right now, they shouldn't be a threat. And quite honestly, if it were traffickers who were responsible for this latest incident, they would have been more effective—put vipers in the bathtub or venom in their G & Ts. They would have killed, not just maimed.

She dried and wrapped herself in a towel. She had laid out black silk pants and a patterned linen shirt for tonight, but somehow, she felt it wasn't dressy enough. She pulled out several outfits, and then put them away. *What is your problem? You are acting like a girl on the first date.*

She froze. *You can't be serious! You're dressing for Evans? You silly goose.* She was so glad Whitt hadn't come down yet. She would have teased her mercilessly. Whitt had a lot of nerve, though. She still hadn't come clean on what happened last night. And knowing her, she probably never would.

Whitt came in a few minutes later. Finley was pulling her jewelry bag out of the safe. She was wearing the black silk pants but had changed the patterned linen for a cream chiffon wrap blouse.

"Am I appropriately dressed? What are you wearing?" she asked as Whitt closed the door. "But before that," she said and approached her sister, "You okay?"

"Yeah, I'm fine. Quite a surprise, but I've recovered." Whitt dropped her satchel on the desk. "I was thinking of that floral slip dress and a shawl. My shoulders will be covered."

"Should I change then?" Finley looked down at her outfit. *Why am I feeling so insecure all of a sudden? This is stupid.*

"No, I love that outfit. It is so you. What shoes?" Whitt asked.

Finley reached into the closet and pulled out the pair of red, black, and purple tapestry stiletto sandals. She held them up for approval.

"Brilliant!" Whitt exclaimed as she ducked into the bathroom.

When Evans walked into the lobby at seven thirty, Finley was deep into a travel guide. He had started for the desk until he saw her in the common room. "Are you okay?" He put down his duffel and came immediately into the side room. His eyes rested on her wrists, now wrapped on only one side. "And your sister?"

"We're fine. A little shaken but generally all right. I have the snake upstairs if you want to see it. But it will have to be after dinner. Whitt is determined not to have her holiday disrupted." She paused and then said sheepishly, "We have reservations at Rick's. I hope you'll join us."

Evans's look of concern faded, and he grinned. "As long as you're all right. And yes, I'll join you. You can tell me what happened over dinner. Let me see if they have a room, and then we can talk." His voice resonated in her chest. The vibrations of his deep, slightly accented baritone unnerved her.

"I booked a room for you already. They'll give you your key," Finley told him quietly.

"Thank you." he smiled again, with a hint of pleasant surprise. "Shall I meet you here in ten minutes?" Finley nodded and returned to her book. From the corner of her eye, she watched him as he went to the desk and got his key. She followed the movement of his tanned hands, the curve of his jaw, the flash of his smile. *Good Lord, woman. Get a grip! You're acting like a stalker.*

Finley was still reading when the inspector came back into the room. He wore the same wheat-colored, double-breasted linen suit that he had arrived in, but instead of the white linen he had worn previously, he had changed into an open-necked, blue dress shirt. The combination of the blue shirt, his greying dark hair, and his slate-colored eyes almost took away Finley's breath. She sighed before she could catch herself. *Lordy, that man is handsome!*

"Are you all right?" Evans stepped toward her.

"Yes. Just too long in one spot." Finley rose from the chair. She noticed that, with her heels, she was almost as tall as him. *He probably likes petite women. Most guys do. That, I am not.*

"You look lovely, by the way. Is the necklace a new acquisition?" Evans said. She reached up to touch the silver and amber Berber necklace and remembered that she had gotten it in Marrakesh years ago. With Max.

RICK'S CAFÉ DID NOT DISAPPOINT. Every detail matched the vision made famous in the movie—the octagonal cupola, the white arches and columns of the main dining room offset by the black-and-white inlaid floor, the potted palms, the marble-topped bar, and most essential, the baby grand piano. It was like going back in time and stepping onto the movie soundstage, but somehow without feeling overly kitschy. The restaurant was running a bit behind, so the foursome was shown to a small table in the bar area. A pianist was playing tunes from the forties that set the mood.

"So, tell us about yourself, Inspector," Whitt started, with a sly smile. "You know all about us, and we know nothing of you. It's only fair."

Evans returned her smile. He paused, seemingly unsure where to begin or how much to tell. Whitt was relentless. She was determined to find out as much as she could about this distractingly handsome police officer. If she ever saw Anna again, Whitt would love to gloat over the fact that she had had dinner with the "luscious" cop and had come away with some delicious tidbits of information.

"Come on. We don't bite," Whitt continued.

Evans leaned back, running his thumb over the cut pattern of his old-fashioned glass. He had ordered a single malt, Macallan, and was warming it with his large, elegant hands. He took his time responding, while he bought himself more time to decide what he wanted to share. "How far back do you want me to go? You know that I'm with Interpol. You have probably guessed from my accent that I am English. What else would you like to know?"

While his eyes were on Whitt, who was directing the conversation, his focus was on Finley, who sat beside him, quietly nursing her bourbon. She seemed distracted, most likely by the snake and the fact someone was still trying to harm her and her sister. She remained quiet while her sister bombarded him with questions.

"Where were you born?"

"Paris."

"But you said you were English?"

"I am."

"So, your parents are English, but you were born in Paris?"

"Yes." Evans gave Whitt a cunning grin, waiting to see what question she would decide to ask next. He rather liked being on the other side of the interrogation. He understood better now why suspects often grinned like Cheshires when he was questioning them. It normally angered him, but he could see the sport in it. Whitt's brow furrowed while she pondered her next line of questioning.

"Was your family in the diplomatic corps, or was your father a businessman?" The voice had come from beside him, instead of across the table. He turned and looked at Finley, who had joined the conversation.

"My father was a diplomat."

"Where were you posted?" Finley continued, warming up to the exchange, and seemingly as determined as her sister to wheedle information out of him.

"Throughout Europe initially and then Northern Africa. His last post was Hong Kong, but I was at university in the United Kingdom by then."

"How many schools did you attend before university?" Whitt had rejoined the inquiry. David sat listening to it all, amused at the intensity of the questioning. He could see that Evans was enjoying the banter as well. *I guess he doesn't get to sit on this side of the table often. He's being pretty laid back about it. Finley's perked up, and Whitt's having fun. It's not every day you get to interrogate an Interpol agent.*

"Not that many, really. I started at the British School in Tunisia, and then we moved to Morocco. By the time I was eight, I was shipped back to Harrow for forming. I saw my family on holidays."

"We thought we had it bad as Army brats getting carted around the country and overseas, but we were always with our family." Whitt looked saddened by Evans's experience.

Evans picked up on the shift in mood. "It is the lot of young British boys of a certain type." He didn't say "class," but it was implied. "Even if my parents had been in England, I would have been sent off to school. It wasn't really that bad. I got baskets from Harrods or Fortnum every two weeks because my mother feared I would starve. That made it quite easy to make friends."

"But you have virtually no accent," Finley observed.

"I fought hard to erase it when I entered the force." He knew the questions about why he had joined the police force would come next. He mentally strategized how much he would say. "The other blokes didn't take too kindly to me being a toff."

Whitt was poised to ask a follow-up question when the maître d' came to show them to their table. It was on the upper level, near the atrium-like opening that overlooked the ground-floor dining room and bar. From that vantage point, they could see almost everything that was happening in the restaurant. It reminded Whitt of another atrium, in Tangier, and she shuddered. She turned back to current company and decided on dinner.

"This is quite nice. It's actually less kitschy than I thought it would be," Whitt opined. "Do you know if the food is any good?"

"Surprisingly good." Evans opened his menu and then leaned over to point out to Finley a few of the selections that were house specialties. "What are you thinking—fish, meat? You're not vegetarian, are you?" Evans raised an eyebrow as if to be vegetarian was the worst of sins. Finley chuckled.

"No, I'm not a vegetarian. I see duck, and I may not be able to resist," Finley replied. Evans looked slightly and pleasantly surprised by her choice.

After some indecision, David opted for the T-bone with caramelized onions and new potatoes, Evans for the lamb with a mint sauce, Finley for the duck with fruit chutney, and Whitt the monkfish in saffron sauce. When the wine had been ordered and poured, Evans waited for them to tell him about what had happened. He knew it had been serious enough for Finley to call him, and that no one had been seriously hurt. Beyond that, he knew nothing.

Finley waded into the silence. "Whitt, want to tell Evans what happened today?"

"Nothing much, except someone tried to kill us again. Finley says the snake bite wouldn't have been fatal, but I'm not so sure," Whitt offered. "You can look at it. Finley brought it to the hotel."

"Walk me through exactly what happened. Was anyone following you that you saw? Was there anyone near you at the time?" Evans asked, trying to keep his voice calm and neutral, even though he was angry that whoever was doing this had disrupted these women's sense of safety.

Whitt and David supplied most of the chronology of events, with Finley periodically adding clarifications. Evans took a sip of an aged cabernet sauvignon, holding it on his tongue for a moment before swallowing. Finley watched his jaw tense up when Whitt described the dusky color of the snake. "Do you know what kind of snake it was?"

"A horned desert viper, according to the men who were there," Finley reported.

"They generally aren't found in the city. Is that why you surmised that it wasn't an accident in your message?" Evans asked as a waiter brought their food.

"That and the hemp sack that was left in front of the tagines. Someone put it there. It didn't hop in by itself."

"You said you have the snake?" Evans arched an eyebrow at Whitt, who motioned with her fork at Finley.

"Apparently, she got some poor man to wrap it up in a tarp for her. I went and had tea." David shook his head.

"Whitt was pretty rattled, so the lady who owned the shop brought her tea. She recovered after a little while. Enough to finish her shopping," David said. Whitt promptly elbowed him, and he stopped talking.

Evans was quiet again. He stared at his plate, his brow growing increasingly furrowed.

"What are you thinking?" Finley asked.

"That my original theory—that this was all trafficking related—was wrong. And that there were two crimes going on simultaneously. Most likely unrelated." He paused and added, "Which means we have a killer who has not been apprehended."

"They may have been unrelated to each other, but they may be related to the hotel," Finley said and looked down at her plate as she spoke. "I think I may have seen Peter."

All three of her dinner companions stopped mid-bite. Evans put down his utensils, turned slightly in his chair, and lasered in on her with hawk-like intensity.

"What do you mean when you say you saw Peter? This is Peter Brown from the movie crew who was supposed to have left for the United Kingdom? You saw him where? When?" Both of Evans' eyebrows were raised now. Finley felt his eyes boring holes into her.

"I'm not sure that it was even him," Finley protested. "He was in a djellaba, and his hair was really short. I just remember thinking he looked like a young Peter. But it probably wasn't him."

"When was this?"

"I guess it was yesterday. Shortly after we got in. Whenever it was that we had lunch at the first restaurant when we went to in the medina. The one with the courtyard. Everything is running together!"

"Did you see him again?"

"No. I don't even know that it was him in the first place," Finley quipped. She didn't like being in the hot seat. She didn't like feeling like she had done something wrong. Evans sighed.

"I'm sorry. I didn't mean to put you on the spot." Evans's face had returned to neutral, and the tension in his jaw had relaxed. "We'll look into it. He is most likely in London just like we thought. But it is worth an extra look."

The waiter had removed the plates and brought the dessert list.

"I can't eat another thing." Finley had managed to finish every morsel of duck that she hadn't shared. David had wanted a taste, as had Whitt. She even managed to convince Evans that it was worth a try. He conceded only because she agreed to take a taste of his lamb. Finley couldn't remember a meal as enjoyable as this one. *And most of the time we were talking about murder. Mama would be mortified!*

"Well, I can." David and Evans said at almost the same time. Whitt and Finley smiled. *Guys!*

"The cheesecake is their specialty, but the apple tart is good as well. Shall we get both?" Evans asked. David nodded. The conversation returned to Ross and Julien's murders.

"Even if it were Peter I saw, how does that connect him to the murders? Maybe he decided to retire here instead of going back to Britain," Finley queried. "There's no sin in that."

"Maybe, but doesn't it seem fishy to you that he said he was leaving, and then he shows up here, and then someone comes after us again?" Whitt asked. It did seem unusual, but that assumed that the person Finley saw was, indeed, Peter.

"Have we covered the snake incident sufficiently enough?" Finley asked, glancing at Evans. She wanted to change the subject. She didn't want the evening to be all about murder. She was ready to move on. "Can we find a less morbid topic?"

Whitt grinned mischievously. "I'm sure Inspector Evans wouldn't mind another round of questions while he and David eat their dessert?" Evans groaned but nodded.

For the next thirty minutes, Whitt and Finley plied Evans with questions about his time at university and his early career. They learned his favorite color (blue) and what was on his bucket list (skydiving).

Whitt noted that a preponderance of men chose blue as their favorite color. She surmised that it was most likely because it was the first color boys saw as babies and so it stuck. Finley guessed that they just said it so that the questioner would move on. At that, Evans coughed slightly and let a subtle smirk slide up his lip.

When they got outside of Rick's, Whitt linked arms with David and was already pointing her body in the direction of the Corniche. "We're going to walk along the water, if you are okay to get back to the hotel," David said.

"I'll make sure she gets back safely," Evans nodded, and the two couples parted company. When they reached Finley's floor at the guesthouse, Evans touched her arm gently. "I'm going up for a nightcap. Will you join me?"

Finley was too keyed up to go to sleep. The incident in the medina, the at-large murderers, the possible sighting of Peter. There were too many questions and too few answers. Besides, she had eaten too much to sleep comfortably—and she was enjoying Evans's company.

"Sure," was all she said and let him lead her to the roof bar.

When they had ordered, Evans turned to look out at the water. "You were awfully quiet tonight." He smiled without looking at her.

"You let your sister lead the interrogation. Were there questions that you wanted to ask but didn't?"

Finley glanced over at him. He really was exceedingly good-looking. And quite self-assured, just on this side of cocky. In another man, that last question might have sounded arrogant, but from Evans it sounded open and inviting.

"No, I learned a lot. About a man who plays his cards close to his chest."

"And you?"

"And me, what?"

"Don't you also play your cards close?"

Finley froze for a moment before picking up the glass of champagne that just been placed on the table in front of her. She took a sip, unsure how to respond.

Evans preempted her, taking a long swallow of his single malt. "Do you mind if I ask you some questions?"

"I've already been interrogated by you!" she protested, with a slight smile.

"But the chief inspector was leading the questioning." He had turned his attention away from the sea and directed his focus to her. Her breath quickened under his gaze.

"Why don't we alternate? Then neither of us will feel like we are under the lights? Fair?"

Evans conceded. "But I get the first question." He paused, and then asked, "Have you ever been married?"

The question caught Finley completely off guard. She drew in a breath and held it. Evans sought to put her at ease.

"If you would prefer not to an—"

Finley cut him off, "Yes." She paused. "I married quite young. Right out of law school."

Her eyes were fixed on a point in the far distance. She wondered why it bothered her to tell him this. Grant Lambert, her first husband, was part of her history and not her present. He was settled in Darien, Connecticut, in a house with a picket fence, two-point-three kids, and a perky blond wife who chaired the Junior League Bazaar every year. She chuckled to herself. *Aren't you a catty little thing? Maybe, but it doesn't make me feel like any less of a failure.*

"And you?" She brought her gaze from the distance to the man beside her. She drained her glass and lowered it slowly. Evans had been watching her. His face softened when she returned to the conversation with her barbed questioning.

"No," he shook his head, a wry smile on his lips. "Confirmed bachelor."

"Ever close?"

He shook his head more slowly this time. "No, not really. This job isn't easy on a wife. It can be lonely. So many nights away, so many things you can't talk about. I suspect a lot of the wives feel shut out. Isolated." He looked at her intently. "I wouldn't wish that on any woman. Especially one I loved."

He was almost whispering. Finley wondered what lay behind the words. The women he might have loved longer if he had been a banker or a poet. Yes, that is what he struck her as in another life—a poet. He reminded her of a tortured artist. A Dylan Thomas. Or a Yeats.

Finley smiled, "Your turn."

One drink had turned into three, and it was creeping up on two o'clock in the morning. The bartender poured them one final glass and signaled good night. "You're welcome to stay up here as long as you like. The guard will lock up after you leave."

They didn't hurry, even after the bartender left. If someone had asked, they probably couldn't have told them anything about the conversation except that they had laughed and good-naturedly debated everything from the absurdity of American politics to whether Jennifer Garner and Ben Affleck would get married again.

"I probably need to get some sleep. We promised David a tour of the mosque tomorrow since we missed it today. A little snake got in the way," Finley said. "You're welcome to join us."

"I think I'll pass. I need to talk to a few people to see if I can't get a bit more information. Why don't we meet for lunch, and we can compare notes? I can pick up the snake then as well."

They agreed to meet at the first restaurant they had gone to in the medina, and then walk to the tagine shop after lunch so that he could see the area. He doubted that there would be anything that she hadn't already collected, but just in case. He would also ask some of the local residents what they might have seen. Speaking Moroccan Arabic might prove to be an advantage.

Evans walked Finley back to her room. Outside her door, he waited, looking like a teenager on the front porch after a first date. He slowly took her hand and kissed it softly.

"I have a confession to make," Evans whispered. He was standing close, still holding her hand. Finley thought he smelled faintly of sandalwood and citrus. It was an intoxicating fragrance, whatever it was. *Drinking a whole bottle of wine would make anything intoxicating. Just don't make a fool of yourself.*

"Okay. As long as I don't have to confess to anything."

Evans smiled. "No, I'll give you a pass this time." His eyes were locked on hers with unnerving intensity. "If ever I were to marry, you'd be the sort of woman I would look for." He kissed her hand again.

Finley returned his sad smile and leaned across to plant a kiss gently on his cheek. "I'm touched."

"Davies is a fool if he lets you get away," he muttered quietly, as he turned and walked down the hall.

Whitt was lying in bed, pretending to be asleep when Finley slipped into the room. She waited to speak until after Finley had brushed her teeth and was sliding into the cool Egyptian cotton sheets.

"You have a good time?" Whitt asked.

"Yeah, he's a very nice man." Finley was pensive. Evans had given her a lot to think about, not the least of which was Max. She had placed the Berber necklace in the jewelry bag with extra care, as if a little of Max was still there on the amber cylinders or the silver beads.

"Does Max have a rival?" Whitt probed.

Finley laughed softly and searched out her sister's form in the darkness. "No, I am not on the market! I have a good friend in Max and a passing acquaintance in Evans. Life's good. Just let me be happy."

"Goodnight then, happy face!"

"Night. Love you."

"Ditto."

E VANS WASN'T AT BREAKFAST. FINLEY didn't really expect him to be, but she had secretly hoped he would make an appearance. She had left a note for the staff on the top pf the burlap sack that was still shoved into a corner of the room. It simply said, "SNAKE. Do not touch!" in English and French. She didn't know how to say it in Arabic, but she figured the large block letters would be enough to keep the curious away. She would pass the sack onto Evans after lunch.

"How was your evening?" David asked, with a slight edge to his voice.

Finley looked over at him wolfing down three croissants with his dish of baked eggs. *What brought that on? He sounds a bit testy. Did he and Whitt have a fight?* She hadn't asked Whitt about her walk with David last night. She was too much into her own feel-good bubble.

"It was enlightening. Evans is a complex fellow," Finley said.

"I heard you shut the place down," David said and looked up at her between bites.

Finley wondered where he had heard that, or if had he been listening when she and Evans got to her room.

"I guess it was a bit late when we headed down. We lost track of time," Finley confirmed.

Whitt tore off a piece of *khobz* and dipped it into her soft-boiled egg. She was clearly amused by the conversation. If she knew what was going on, she wasn't telling. Finley arched an eyebrow at Whitt, who shrugged and went back to her breakfast. So this wasn't about Whitt and David. If that was the case, then what was it about?

David grunted in response, staring grumpily into his coffee. Finley decided a change of subject might be in order.

"So, are we going anyplace besides the mosque this morning?" Finley asked. "Evans suggested that we meet for lunch near that place in the medina. After we eat, we can show him where we saw the snake. Then he'll come take that ghastly thing away."

"You know he's almost ten years older than you," David sneered. He was staring angrily at Finley, but his voice was almost pleading. "Max deserves a second chance."

So that was it. David was upset with Finley, not Whitt. He was protecting Max's "territory" in his absence. Finley smiled and reached across the table to touch David's arm.

"He's also a confirmed bachelor! And Max will always be my friend," Finley said softly. She withdrew her hand and reached for more coffee. "So, are we good?"

David laughed sheepishly. "Okay, so I feel for the guy. Max is good people. And yes, we are good. Sorry to have gotten involved."

"Max *is* good people," Finley agreed. "And you have no reason to be sorry."

Whitt shook her head and laughed. "Y'all are too deep for me this morning. After the mosque, I do want to stop in a textile shop I saw when we were walking last night. Large kilim pillow slips would be nice for that reading nook I have off the den. David, any place you want to go?"

"There was a map shop on that same street, so I may drop in there while they are plying you with tea to encourage your pillow cover decision." David scoped the plan of action. "We'll just cut through the park to get to the medina. We should make it back in time to meet Evans for lunch." He cast a sly glance at Finley.

"Then, I think I'll just come back here after the mosque and go through all the frames that I shot. I haven't had a chance to see what's working or not," Finley said. "It still gives me time to reshoot some areas if I need to after lunch."

The Hassan II Mosque was not far from the hotel. In fact, Whitt and David had walked past it at least a dozen times on their way to the Corniche or to Whitt's favorite shopping haunts. That said, a brief walk past didn't do justice to the exquisite mosaic tile work and elaborate painting and gilding that graced the elegant arches and decorated walls of one of the largest mosques in the world. Situated on a promontory looking out over the Atlantic, the building was a blend of Islamic and Moroccan design elements that could amazingly hold up to 25,000 worshippers within its walls.

The burlap bag was still where she left it when Finley came back into the room after the tour of the mosque. Seeing it grounded her a bit. She was in a strangely euphoric state after seeing the magnificent handiwork in the elaborately decorated rooms. It was the same feeling she had had after wandering around the Taj Mahal. A sense that love—whether of Allah or of a woman—had allowed human hands to transcend their earth-bound limitations and achieve such mastery of stone that they created the sublime.

To be able to capture half that imagination on film would be her ultimate wish. To let people see in three dimensions an image that was really only captured in two because of her vision, composition, and artistry. *One day. Just keep slogging, kid. Then, one day.* She reached inside the safe and pulled out her cameras. She hadn't looked at much of what she had shot since the quick glance she took on the road to Casablanca. That was a few thousand frames ago.

She turned on her favorite playlist on her phone and started flipping through the pictures, deleting the "butt dial" frames that she had accidentally taken. She paused on one of Whitt and David snuggling. She hadn't planned on capturing that, but they were there in the frame when the shutter clicked. It was a sweet shot of them.

She would have to get it blown up and framed. *Maybe as an engagement gift. Okay, stop getting ahead of yourself. That's what killed you and Max. Don't do it to Whitt. Leave them alone. Let it evolve.* She sighed at the thought of Max and kept moving through the frames.

Finley was almost finished with the pictures from Rabat when something caught her eye. She scrolled back a few frames, plugged her camera into her computer, and advanced slowly frame by frame. She enlarged one image and sat staring at the screen. One particular figure showed up in three of the next several frames shot in the Kasbah des Oudayas.

She visualized where they had been, near the top of the hill, just before they had gone through a portal that led to the terrace where they had tea. There were a few shops filled with shoppers that had been crowded, some narrow passageways that she assumed led to houses. The colors and the light had prompted her to take a few shots before they reached the top of the battlements. She hadn't composed the shots, just focused and clicked.

She marked the sequence and started scrolling through the frames again. She was now in Casablanca in the medina the first afternoon after their arrival. Whitt and David had left. It was just her and the boys. After seeing the man who looked like Peter pass the restaurant courtyard.

She slowed her pace, scanning each frame for men, and then tall men, and then tall men that looked like Peter. She enlarged several frames looking inch by inch. She saw nothing until she reached a sequence of shots of the boys. She remembered they had gotten bored, and she feared that they would leave her before showing her the way out. She had had them pose in front of different doorways and passages in the filtered light of the medina. In two shots she could just make out what looked like the same figure. How had she missed it?

Finley got up and opened the blinds so that additional light would flood into the room. She returned to her computer and scrolled forward. She was now on the following morning when she and Whitt had gone into the Central Market and then back into the medina. She was breathing rapidly, her eyes flicking across the images in the frames, looking for the figure. It was becoming clear that they had been followed, at least from Rabat, and perhaps from Tangier. She needed to talk to Evans.

"Hello, Inspector Evans."

"Hi, this is Fin—"

"Where are you? Are you okay? Where's your sister?"

"Slow down. We're fine. At least as far as I know." Finley didn't know exactly where Whitt was, now that she was saying it. "I need to show you something. On my camera."

"I'm over with the Casablanca police. I've got additional information that I need to talk over with you." Evans shouted over the ringing of phones and people talking in the background.

Evans continued. "Let's meet upstairs. On the roof in an hour. There're fewer people there, and we are less likely to be overheard. Can you get in touch with your sister?"

Whitt had a dual SIM, so she could call her. Evans had moved up the time and told her not to leave her room until he texted her and then knocked. Seemed like a lot of precautions, but after everything else that had happened, she didn't argue with it.

"Whitt? Listen, where are you guys?" Finley waited for the answer. "As soon as David gets his map, you need to head this way." She heard her sister start to protest, talking about yet another store that she saw with textiles.

"You can do it after lunch." Finley's voice was firm. "I need you back here. Now."

David and Whitt arrived in the room only some twenty minutes later. Whitt was wide-eyed.

"Are you okay? What happened? Did someone try to hurt you?"

"No, Evans is coming over, and you all need to see these." Finley pointed to her computer screen. "Seems like Evans also has more info and didn't want us discussing it out in the medina."

David had moved over to the desk and was looking at the computer. "Who the heck is that? They show up in several of your shots." Whitt came over to join him.

"That makes no sense." Whitt stared slack-jawed at the pictures that Finley had storyboarded across the screen.

Finley's phone pinged. She moved to the door just as Evans knocked.

"So, what do you have to show me—besides the snake?" He entered, his eye catching the burlap sack with Finley's handwritten warning.

"These," Whitt gestured to the screen, and the array of pictures featured one face that Evans readily recognized, even with the changes in hair and dress.

"This is starting to mesh a bit better now," Evans started. "Describe the interaction between Anna and Peter when they were together."

Finley and Whitt tried to think. They had never imagined them "together" per se, so they had to remember those times that they had seen them in the same room or near each other. Whitt had to admit that she could count on one hand the number of times she had interacted with any of the crew. Finley might have had a few more conversations, but not many more, and David had never met any of them as far as she knew.

"It's hard to say. The times that I saw Anna, she was with Taryn or Stacey. I can only think of one gathering on the terrace. Right before we found Ross," Whitt recalled.

"And then they were together at breakfast the morning after. Remember?" Finley was looking in the direction of her sister, but her focus was somewhere past her, using that visual marker to help her wind back time. "Also saw them the first night I was at the hotel. As I recall, they were sitting together then, but I didn't think anything of it. Why?"

"It appears they have a history," Evans reported.

"That's true of a lot of them in the crew. They've worked on several projects together over the years. Both Stacey and Peter mentioned it."

"How many of them ever worked in Hollywood? Do you know?" Evans asked.

"I haven't the slightest," Whitt shrugged.

"Let me think," Finley said, and closed her eyes as she tried to go around the table on each night, remembering who had said what. "Peter, he had tried acting there. Anna, she mentioned that she had worked both in New York and Los Angeles. In addition to London." She paused, eyes still closed.

"Gavin, no. Julien, no. Thomas, I can't recall. Stacey, no. Ross, yes—he said he had been in California. I assume it was Hollywood, but I don't recall ever clarifying that. And I didn't ask any of them the time periods, so I don't know if they knew each other then or not. Does it matter?"

"It might." Evans was scrolling through the pictures that Finley had pulled up on the screen. "From what we can tell, Ross was blackmailing a lot of people. We initially assumed that he tried to go after Sayeed and his operations, and that was why he was killed. But the intelligence on the Hollywood connection—especially now that we've arrested or have tails on most of those connected with the traffickers—points elsewhere."

"And these pictures seem to confirm it," Whitt said as she pointed toward the screen.

"We have put out an all-points warning." He looked up to see confusion on their faces. "Ah, an APB in your vernacular."

"There're a few possibilities—they can both be here. They could have headed back to Tangier once they figured they'd scared us with the snake. Or one could be here and one in Tangier," Whitt outlined.

"Or Anna could've headed to Agadir, and Peter could be any-where, even out of the country by now," Finley added.

David had been quiet until now. "But do you know how the two people you were talking about are connected? I never met any of them, so I'm just guessing. You guys said Peter was older than the rest of the crew. So, maybe there was something between Anna and Ross, and somehow Peter got involved. But why would Anna and Peter be working together now? Confusing."

Evans concurred. "And there is the crux of the matter. What is it that connected Anna and Peter? We now suspect that Ross was blackmailing Anna, and Peter tried to help her out. But why? I don't think Anna would be strong enough to break Ross' neck. And she definitely couldn't have tossed him that far over the rail."

"So, we're back to where we started," Whitt commented with a frown. Her lips pursed.

"Not really." Finley's brow was furrowed. She was still looking at the screen. "We've narrowed the players. We just need a how and a why."

"Can we ponder those over lunch?" David was, of course, hun-gry. The others were too. Finley closed her computer and headed for the door behind Whitt and David. Evans pulled her back.

"Is there someplace we can lock these up? I don't want to lose what little evidence I have of some connection," Evans asked. Finley collected the cameras and the computer and put them in the safe. "Better."

Lunch was a quiet affair. They were alone in the restaurant and settled on mezze again—*briouat, kefta,* egg tagine—a Spanish tortilla-like dish—and cheese. While they ate, they each played out scenarios in their mind, throwing possibilities out to the others when something began to gel, only to have those possibilities turn improbable under further scrutiny.

"We're thinking too hard," Whitt finally said. "We need to fin-ish our little excursion, head back to Tangier, and mull it over there.

The answers aren't here in Casablanca. Unless the snake knew the answer. And Finley killed it!"

Finley laughed. "I didn't kill it."

"But you both almost got killed. Twice. I suggest you let us handle it." Evans frowned. "Thank you for your assistance. I couldn't have gotten this far without your insight. But I think it's best that you leave it be. Head back to Tangier tomorrow as you had planned and leave it alone."

"I couldn't agree more." Whitt was looking at her sister. "Let me show you that textile shop I was talking about. And David should show you the maps he got. They had architectural drawings as well. You like those!"

Finley knew when she was beat. The consensus was that she should return to holiday mode. She was fine with that, as long as Evans had the pictures—and the snake. And whoever was following them played nice and didn't come after them again.

She still had an article to write and pictures to sort through. Interpol and the police would find Anna and Peter and figure out the why and the how. And they would have Taylor to keep them safe. *He was doing such a bang-up job! She shouldn't, but she would, rib him if she ever saw him again.*

Evans escorted them back to their room, picked up the snake, and waited until Finley had loaded the pictures onto a thumb drive for him. He planned on taking the train back to Tangier that evening and would let them know if there were any developments. Finley knew what that meant. He was hoping that they would be long gone back to the New York or Manila or Tbilisi or wherever before this thing broke wide open.

"Let's get going, then. There is a lot of shopping left to do," Whitt said after Evans left. "Have you bought anything here in Casablanca?"

Finley had to think of what she had bought. To Whitt's point, it was very little. "Not much. Let's go. I have shopping to do," Finley said, to which David sighed. The prospect of being Sherpa to both sisters was daunting. He wasn't sure he was up to it.

The map shop on Rue Dahiri was more like a mini museum. Finley could have stayed three or four days pulling out browning maps of the Magreb and places beyond. David was glad for the chance to return and gave her a short tour of the many alcoves that held racks of old maps, reproductions, and lithographs of architectural designs.

Whitt sat looking at old fashion and interior design coffee table books. The dust stirred up by the opening of the map racks and the turning of pages created a sunlit fog in the treasure-packed space, but Finley didn't mind. It took her almost an hour to select her maps and prints. She was in her element.

"Who'd you buy the prints for? And what about the maps? The one with the watercolor was quite well done," Whitt asked as they were leaving.

"Friends. They have all the jewelry and housewares. From our other trips. This is a little something different." She turned to David. "Thanks for showing me the shop. When you go to Hong Kong with Whitt, get her to take you to our favorite map shop in Kowloon."

Whitt smiled. *She's got him going all over the world with me. Wouldn't be a bad thing. He's a pretty nice traveling companion. He's a pretty nice companion, period.* They wandered over to the artisan's studio Whitt had visited earlier. Finley bought some silver bangles while Whitt and David looked at necklaces and more rings. Whitt couldn't resist adding to her stash of jewelry, and soon she was adding to the packages David had offered to carry.

"Are we leaving this afternoon or tomorrow?" Finley asked. They had stopped at a café not far from the water for mint tea. She was starting to get tired. She could use a hot shower and a glass of wine if they were going to stay the night.

"Let's go in the morning," Whitt said while looking at David. "What do you think?"

"Makes sense. Let's just enjoy the city this evening and tackle the trip back tomorrow," David said. "Besides, I haven't booked a room in Tangier. I'm sure Max would let me crash, but I don't want to impose."

"Max likes you. He'd be glad for the company, I'm sure," Finley smiled. Even as she said it, she wondered whether he indeed would welcome the company or whether the woman he was with the other night would view it as an imposition. She hadn't found out who she was or how well Max knew her. *It's none of your business, so just get it out of your head.* But she couldn't.

20

THE TRIP BACK TO TANGIER was faster than the one down to Casablanca. The evening before, they had gone to Porte de Peche, a seafood restaurant in the harbor. David had been hungry, as usual, and they had walked the short distance to the restaurant after having drinks on the roof. Evans had apparently already left. Without the murders to direct their conversation, they fell back into a more normal range of conversation topics—politics, religion, and sex. *Good Lord, this boy must think we are crazy. Welcome to the family!*

On the way back to Tangier, Finley drove. The traffic was surprisingly light and the scenery pleasant enough when she bothered to observe it. Her mind was a tornado, with ideas and questions and snippets of conversations whirling around. *Leave it alone. This is not your battle anymore.*

Whitt rode shotgun for the first half of the trip and then switched with David. "I don't mind if you both want to sit in the back," Finley smirked. "As long as you don't do anything nasty." Whitt punched her sister's shoulder. David just blushed slightly.

"Nah, I want to experience your driving," David chuckled "Whitt says you go so fast that the trees seem to bend in."

Finley caught her sister's eye in the rearview mirror and laughed. "It's not quite that bad. But I do like speed."

Finley managed to get them back to the city around noon—in under three hours and without a ticket. Max had texted her the night before asking when they were getting back in town and suggesting that they all stay at his place. She messaged back with their expected arrival time, but she declined the invitation to stay. David, however, had taken him up on it. So, Finley directed the car to Max's and pulled up in the alley near the garden. Max greeted them at the side door.

"Come on in." He was in jeans and a T-shirt—and barefoot. Clearly, he was working from home. "I didn't know if you had eaten, so I made something for you guys to snack on while you tell me about your trip."

They followed him into the dining room. David went into the hall and dropped his bag at the bottom of the stairs. Max had pulled a couple of bottles of wine out and had a crisp Alsatian white chilling in a small blue-and-white wine bucket. He had laid out an assortment of cheeses and breads, mounds of three different types of olives, and a big fat *bastilla*. Whitt beamed. All was good in the world.

"If we eat all this, we won't need dinner," Whitt observed.

"Speak for yourself," David mumbled as they grabbed plates of food and glasses of wine. They settled in the living room with Whitt and David on the couch and Max and Finley across from each other in the easy chairs.

"What did you think of Casablanca?" He directed his question at Whitt and David. He knew Finley had been before. The two of them had gone there a few times when she used to live in Tangier. He recalled one particular trip, right before she had headed back to the States. He had almost asked her to marry him then. But he hadn't. He shot a glance at Finley before turning to Whitt. "How'd you like the shopping?"

Whitt knew not to minimize the dent she had put in her wallet. The evidence of her shopping safari was strewn all over the back seat since the car's small trunk wasn't big enough for both the duffels and her purchases.

"Abundantly," Whitt stated. She remembered the last time she had sat on that couch, in that very spot. It had only been a few days, but it seemed like a lifetime ago. *I guess that's good. Maybe that means I am putting some distance between me and what happened.*

"What did you do besides shop?" Max asked.

Finley described the side stop in Rabat and their wanderings through the Kasbah des Oudayas. She commended him on the list of photo locations that he had suggested and recounted some of the types of lenses and angles she tried. No one wanted to bring up the snake.

"Whitt, did you find your tagine?" Max had made it unavoidable now. Finley glanced at Whitt. She stopped mid-bite and smiled graciously before responding. David and Finley waited to hear how she was going to spin this.

"Yes. I got a beautiful blue-and-white one with bright blue inside," Whitt explained concisely.

"How many shops did you go to before you found the right one?" Max asked with a smile. "David, I know you must've traipsed around at least ten shops before she decided."

"No, she only went to one shop, but they had a nice selection," David said. He decided to bite the bullet and went on. "She did pretty well, narrowing it down to three, until she saw the snake."

Max stopped. He said nothing. He looked at Whitt, then at David, and finally at Finley.

"Why don't you tell me about the snake that you failed to mention in your text?" His voice was even.

"Whitt didn't get bitten. She was just shaken up," Finley began. "It was a horned desert viper, and a man nearby took a shovel and killed it. It wasn't an accident. Someone put it there for us. Evans came and they are investigating it."

"Interpol is investigating this?" Max asked, his voice rising.

David provided the response, "It seems that it wasn't the traffickers that killed those two men. Evans thinks that there's something else going on. And then Finley found pictures of people who seemed to be following us, and that pretty much confirmed it for Evans. So, it's with Interpol again."

Max got to his feet. "That does it. You all are staying here until they find out who's doing this. No one knows about this place, so you're safe here."

He was starting to pace. Finley had seen him do this pacing thing before, whenever he was frustrated or angry and didn't want to lose control.

He moved toward the side door and the car. "David, can you help me get their bags and the packages in?"

"Hold on. We didn't say we were staying," Finley challenged. She stood and headed toward Max. "I understand and appreciate your concern, but I think Whitt and I should have some say in this. We were okay staying at the hotel after the raid."

"But things have changed. You thought it was resolved, but it's not. Are you going to tell me you think you're safe there?"

"No, but I don't like the idea of someone else deciding things for me and my sister," Finley said. "Whitt, are you okay staying here?" Finley turned and looked at Whitt, who was trying hard to hide a smirk. *They're fighting like old, married people. He should know by now that you ask, you don't tell anything to Finley Blake.* Whitt recovered enough to nod.

Finley walked into the kitchen and stopped in front of Max, who still stood with his hand on the side door. "If the invitation is still open, we will graciously accept your offer to stay. But only for one night," she stated. "We have to go back to the hotel at some point. All our things are there. The police will figure it out, and we'll be okay." She held his gaze until he conceded.

"I just want you to be safe." He whispered softly under his breath, before opening the door and walking outside. David slipped past her and into the yard.

Finley took the packages from David as he brought them inside. "Where shall I put these so that they are out of your way?" she asked Max as he came in the door with the last of the bags.

"I think if we stack them there, you won't forget them." He pointed to a small nook in the living room behind the couch. He gave her a sideways glance as he passed to start the pile of Whitt's finds. When he had finished, he headed toward the kitchen and started making coffee.

"Anyone besides me want coffee or tea?" he inquired. Finley nodded, but Whitt shook her head.

David had returned to his place on the couch, bringing what was left of the bottle of white with him. He topped off Whitt and refilled his glass.

"You handled the introduction of the snake quite deftly, if I dare say so," Whitt said.

"Thanks. Seems I lit a fuse, though." David was looking past her to Finley and Max, who were clearing the table in stony silence. "This is going to be awkward if it doesn't pass soon."

"Never fear. Finley will take care of it." Whitt followed her sister's movements in the kitchen. "She hates being controlled, and he knows it."

Whitt went back to her wine and her conversation with David. She would leave her sister to clean up the mess she had made. *She can be so bull-headed. But she's right—he never asks. He just "takes care of it." And how's that working for you, Max?*

Finley placed the last of the platters on the counter and reached in a drawer to get some foil.

"Still remember where things are, eh?" Max said, just over her shoulder. She turned to face him. She took her time, careful of what words she chose. This was a balancing act, not the high dive.

"Look, I'm sorry I got angry. You know me. I'm mouthy." Finley raised an eyebrow. "Thanks for letting us stay."

"No problem," Max replied. "I'm the one who should be apologizing. I overstepped. Again." He laughed, breaking the tension that connected them like a cord. "Forgiven?"

Finley smiled, "Only if I am." She extended her hand to make a truce.

"Done." Max shook her hand and held it. He tilted his head slightly so that he could look her in the eye. He started to say something, but stopped himself, dropping her hand and instead planting a kiss on her cheek before heading back into the living room.

"I have another couple hours of work left to do, and then I can join you for whatever you have planned for the afternoon and evening," Max announced.

"We're good. I think I am going to head into the garden and read while my lunch settles, and then we can decide on whatever else we want to do." Whitt motioned toward the back of the house. She and David had discussed going to the American Legion Museum since they only had another couple of days before they left. Whitt was pretty shopped out, surprisingly.

"What're you up to, Fin?" Max asked. The war between Max and Finley was apparently over. Whitt glanced knowingly at David. *See? I told you she would douse the fire.*

Finley was opening her backpack. "I'm going to finish going through my frames to see what I have that I can use for the article. That should take me, like, forever!" She smiled at Max who understood her tendency to get sidetracked or zone out before a task was done. "Is it okay if I work in the den upstairs?"

David looked at Whitt, who was rummaging in her satchel for her book. He knew there was unspoken history between Max and Finley, but he didn't know it ran this deep. *She knows his house, his moods. What else does she know? Does she know he still loves her? If so, she doesn't act it.* He mentally acknowledged that he only knew one side of the story and even that had been implied, not spoken.

"Sure. Let me be sure it's cleaned up," Max replied.

He headed up the stairs with Finley on his heels. Assured that the room was habitable, Max left her in peace to review the rest of her pictures. She marked several that she wanted to consider for her article. Ones in which the subjects or the colors might play well in a magazine spread. But the ones she stayed looking at the longest were those in which she had succeeded in capturing a feeling, not just a face. There were only a few like that, but they held her attention.

She was almost through the sequence she had taken of the boys playing soccer when she caught what she thought was another glimpse of Anna dressed in a man's djellaba. Like the earlier snapshot of her that Finley had seen in the pictures from the medina, her blunt Cleopatra cut had been replaced by a short boy cut, but the features were the same.

Finley advanced through the frames slowly. She had been snapping pictures quickly, she recalled, hoping to catch a good action shot of the match. She hadn't been concerned about the framing or setting. It was only now that she was dissecting the background in these frames, that she was starting to understand what she was seeing.

If the picture of the boys in the medina had yielded the figure of Anna, this sequence was revealing far more. Definitive proof of a connection between Peter and Anna. At least two frames in this sequence had images of Anna and Peter together. Maybe not talking but standing or walking close enough to be caught in the same shot.

Finley's hand froze. She touched the camera face to enlarge the image. She needed to blow this up. She ran down the stairs to grab her computer. Whitt and David were outside, but Max was sitting, head down, shoulders hunched, typing on his computer.

"What's wrong?" Max looked up, focusing on the urgency of Finley's movements and the frown on her face.

"I just need to blow a shot up," Finley said.

"May I see?" Max rose and followed Finley who was already halfway up the stairs.

"Sure," she called over her shoulder and kept ascending.

"If you want to enlarge it, use the big monitor. Here, just give me your cable." Max reached for the USB cable that she had plugged into her camera and connected it to the monitor.

In the split second before Finley's pictures appeared, the face of a stunning woman with flowing dark hair flashed across the screen. Finley flinched. *Who was that? Is it the same woman she had seen at the restaurant? She must be someone special. Not your business, girlfriend. Not your business.*

Her attention returned to the pictures. She scrolled back a few frames and then advanced the pictures slowly, pausing to scan each frame for what she thought she had seen earlier.

"There!" she cried, pointing at an apparent exchange between two men. The older of the two seemed to be passing something to the younger, both faces in silhouette. It was Anna and Peter. "Can we enlarge it more?"

"Yes," Max moved to the keyboard and zoomed in. "What are you looking for—or at?"

"That!" Finley pointed at a small hemp bag. The same one that she had handed over to Evans. The one that in this shot held a poisonous snake. "Now if I can just find something that has her near that pottery shop."

Max was fixated on the bag. "Did she try to kill you?"

"Well, it was Whitt that got the worst of it. If this is Anna, it's probably payback for Whitt talking to her boyfriend." She remembered the look in Anna's eyes as she watched Thomas talking to Whitt. Innocent enough, but Anna had seemed peeved. No, peeved was too mild; she was seriously pissed. "Now to find her on that street, if not with the tagines."

"You think she's the one who put the snake in the tagine?" Max's face was incredulous. "But why?"

"Don't know why. That's for Evans. I just need to help him establish that there was a direct connection. Enough for him to go pick both of them up and hold them."

Finley was hyper focused on the frames that she took near the pottery shop. She had been trying to construct a visual composition with the angles created by the narrow street, the jutting doorways, and the shadows of the rooftops on nearby buildings. Once again, she had just shot, barely focusing, and definitely not composing, once she had found the right part of the street on which to shoot.

"Is that you? Come to me, my pretty," Finley was leaning into the screen, squinting to make the blurry images sharper. Max was hanging over her shoulder, scanning the frames too.

"Hold on," Max had his eye on a tall figure walking toward the camera from a side street holding something. "Go back a couple—" Finley was already moving the cursor back and then slowly advancing it.

"See," Max was pointing at the screen. "Here, there's no one on that section of the street. If you move forward, you see a person, dressed almost exactly like the person in the bag exchange, come out of nowhere and come toward the camera."

Finley kept her eye on the screen. She remembered that she had switched to auto for this sequence because of the little girl in the doorway. And the shots switched from landscape street scenes to portraits of the little girl.

"Damn, just when I needed a panorama, I go to close-up!" Finley sat back in the chair, disappointed. She kept advancing the frames, hoping for a reprieve.

"Keep going forward. See that figure on the far edge of the frame?" Max was trying to refocus the shot so that the peripheral image became clearer. "That looks like the same djellaba—see the border on the sleeves—but the person is now walking away, and they aren't carrying anything."

Finley grabbed a screenshot of the frame and grinned. "I think we got them." She turned to Max and kissed him on the cheek. "Thank you. Good teamwork."

She continued, "Sorry I kept you from your work."

"I was just finishing actually," Max said. "And this was fun. You had better run off now and call your inspector."

Before Finley could say that Evans wasn't "her inspector," Max had gone back down the stairs.

THE SUN FILTERED THROUGH THE leaves, creating a dapple effect on the plants in the garden. Not an expansive plot by any means, but it somehow had the right mix of greens and yellow, red and blues, and oranges to make it feel complete. Compact, yet complete. David sat on the woven reed settee, which took up a good portion of the garden space, with Whitt's head on his shoulder. They had left Max and Finley working inside. Both had brought a book to read. Hers was a travel history by William Dalrymple—one of her favorite authors—his, a novel he had picked up in the airport in Dubai during his layover. He didn't really know what it was about. He had picked it up because of the alluring cover illustration featuring an enormous orange sun over a desolate brown desert.

He used the book as a blind to allow him to think without being caught daydreaming. In reality, he wasn't daydreaming as much as puzzling. He was both intrigued and saddened by the relationship between Finley and Max. He didn't—couldn't—understand it. Maybe it was because he felt compelled to say what he felt. To put it out there, to see if it would float. If it didn't, he had always licked his wounds and set his sights on another target.

He looked over at Whitt. Was she like him, or a puzzle like Finley and Max? They had never talked about a relationship per se. They were still getting to know each other, but he figured this trip had changed the tenor of their relationship. At least he hoped it had.

He wanted Whitt in his life. He knew that, without a doubt. He had to admit, though, that he was unsure about what she wanted. She seemed to like being with him. She had leaned on him when she was frightened. They talked easily and laughed readily. That was a pretty good start. *Right?* Whatever "this" was, he wanted to play it all the way out.

"What're you thinking? You look pretty serious. Is the book that thought-provoking?" Whitt squinted slightly as she held her hand up to shade her eyes.

"Just thinking. Nothing in particular. Your book good?"

"Yeah. I like Dalrymple's style of writing. It's historically informative and insightful, yet interesting. But I really like him because he makes me laugh." She paused and added, "Like you."

"Do you think I am going to keep you laughing twenty years from now?"

"Hmmm . . . probably not. In all likelihood, I'll find you trite and roll my eyes at jokes I have heard more than a hundred times."

He leaned back, closed his eyes, and let the sun warm his face. Whitt continued to look up at him. His tan was darker now after walking in the sun the past few days, and his hair had streaks of light blond. What was he thinking about so hard? He was less of a thinker. More of a doer. What he thought, he said. Maybe she should try the same.

"But I promise to keep loving you no matter how tiring your jokes get." She went back to her book.

David's eyes opened, and his head shot forward with bafflement all over his face. He looked at her, not sure that he had heard what he thought he had heard. His face softened. He smiled and gently moved a strand of hair that had flopped over her forehead.

"You promise?"

"Promise," she murmured, without even looking up from her book.

Despite what she had said about being shopped out, Whitt had a bit more shopping left in her after the tour of the American Legion Museum. The extravagant array of carpets, weavings, and paintings in the museum made her realize that she might have just a little more space in her suitcase.

Whitt thought back to a movie she had seen as a teenager about the kidnapping of an American widow by a dashing sheik during the Teddy Roosevelt era. *The Wind and the Lion*. The movie starred Sean Connery and Candace Bergen, so it hadn't mattered whether there was even an ounce of truth in the storyline. The visuals of those two made the movie worth watching in any case.

It was the carpets in the museum that had her back at the rug merchant in a small shopping arcade near the museum. Finley and Max had decided to come along. It was a good thing too, since Whitt never would have found the rug shop without Max.

When they walked in, the owner, Naim, welcomed Max like a brother—with three kisses on the cheek—and greeted the rest of them as if they were long lost family. He was a handsome man about Max's age. Though several inches shorter, he had a similar runner's build too. His rug selection was one of the best that Whitt had seen yet. *Leave it to Max to find the best. He's still sweet on my sister, so he has to have good taste.*

Naim laid out six or seven different rugs that varied by pattern and color. As Whitt began to gravitate toward a particular design, he would signal to a couple of younger men that stood behind him, and they would remove all but the three carpets she admired the most. Naim would then pull out more rugs with similar patterns or a slight difference in color.

He did this a couple of times until he had helped Whitt narrow down both the pattern variance and the color. In the end, she decided on a red-hued Beni Mguid from the Middle Atlas, which had a slightly plusher pile than the flatweave kilims that she had purchased earlier in the trip.

While Whitt had been going through the selection process, Naim's father had been giving Finley and David a lesson in the types of Berber tribal rugs while his wife poured fragrant mint tea into their glasses. Several times, Finley caught Naim looking at her, then catching Max's eye and smiling. Even so, he never missed his cue with Whitt, always switching out the rugs at exactly the right moment.

"Goodness, that was tiring. It's so hard to decide. Maybe I'll switch out the whole downstairs to a Moroccan theme for a year or so and change everything out." Whitt sipped her tea while they packed her rug. "I could easily do it with what I have bought."

No one challenged her. They were afraid that if they did, she might think of something else she needed to complete the theme and head off to yet another shop. It was already dark outside. Naim's family had kept the shop open just for them. David picked up the wrapped rolls that held Whitt's rug, and apparently, a small token of appreciation for each of them from Naim's father. When they headed into the street, Max stayed back to add his thanks to Naim and his family in Arabic.

"They seem like a really nice family. Have you known them long?" Finley asked when Max had joined them again. She was still curious about the exchange between Naim and Max. *Why did Naim keep looking at me and smiling at Max?*

"A few years. In fact, you were the one who introduced me to the shop. His brother used to run it. They were in the medina then," Max said.

Finley looked puzzled. "That's Kamal's brother?" Kamal used to be Finley's Arabic tutor when she had first arrived. He ended up marrying Aliyaa, the owner of the fish restaurant where Finley had run into Max. He now helped her run the restaurant with her family.

"One in the same."

"Small world."

"And about to get smaller. Naim's sister is married to the owner of the restaurant I'm getting ready to take you to. Really good farm-to-table food. Traditional food with an edge." He looked to see if he saw any objections. "Are you in?"

Everyone nodded. Whitt and David fell in behind Max and Finley, who walked side by side down the narrow street.

"I bet you can't remember how to get to Rue Moulay Abdellah from here," Max teased and glanced at her with a mischievous smile.

"You mean near the Rembrant?" Finley asked.

He nodded. She had to think for a moment. It had been a long time since she had been in Tangier, and some things had changed in the city, even in the older parts. She recalled that it was near the Rue de la Plage, not far from the fish market.

"Bet I can!"

"Without GPS!"

"Of course, without GPS. Follow me." Finley struck off toward Rue Amerique de Sud, and Whitt and David followed. Max sniggered and joined in. She took a left when she reached Rue de la Plage and stopped for a moment when she got to the next major street. She remembered a short cut and took the next left, which connected her in time to Rue Moulay Abdellah.

"Okay, now where?" Finley asked. Max was impressed. She had come directly to the street. *Even remembered the short cut.*

"I'll take it from here. The restaurant is tucked away and can be a bit hard to find." Max took her by the arm.

Finley let him lead. Soon they were in front of a quaint restaurant with a whitewashed front and large blue retracting doors that opened right onto the street. The street was redolent of onions and spices, which was almost overwhelming, taking her back to her grandma's kitchen—a gathering place for the women of the family. Aunts and cousins, who despite doctorates, law degrees, and medical degrees, found comfort in the hearth of that old house that had raised Mama and her siblings.

The calm interior of the restaurant was surprisingly modern. The rough, whitewashed walls continued inside with hints of blue from the doors highlighted in the prints on the walls and the napkins. The waiter greeted Max warmly and led them to a table along the wall that looked out onto the street.

Shortly after, a slim woman in a stylish lightweight print dress came up to Max and kissed him on both cheeks. Max made introductions all around, saving Finley's until last. The woman had shaken Whitt and David's hand, but had kissed Finley when she got to her. Finley's Arabic was long forgotten, so she couldn't understand what was being said or even intuit from the woman's face.

"Are you okay with letting Fazia decide dinner for us?" Max asked. They all nodded in agreement. Being foodies, they all knew that they were more likely to get something special letting the chef decide what to bring out. Max ordered one bottle each of the local white and red wines. When the wine had been poured, Max turned to Finley.

"Did you tell them what you found?" he asked.

"We found it, not just me," Finley answered. "We found proof of a connection between Anna and Peter as well as some indication that Anna put the snake in the tagine." Whitt's mouth dropped open, and David smiled in silent triumph.

"Did you call Evans?" Whitt asked.

At the mention of the inspector's name, Finley noticed Max's jaw clench slightly. *What does he have against Evans? He was fine letting him into his house when I thought he and Taylor were thugs. What's up with him now?*

"Yes, I called him shortly before we left for the museum," Finley recounted. "He said they were going to arrest Anna in Agadir. They were still looking for Peter."

"He could be anywhere by now," David remarked. He was attacking the olives and cheese that the waiter had brought out. The mezze was enough for a meal, but Finley knew that more food was coming. The key was to pace herself so that she could taste a little of everything. She decided to change the subject.

"When did this restaurant open?" she asked.

"Shortly after you left," Max said. The air stilled between them. Neither really knew what to say to break the tension, to ease the awkwardness. David jumped in.

"Do you know what time we need to leave for the airport if we have an eleven o'clock flight?" he asked.

"Probably around eight o'clock. It'll be a Sunday, so there won't be a lot of traffic," Max answered without missing a beat. The awkwardness was thankfully behind them. "You should be there by half past eight."

"Where do you connect?" Finley asked." Do you have a long layover?"

They established that they had a significant layover in Casablanca. If Whitt hadn't had so many packages, it would have been faster for them to take the train to Casablanca and fly directly to Tbilisi. Whitt looked so sheepish that all they could do was laugh.

"You got what you came for," Finley noted. "You said you wanted jewelry and rugs—and a tagine! And you got that and more."

Dinner was a gourmand's paradise. Naim's sister, Fazia, had unleashed the culinary genius of the chef, who happened to be her husband. They feasted on dishes that no one but Max had ever tasted before. Fazia brought out two more bottles of wine for them from the reserve cellar as well as a selection of desserts that weren't on the menu. Other diners craned their necks to see what Fazia was going to bring next.

By the time they left the restaurant, the streets were hushed. They decide to walk the short distance back to Max's house. They needed to walk off all that food—and the alcohol. No one was drunk, but they all were enjoying the evening. David had his arm around Whitt's shoulders. Finley and Max followed, side by side, quiet and pensive. It took no more than twenty minutes to make their way back. Whitt and Finley said their good nights and headed upstairs. Max had made up the beds and put their bags in their room.

"I owe David one," Finley said quietly, once in her room. "That could have gone any number of ways."

Whitt stood looking at her. "Before you head home, you need to clear the air. You have to talk about it."

"He asked for a 'talk' before we headed to Casablanca."

"Well?"

"What is there to talk about? What's it going to achieve? It's just picking at a scab. One that has almost healed over."

"Your call, but I don't think it's going to fully heal until you talk." Whitt had finished brushing her teeth and braiding her hair. She headed to her side of the bed and slid in. "Good night."

"Thanks for being my sister. Love you. 'Night."

Finley didn't know what time it was. The house was as dark and quiet as a church between masses. She had had a hard time getting to sleep, and when it came, it was brief. She reached for the glass she had brought up for water. Empty. Maybe some more water would help. Maybe warm this time. She slipped a shawl on over her light-weight sweats and T-shirt and let her eyes adjust to the dark before heading down the stairs.

She thought she would be alone at this time of night, but Max was there at the dining table, ostensibly working, in partial light with a large glass of wine, full almost to the top, and the rest of a bottle of red beside him.

"You okay?" Max saw her in the shadows and a look of concern crossed his face.

Finley held up her glass. "Couldn't sleep. I thought more water might help." She headed into the kitchen and pushed the red tab on the filtered water container.

"Can I get you something else? Coffee? Herbal tea?" He held up his glass. "Wine?"

"Are you drunk?"

"Not yet but trying hard to get there. You know me. I savor too much to get enough volume in me to get drunk."

"Want to talk about it?" Finley asked. She was genuinely concerned. He looked unhappy, unsettled. She moved to a chair beside him and rested her chin on her palm. She sat looking at him, sipping on her water as he nursed his wine. "Friend to friend."

Max laughed ruefully. "Friend to friend," he muttered under his breath.

He thought about how sad it was that it had come to this. Only friends. Or maybe he should be happy that he at least had that. She didn't seem angry with him. She wasn't lashing out at him. She had probably moved on. Maybe he should just be thankful that he had a chance to see her again, enjoy her company for as long as she was in Morocco, and leave it at that. *But I can't. I need to hear it from her. I need to know.*

"It's a woman, isn't it?" Finley gave a small joking smile. "The woman at Aliyaa's restaurant? She was very pretty. What's her name?" She was trying to keep it light even though she felt a vise squeezing her heart as she spoke.

"No, Amina is a colleague." Max looked at her under lidded eyes and took another slow sip of wine. "Nothing more."

"Then it must be the woman on your screen saver. I only caught a glimpse, but she's a stunner," Finley said, teasing him gently about his stable of pretty women.

Max tilted his head to the side and smiled at her, a hint of puzzlement on his face. His voice was heavy with drink, but his focus was targeted, "She's also on my phone."

"Who is she?" she chuckled and reached for the phone he held out to her. Glad that he was willing to share his feelings with her about this woman, whoever she was. *You can handle it. He's moved on and you should too. You couldn't have had this conversation a year ago. So, that's progress. But why is he so heavyhearted?*

She touched the phone screen and a picture of a woman with a cascade of long, coffee-colored curls came up. Her smile and the look in her swamp green eyes reflected the heart of a woman so deeply in love. The man beside her looked at her in awe. Finley's face fell. Her heart seized.

"Where did this come from?" Her voice was tight, tortured, hollow.

"We took it in Casablanca, that last trip before you headed home. The one when I almost asked you to marry me. But I didn't." The words were soft, barely audible.

She looked up from the picture, and their eyes locked. Her intonation was hard. "And why didn't you?"

"You were in the window for partner. I couldn't do that to you. Distract you." Max poured more wine into his glass.

"Shouldn't I have had some say in the matter?" her pitch rose. Her eyes narrowed.

He looked at her sadly. "I suppose you should have. But you know you. You would have forgotten yourself and done what was best for us, even if it meant you giving up something you loved. I didn't want you to do that."

"So, you made the decision for me?" She was angry now. Three years. All that hurt. All because he didn't trust her to make a decision? She closed her eyes and tried to steady her breath. *If this is love, he's got a funny way of showing it.*

"I know now that I overstepped. Again." his tone was so soft, so sad, almost forlorn. Her anger subsided. She opened her eyes and reached for his glass, taking a long swallow.

"What would you have done if I had asked?" he queried.

"I don't know. I never got the chance to consider it," she said slowly, pondering the question and putting aside the answer because it was a moot point.

"We could pick up where we left off," Max offered hopefully, his eyes never looking away from her face. *Whitt was right. He does still care. Do I?*

Finley took another sip of his wine and sighed. She looked at him with a wistful smile. "We're different people now."

"Is there someone else?"

Finley shook her head slowly, and her smile grew even more contemplative. *You didn't leave much space for anyone else. I guess neither did I.*

"What about your inspector? He certainly seemed interested."

Finley allowed herself to laugh at this. He and David must have had a conversation about Evans. Poor guy wouldn't have stood a chance even if he had made a move. "He's a confirmed bachelor!"

There was a long pause. Finley wondered what was going though Max's head. She thought the wine might have caught up with him. She didn't know what else to say, so she waited.

"Then let's start again." He was staring at her, his eyes roving her face for some indication of what she was thinking, how she was feeling. Something.

"What does that mean?" She half-laughed and shrugged, her brow knitted in confusion.

Max extended his hand and offered her his most engaging, endearing smile, one that reached up to those gorgeous eyes. "Hi, I'm Max Davies. What brings you to Tangier?"

She paused and looked at him. Hard. His face was almost beatific. His teal eyes imploring, the laugh lines around his mouth so appealing. She knew she was staring, but she was also thinking.

Hard. Did she really want to do this again? There was no telling if it would end any differently. And then she would have to endure all the heartache a second time. Maybe it was best to just leave it alone. They could stay friends—special friends—but just friends.

Instead, she shook his hand and introduced herself, "I'm Finley Blake. I'm here doing a travel story." And for the next three hours, they talked about everything and nothing. They finished the bottle of wine and started on another. Finley recalled her easy conversation with Evans. This one had the same level of comfort, but with deeper meaning. This one had a future.

MORNING CAME TOO QUICKLY. NEITHER of them had gotten any sleep, and both of them were working through hangovers. Max had left her around six o'clock for his run, and Finley had gone upstairs for a shower. She needed that shower, strong coffee, and some aspirin.

When they were all up and dressed, she and Whitt needed to take the car over to the hotel and get the rest of their clothes. They had two more days left on their reservation, but she would just eat the cost and check out early. Whitt and David were leaving the next morning, and she could head to Fes sometime tomorrow afternoon. Then Max would have his house back. His project was almost wrapped, and he would pack his bags and head back to London.

They had talked about how they might make this work long distance. They both had international jobs with some flexibility in terms of the projects they selected. If they worked it right, they might be able to find assignments in the same city for at least some periods of time. They had managed it for two years in Tangier not so long ago. They both knew the risks, but the alternative was worse.

That they had already seen, in bold relief. Even if it didn't work, they could honestly say they had tried.

Finley was putting coffee on when Max came back from his run. He came through the side door, stopped to refill his water bottle, and took a long drink of water.

"What do you want for breakfast? Let me grab a shower, and I'll fix it for you."

"I'm fine with coffee right now. I need to let my head level off before I can think of food." She leaned on the counter and watched the coffee brewing. "Your head doesn't hurt?"

"Nope. A run generally clears it up."

"You drink like this often?" Her face was quizzical. She couldn't imagine drinking that much on a regular basis and staying sane. She couldn't imagine drinking that much ever again, truth be told.

"I used to." His voice was quiet, remorseful. "And then you came back, and I stopped. But then I thought I might lose you again, and I went into a spiral, like last night. Now I think I can stop." He paused. He gave a short laugh. "I bet you didn't know you had that effect on me, did you?"

He was facing her. He looked so vulnerable, so bare that it startled her. He was always in control, taking care of things. She had rarely heard him be so honest. She reached over and touched his face. He hadn't shaved, but the scruff looked good on him.

"No," she said softly. "Go take your shower." She reached past him, grabbed a mug from the rack, and poured herself a cup of coffee. "You want some?"

"Can I just take a sip of yours, and then I'll get some when I come back down?" he asked.

She held the cup out for him to take. It seemed like such a small gesture, but it told her volumes about the chasm that they had managed to cross in the last few hours. He took a gulp of the hot coffee and kissed her forehead before heading up the stairs.

By the time Whitt and David had come downstairs, Max and Finley had prepared a veritable feast for breakfast. Finley had put a red pepper and chorizo frittata in the oven, and Max was flipping buckwheat pancakes. Another pot of coffee was on, and the table was set. Max had put a bottle of champagne on ice, and he had pulled a jug of fresh-squeezed orange juice from the fridge.

Whitt and David stood and watched. They had both heard voices late last night and assumed that Finley and Max were talking, but it sounded intense so the homey scene playing out in the kitchen wasn't what either of them had expected.

"Morning!" Whitt said brightly. "Smells good. What are you making?"

Finley pointed to the oven and then Max. "Frittata and pancakes. Want coffee?"

She held out the pot. She had just refilled Max's cup and hers. Finley could tell her sister sensed a sea change but wasn't sure which way the tide had turned. David grabbed a mug and took the pot from her with an eyebrow raised. She smiled, which should have told him all he needed to know.

"So, what are the plans for today?" David asked nonchalantly. "Besides us packing up."

"I figured that Whitt and I should probably run over to the hotel, check out, and bring our stuff over here," Finley replied.

Whitt didn't even attempt to hide her surprise. After Finley's protest yesterday and her insistence that their stay at Max's be for one night only, she was wondering what had brought about the change in plans.

Max finished flipping the last pancake and turned off the burner. He passed the platter to Finley and went to the cabinet to pull out a container of local honey and a bottle of syrup. He picked up the frittata pan with a bright blue oven mitt and brought it to the table. Whitt had put the coffee carafe on the counter and pulled out a chair beside David.

"David and I can go with you. Might make the packing up go faster and leave you more time to do one last thing in the city."

Max had taken a seat and was opening the champagne. "Anyone for mimosas?"

David and Whitt nodded. Finley shook her head. "I'll stick with coffee for now."

"Late night?" Whitt asked, casting a glance across the table at her sister. "I thought you went to bed when I did?"

"I did," Finley stated, "but I couldn't sleep, so Max and I sat up talking. I think we lost track of time."

Whitt smiled. *I think I heard that excuse a few days ago with a different guy. Looks like whatever she was afraid would happen if she talked to Max didn't. I hope something good did.*

Breakfast turned into a raucous affair with a return to the topics of global politics, despotic leaders, celebrity couples that seemed ill-matched, and bucket list travel spots. One would have thought that with all the travel the four of them did, there would only be a few places on earth left to explore. But each of them had places on their lists that, not surprisingly, one of the others had visited, so the conversation soon turned back to good places, good food, and good wine. Good times with good people.

"That's what we should do. Quit our jobs, empty our savings, and go in on a restaurant that fixes all the food that we like." David seemed excited at the prospect.

"We would have to switch out the menu and the wine list because we like so many different types of cuisines," Finley added. She and Whitt had often talked about opening a breakfast and lunch place in Charleston that served a changing menu based on what they called comfort foods— phở, grits and salmon croquettes, *ropa vieja*, Korean short ribs, and sausage with polenta. Maybe they would just have to add a couple of nice guys as investors.

It was early afternoon when they finally got to the Sultan. The hotel had not lost any of its luster in the days that they had been gone. The lobby was quiet. The movie crew, including Taryn but minus Anna, who had already been picked up by the local police, was far away in Agadir. Whitt hoped that they had found Peter too and put him in jail.

Finley packed her clothes, shoes, and camera equipment far faster than her sister. Once she had packed, Finley stacked her bags near the door and waited to see if her sister needed help. David had been enlisted to tote Whitt's things from the closet to her meticulous piles on what was once Finley's bed. Max shook his head at David's patience. He knew what it felt like to be willing to do anything for someone you cared about.

"I am going up to the roof." Finley stared at the mounds of clothes on the bed. "You guys are taking too long."

Max moved toward the door. "I'll stick these in the car—so you can claim your space—and I'll meet you upstairs."

Whitt shot him a look and smiled, "We'll be up in a bit. It won't take long." She looked at all that remained unpacked, "I don't think."

Finley passed her suitcase and satchel to Max and slung her backpack over her shoulder. She took the back stairs to the upper floor and stepped into the bright sunlight on the terrace. The bar and restaurant were empty, except for the bartender who looked up when she came in. She asked for a glass of white wine for herself and a glass of red for Max. She'd let Whitt and David put their order in when they got upstairs.

She fixed her eyes on the sea and the almost blinding light of the ripples forming as the boats in the harbor went by. She didn't see the bartender leave or hear Peter when he came in, but when she turned toward the door, there he was, gun in hand, walking toward her.

She pushed back from the table and slowly stood up. She wanted to be able to run or throw something if the opportunity arose. She refused to die sitting down. Peter stopped as she moved away from the table, his back to the door—between her and any way out.

"Surprised? Probably not," Peter said. He was agitated. "You just couldn't leave well enough alone. Between Ross digging into the past, and you with that bloody camera. Always snapping photos. You saw too much. You have to go."

Finley decided to play for time. Max would be up soon. If she was loud enough, he would sense something was wrong and go get help. She prayed that he wouldn't try to be a hero. After all this . . . She put the thought out of her mind.

"I didn't see anything. I wouldn't have even known what I was looking at. I was taking pictures of kids in the medina for my article."

"So you say. But you are too smart for your own good. They picked up Anna, you know. So you had to have seen something. Known something. Do you want money too?"

He was getting angrier and began to rant with his eyes fixed on some object in the distance. He hadn't shaved in a while, his djellaba was dirty in places, and the hair he had cut short to hide the grey was starting to grow out at the temples. She wondered where he had been since they left Casablanca. Had he stayed there until Anna left for Agadir, or had he left before and let her do the dirty work?

"Ross wanted more and more and more. Poor Anna was desperate. She hadn't meant to kill her. It was an accident. She was just a kid. Her mother could be cruel when she was drunk."

He was getting more erratic, swinging the gun around, and then stabbing the air with it like he had a picture in his mind of something that he wanted to kill. "She just snapped and hit her and then she couldn't stop hitting her. Again and again and again. I couldn't stop her. I could only help her."

Finley was so focused on Peter and making sure that he didn't start shooting at her that, at first, she didn't see the bartender come back. He moved quietly and purposefully to position himself, so that he was hidden from Peter's view. She focused hard on not looking in that direction.

"I understand that Ross was blackmailing Anna and you, but did you have to kill him?" Finley asked, trying to keep her voice neutral. "Couldn't you have just turned him in?"

"Then it would have all come out. Anna. And me helping her bury the body. No, he had to be taken out. He was a cancer."

"But why did you kill Julien? Was he blackmailing you too?"

"He saw me." Peter had refocused his eyes on Finley. He either was deciding or had decided what he was going to do with her. She needed to think fast about ways to minimize damage if he started shooting.

"He saw me. And so did you." Peter's voice was almost apologetic. Finley understood the implication and went silent. They stood looking at each other as Peter raised and steadied the gun.

From the corner of his eye, Peter must have detected movement. He spun around, ready to start firing at whatever had moved, but before he regained his balance, Finley had grabbed one of the painted stone napkin weights that graced each table and hurled it at the back of Peter's head. In that split second, the bartender rose from his position and fired. Peter lurched forward. Finley didn't know whether it was from the force of the stone or the bullet, but he dropped to his knees and then fell, facedown.

Evans rushed up the stairway, taking two steps at a time. He heard the shot as he was nearing the last landing. He saw Peter fall, but he didn't know what had occurred before the shot. All he knew was that a shot had been fired, Peter had fallen, and Finley was still standing. That, in itself, was a miracle.

"Are you hurt?" he approached her almost at a run. He scanned his eyes over her, looking for any sign of blood. Finley was so intent on watching the bartender—whom she now recognized as Taylor— pull off the djellaba, grab a set of handcuffs, and secure Peter's hands behind his back, that she didn't hear what Evans had said.

"Finley, are you all right?" Evans asked again, taking her by the shoulders to get her attention.

Finley nodded.

"Why don't you sit down? I'll get Davies." Evans motioned to one of the several police officers who were swarming the terrace. Within minutes, Max, Whitt, and David had joined her on the roof.

"Fin, dear God! Woman, you scared me bloodless. I couldn't do a damn thing to help you but call Evans." Max dropped to his knees and pulling her close. "Thank goodness he was already outside the hotel. One of his agents had seen Peter this morning, and they were staking out the place."

"Is he dead?" Finley's voice was quiet. Her eyes never left Peter, as if she wanted to be sure he didn't rise and start killing people again.

"I don't know. I don't think so. But let's get you home." Whitt was standing beside her sister, a glass of bourbon in her hand. In the absence of a real bartender, she had moved behind the bar and poured out a measure.

"I can't leave, yet. They need to take statements, I suppose."

"Then I think we all need a drink." Whitt set the glass of bourbon in front of Finley and went to the bar to get the bottle and some more glasses. She poured shots all around. "So, what happened? All we know is that Max came flying into the room, called Evans on his phone, and said we had to stay put."

Finley took a slow sip of the bourbon, her eyes focused on the clear dark liquid as she tried to piece together what Peter had said.

"Peter confirmed that Ross was blackmailing Anna." She paused. "Anna killed someone, and Peter was there. A woman, but I don't know why Peter was there, where 'there' was, or who the woman was. But Peter helped Anna bury the body." Whitt gasped, and David sat back, slack jawed. Max had gotten up and taken the seat next to her. He listened, letting her shock run its course.

"I don't know if Peter or Anna killed Ross, but Peter said he killed Julien because he saw him." Finley furrowed her brow. "I don't know what he saw Peter doing. He thought I saw him too, and he said I had to die so I couldn't tell anyone what I saw."

"What did you see?" David asked.

"Nothing besides Anna and Peter together doing something. I guess he feared that all their secrets were about to be exposed." Finley was still confused. "But even if Peter did kill Ross, how did he get him over the rail and onto the chandelier? There's still something missing."

The ambulance arrived, and the technicians were loading Peter onto the gurney. The handcuffs had been moved to join his hands in front of his body. His eyes were still closed, but they hadn't put him in a body bag, so she supposed he was still alive. Evans and Taylor were talking. Evans soon joined Finley's group at the table.

"We're going to need to get a statement from you," Evans stated. "I would prefer getting it now while the incident is fresh in your mind. If you don't mind." He had turned to address Max, "I also will need one from you. Just about what you saw when you came up the stairs." Max nodded.

Evans continued, "I know that you're planning on leaving in the next day or so, but we're going to need you to stay in Morocco at least until we have all the facts sorted out. Your sister and her friend are free to go once we get a preliminary statement from them. Just to be thorough."

"If you step over here, one of the officers and I will take your statement," Evans motioned to another small table.

"Then will you tell us what the hell Peter was talking about?" Finley asked. "About Anna murdering some woman. It's like musical bodies—I don't know who killed whom, and it's driving me crazy."

"Let me get the statements first, and then we can compare notes." Evans signaled for Finley to head to a nearby table. When she and Max had each finished speaking to the officer under Evans's supervision, he called for Whitt and David in turn. Finally, he spoke briefly to the officer, who had taken the statements, and then rejoined them at the table.

"Mind if I sit?" Evans asked. He pulled out a chair, slid his long body into it, and sighed. "I am so glad we got to you in time. We assumed that you were still at Mr. Davies's this morning. We had tracked you back there yesterday morning and checked with our agents in the hotel again today to be sure you hadn't returned. They said they hadn't seen you. They even rang your room to be sure."

Evans looked at Finley and shook his head, acknowledging how lucky they had been. "He planned to kill you, no doubt. He felt trapped. He was desperate after we arrested Anna." He paused, "If I had known how desperate, I would have picked him up first."

He continued, "It appears that, some years ago in Los Angeles, Peter was involved with a woman. Anna's mother. We still don't know what prompted it, but Anna killed her mother."

"That was the woman Peter was talking about. He said she was cruel, and Anna hit her with something to kill her. He looked crazed when he was talking about it," Finley confirmed.

"Well, apparently, he helped her get rid of the body because it was never found. In fact, the woman's disappearance was never reported. Peter and Anna just changed their names and melted into the film industry," Evans stated.

"Until Ross," Max added.

"Our information was that Ross was blackmailing Anna and Peter over this. How he found out, we may never know," Evans sighed and shook his head.

"How did he and the guy he stabbed come upon each other? He was only out of jail for a short time before he was killed." David was trying hard to fit the pieces together and was getting more confused by the minute.

"Julien appears to have left the hotel after we released him and dropped him off. He may have been taking a walk or going for cigarettes. Again, we don't know. In any event, Peter saw him, thought his disguise had been compromised, and decided Julien had to be silenced," Evans said.

"I guess once you kill or cover up a killing, additional lives don't matter much," Finley muttered quietly. "I was just going to be collateral damage."

Finley turned to Evans, "But that still doesn't answer how Ross got on the chandelier. We have been trying to answer that since we found him."

"Turns out that was fairly easy. Anna lured Ross into her room. Peter killed him. Broke his neck. And the two of them together waited until just the right moment to toss him over. They wanted to get him hung there so that he would be between floors. That would give them more time to establish alibis before he was found," Evans recounted the facts without commentary.

"Okay, so what was with the snake?" Whitt asked. "Why go to all that trouble to sicken someone, when you planned to kill at least some of them anyway?" She looked at Finley's pale face and realized how much the two of them had been through during the past two weeks. *Crazy as it is, all of this has brought us closer together. Not just Finley and me, but David and me. Finley and Max. Too bad you have to almost die to value the things you have.*

"Again, Peter and Anna were trying to buy time. In this case, it was more time for Peter to blend into the background here in Morocco. Anna said that the plan was for Peter to get himself fired and pretend to go home to the United Kingdom. Anna would finish the film, break with Peter, and live out her life in Britain or wherever, since no one, but Ross, knew of a connection between the two of them," Evans explained.

"Peter had decided to see if he could settle in Casablanca. Anna got spooked when she heard that you all were heading there. Peter had her follow you—first to Rabat and then to Casablanca. When they thought they had been spotted, they had to find something to slow you down," Evans continued. "They came up with the snake. Don't know whose idea it was. They hadn't planned to kill you, just hospitalize you to redirect attention."

"But the snake was what started Finley focusing attention on them. Before that, it was only Finley's suspicion that she had seen Peter. She wouldn't have gone looking for the proof if the snake incident hadn't happened," Whitt noted.

"I don't think Peter planned to kill any of you until we picked up Anna. He realized then that it was all coming apart. That he might be able to save Anna if he could get rid of you—and all the pictures," Evans remarked. "I don't think he would have killed you here. He also wanted the pictures so he would have threatened you until Whitt turned them over."

"And then what?" Finley murmured under her breath.

"Luckily, we didn't have to find out," Evans responded, smiling softly at her. He stood and reached to shake Whitt and David's hands." I need to go, but I hope all of this hasn't put you off about Morocco. It is a beautiful and exciting place. Travel safely."

"I'll be in touch," He nodded to Max and then to Finley. "And you, get some rest."

The remaining foursome sat in silence, staring into their glasses. It was Finley who spoke first.

"So where are we going now? This is your last night in Tangier. We need to do something fun." Finley turned to look at Max." What would you suggest?"

Max laughed. "I know David is hungry. And so am I. If you are sure you're up for it, why don't we figure on dinner and then maybe we can find a little music to end the night? You guys have a fairly early start time tomorrow."

David put what was left of the bourbon back behind the bar and came back to collect Whitt. Max and Finley had already started toward the door, nodding at the few remaining policemen who were still taking pictures. Among them was Taylor. Finley pulled away from Max and approached the young agent. When she reached him, she took his hand and kissed him lightly on the cheek.

"Thank you. And if you're ever in New York, look me up. I'll try to make your time there as exciting as mine has been in Tangier," she smiled at him as she left and headed down the stairs.

Max's choice of restaurant for Whitt and David's last night in Morocco defied imagination. Max had indicated that the attire was more formal than they had worn in Tangier to date. Whitt thought that David might need to borrow something to wear from Max, but to her surprise, he had pulled a navy brushed-linen two-button jacket from his suitcase and matching buff-colored linen trousers, which he paired with a powder blue shirt. He stood at the ironing board, pressing the travel creases from his jacket, when Whitt came down to get something to drink.

"You know how to iron! I am impressed," she joked.

David grinned proudly. "Been doing my own ironing since Junior ROTC. Wouldn't let anyone, not even my mom, iron my uniform."

"What are you wearing?" he asked slyly.

"It's a surprise!" Whitt called over her shoulder as she headed up the stairs.

In their room, Whitt agonized over what to wear. Max had said that the restriction about covering her shoulders was lifted at this particular place but gave no more information. It appeared that David knew where they were going and what they were doing, but he wasn't telling either. The only other hint that either Max or David gave was that they might want to wear or bring their dancing shoes.

Finley seemed less anxious about her attire now than she had been when she went to dinner with Evans in Casablanca. She had wondered why and had decided that it was because Evans was an unknown. With Max, there was familiarity even though both were excited about discovering each other anew.

At Mooney's insistence, she had packed a red halter-collared silk jersey jumpsuit with a T back. The lines were so simple and classic that it was easy to dress it up with her tapestry stilettos and a pair of gold and green crystal tassel earrings. More than anything, she liked the way it accentuated her toned shoulders. She had packed her antique gold mesh evening bag just in case. Now was just the case. She played up her eye makeup to offset the simplicity of the jumpsuit but left her lipstick neutral and understated.

Whitt had finally decided on a sleeveless black-and-white geometric cocktail sheath that hit just above her knee. It was the length that played best with her long, lean legs. The sheath hugged in just the right spots to give her angular figure nice, rounded curves. Her black strappy sandals with a kitten-heel lent an air of sophistication to her outfit. She always felt pretty when she wore this dress. She had decided to part her hair in the middle tonight and leave it dead straight to counterbalance the natural curves of the dress. She kept her makeup minimal until it came to her lips. A bold matte brick provided all the color she needed.

When Whitt and Finley went downstairs, David was the only one in the room. He paused to take in the full effect of both women's entrance, but especially Whitt's. It was clear that he fully appreciated the beauty of the woman he got to escort to dinner that night. And he was dressed to play the part. The blue of his eyes brightened against the blue of his shirt and held Whitt's attention. She grinned. *Good Lord, kill me now. It can't get much better than this.*

Max had gone to clean out the car. While they had tried to be tidy, he wanted to be sure that nothing got on his guests' evening clothes. He had just dropped the trash from the car in the container and was moving to the sink to wash his hands when he caught sight of Finley.

Whitt and David were sitting on the couch talking, and Finley was standing by the dining table flipping through the *Economist* that he had brought in earlier. He was glad she didn't see him looking at her. His hunger would have embarrassed her. He had never wanted to touch something so badly in his life. *Slow down there. You got a skittish filly. Don't want to scare her away.*

"You guys ready?" Max asked. He swallowed hard as he entered the dining room. He gave Finley a mock catcall. "My, don't you look lovely."

Finley looked up from the magazine and smiled. "You cleaned up pretty well yourself."

He had indeed. He had changed into a marine blue suit with a white linen shirt, open at the collar. The suit material looked like a silk linen blend, giving it texture and dimension. It also looked soft to the touch. *I hope I get to take his arm at some point tonight,* Finley thought. He looked like he had stepped out of the pages of European *GQ*. His laugh lines were more pronounced, the sprinkle of grey in his hair adding just the right seasoning. But it was his eyes—those gorgeous, indescribably delicious blue eyes—that had always caught her breath, just as they did tonight.

Outside, Max let Whitt and David get into the car and then stood to hold the door for Finley. He wanted an excuse to get close to her, even if it was to be polite. He noticed that when she passed him to get into the car, she took in a whiff of his cologne. She turned and looked at him for just an instant. "Armani," she said under her breath. *She remembered.*

The restaurant was less than a fifteen-minute ride from Max's house, but in many ways, it was worlds away. Set in the hills of Tangier, the Villa Josephine offered a spectacular panoramic view of the city below. The hilltop setting, luxurious appointments, and old Hollywood ambiance of the mansion, built in the 1920s by a newspaper magnate, hinted at an era of elegance long since forgotten.

Walking up the elegant pathway to the entrance, the foursome was greeted with smiles and a few open stares. Finley had taken Max's arm on the uneven stone path. In her heels she was only an inch or so shorter than he, but they paired well, as did Whitt and David—she was dark and sultry, and he was as bright as California sunshine.

They were taken to their table on the terrace just as the sun was lowering in the sky. *Max couldn't have planned it better. Glad Whitt didn't fret with her outfit too long.* The champagne was on ice already, and the waiter came immediately to pour. When they all had been served, Max raised his glass.

"Here's to family and friends, to old loves and new beginnings. And to meeting—again—the most exciting woman I have ever known."

David raised his glass, thinking over the events of the past several days, and added, "I know we are talking about different women, but the same applies. To the Blake sisters. We sure as hell will never be bored."

They laughed and clinked glasses.

Whitt raised her glass and looked at David. She remembered a toast her mother had once made. "And to the men who love them."

It was now Finley's turn. She stared at the sinking sun through the tiny bubbles in her glass and tried to think of something witty to say. The past few weeks had been unsettling. Unnerving. Scary. They had tested her physically, mentally, and emotionally. And yet her heart was full. She had no idea what would happen in the future, but tonight she had all the things she wanted in life—family, friends, someone who loved her, the prospect of an abundant future. What she wanted was for this to never end.

Instead, she met Max's gaze and said, "To a lifetime of nights like this."

The End

If you enjoyed this book and want to learn
more about Finley and Whitt Blake
join our mailing list at www.mcarterfielding.com or
drop me a line at carter.fielding6554@gmail.com.
I'd love to hear from you.
Talk soon!

**Read on to get a sneak peek at the next in the
Blake Sisters Travel Mystery series**

ACKNOWLEDGEMENTS

When I started this journey a year ago, I knew I was still testing out my wings as a writer. There was a chance I would crash and burn. A real chance. And yet, over the past several months, I have taken flight—granted at heights that barely qualify as being aloft—but I have started to fly on the wings of words, and it is a high like I have never known. A whole flight crew of folks had a hand in this mini miracle:

- My cousins, the crazy sisters who are never home and are always looking for a place on the map where they haven't been. Thanks for the travel ideas—and all the *tsatske*.
- My parents, who had never read these kinds of books before but are starting to dip their toes into the waters of cozies. Thanks for not calling the shrink when I talk to myself—I'm just testing out dialogue.
- The wonderful people I meet when I travel, who open their homes and their hearts to me. Thanks especially to Layla and Matthew. And Ali and his wonderful family in Marrakesh.
- The team at Bublish—my team manager, Shilah, the creatives, the tech guys, and my amazing editor, whom I only

know as "SJ." Thanks for charting the course, so I make it to my destination each time and land without incident, however bumpy the flight.

- And finally, the growing league of readers who met Whitt and Finley in *Murder in Montauk* and decided another adventure was in order. Thanks for coming aboard. The journey has just begun!

AUTHOR BIO

New author Carter Fielding is a millennial with an old soul. She likes old maps, old photographs, vintage records, and vintage champagnes. A Southerner, with roots in Anderson, South Carolina, she likes a good bourbon, a day that calls for wearing a barn jacket and a pair of wellies, and the smell of wet earth after a good rain. She started writing the Blake Sisters series during lockdown to tame a wanderlust that couldn't be satisfied by a trip to Harris Teeter and ended up building a relationship with the whole cast of characters that has taken on a life of its own.

She lives in Northern Virginia with her Boykin spaniel, Trucker, and uses her passion for books and travel to create characters she hopes readers will come to love.

A Blake Sisters Travel Mystery
Book 2
Murder in the Tea Leaves

Carter Fielding

CHAPTER 1

"**Y**OU HAVE GOT TO BE kidding me!" Finley Blake was wearing a hole in the flatweave Berber rug she had bought during her last assignment in Morocco. That trip had brought a lot of changes, not the least of which was Max.

"You just had me book my flight. Last night, in fact!" Her voice reflected the agitation she felt. Her shoulders were creeping up to her ears. Her jaw was moving back and forth, a sure sign she was upset. "So where am I off to now?"

Finley was back home in Manhattan, talking to Dan Burton, her editor at *Traveler's Tales*, a high-end travel magazine that had hired her as a freelancer for the past several months, ever since she wrote her first "48 Hours in . . . " article for them. That article focused on the exotic wonders of Casablanca, complete with descriptions of all the best food, shopping, and historical sights that could be absorbed in two days.

The success of the Casablanca article, and the eye-catching photos that had accompanied it, had assured her of work for the last few months. Dan had kept printing her stories, both the short "48 hours" pieces that she had done on Fes, Barcelona, and Tangier as well as some more in-depth reporting on Sienna, Dubrovnik, and Bruges she had done just a couple of months ago.

Truth be told, Dan was more than her boss. He was also her friend and had been since their early days in law school. They had often sat together in class because of their last names, Blake and Burton, and had remained friends over the years. They both had abandoned the law long ago and taken up other careers, Finley in consulting and Dan in journalism. When Finley decided to leave the consulting firm where she was a senior partner, Dan was the first person she called.

He had brought her onto *Travelers' Tales* on a provisional basis initially, but the sales worthiness of her stories and photos had earned her a regular slot. Dan would have loved to have hired her for the permanent staff, but Finley had wanted the freedom to pick and choose which assignments she took. And that was what had her so riled now.

The original assignment she had opted for had her in India, working on a piece on preserving the cultural heritage of tribal peoples in Bihar, Jharkhand, and Orissa. Finley would get to see Max who was now in Delhi. Their relationship had been a complicated one, started years ago during an earlier stint in Morocco and interrupted for almost three years because of a profound misunderstanding that had nearly broken them both.

"If we hadn't reviewed the assignment and all the travel logistics just yesterday, I wouldn't have had this reaction," Finley continued. "But I literally booked the flight, hotel, and driver last night because I thought everything was a go." Finley knew that this was only a half truth. *He doesn't have to know the real reason I'm pissed. I told Max I was coming. I really want to see him.*

"I know, but I have a new staff writer coming on and we're shifting the focus to Delhi, which is an easier story. We'll hold the tribal angle for another issue." Dan could hear the frustration in Finley's voice. And while she didn't talk about her personal life much, he had seen how devastated she had been four years ago when she returned to New York. How she had thrown herself into her work to fill the void created by the loss of something precious.

He had met Max socially before, when all three of them had worked in Manhattan. He had known that Finley and Max had been close in Tangier all those years ago and that something had happened, but he never knew what had caused her to come home so broken. What he did know was when she returned from Morocco this time, some eight months ago, whatever hurt there had been was healed and that she readily spoke Max's name.

"I need a more experienced writer on this story, and I think you'll do it justice."

"Don't start buttering me up," Finley's voice was tight, but she masked a smile. "You know I can still refuse it and sit this one out."

"I don't think you're going to want to, though." Dan could tell she was warming to the potential location, even without knowing where it was. "It's politically complex, and you'll know how to balance the perspectives and still get travelers to want to go."

"You going to tell me where it is or just keep me guessing?"

"You want to guess?"

"No, just tell me so I can say no."

"You'd say no to Sri Lanka? As I recall, you called it "paradise on Earth.""

Finley was quiet. As much as she wanted to say no, she knew Dan had her trapped. She sighed and then gave a small laugh.

"I give. You got me," she said. "I can't say no. When do I leave?"

Dan explained the Colombo focus of the assignment and reviewed the logistics.

"I managed to swing a bit of budget. But . . ." Dan started.

". . . don't expect it every time." Finley interrupted. Dan always said that, but still managed to find money to fund her assignments. She wasn't hurting for money. The buyout from the consulting firm had been generous and positioned her well for the future. Still, why pay for things out of pocket when someone else was willing to cover the cost upfront?

It was still midafternoon when she hung up with Dan. She dreaded calling Max, so she put it off. The less she thought about it, the less she would be filled with a longing for Max that she had been burying for months now.

She had seen him in New York for two weeks, when he had met with a potential client there instead of in London so that they could spend some time together. Besides that, there had been a long weekend in Barcelona, while she worked on a story about the rise of tango bars in the city. She and Max had taken a class and danced a *tanda* or two at Centro Gallego, never progressing to the faster-paced *milagro*. That was almost two months ago.

Instead of calling Max, she quick dialed her sister, S. Whittaker Blake, known to all as simply Whitt. *Or Half-Whitt. I haven't called her that in years.* Whitt lived in Manila most of the time, but because she worked for a development bank, more often than not she was on the road. Finley and Whitt saw each other a couple of times a year back in the US, when Whitt had home leave. In between, they tried to work their travel schedule so that they could meet in some location equidistant to wherever they were working. Morocco had been a bit out of the way for Whitt, who had been on her way to Tbilisi for meetings last time, but it had proven to be worthwhile trip in so many ways.

"Hello, Whitt Blake," Whitt had her work voice on today.

Finley laughed. Her little sister, all grown up. Whitt was almost six years younger and had settled into her career as a Young Professional at the bank. She was also settling into a relationship with a deliciously handsome young entrepreneur who was building export relationships with wine and walnut vendors in Georgia.

Whitt had met David a year ago through mutual friends in Tbilisi and they had been together since. He had had a hand in Finley and Whitt's adventures in Morocco—and still had stuck around to see how his relationship with Whitt might play out. Finley had to give him credit. He was made of stronger stuff than she had thought when Whitt first started talking about him.

"Hey, what are you up to?"

"Not much. Just doing revenue projections for that same micro-finance project that I've been working on for months." She tried to sound frustrated that the project was taking so long to get structured, but Finley knew she was glad to be in Tbilisi as long as David was there. "When do you leave for Delhi?"

"I don't," Finley heard her sister take in a breath. *She's probably waiting for curses or tears. Let's see how long she holds her breath waiting for me to start screaming.* Finley waited.

She stared at the early rush hour traffic that was building up on Amsterdam. The double-paned windows muffled the honking and noise of an impatient city. Pedestrians wove in and out of the stopped cars, taking advantage of the suspended animation to hurry home to take the kids to ballet, or to make it to a nail appointment. *Welcome to New York.*

Whitt chose her words carefully, "Is your trip delayed?"

"No, cancelled. The assignment was given to a new writer," Finley looked away from the window and paused.

Whitt was quiet. The silence was heavy. Finley could imagine Whitt's brow furrowing, her hand moving slowly to release the mouse and pick up her ginger tea from the mini-warming plate. *I should put her out of her misery. She's thinking too much. Her brain is going to hurt trying to figure out what to say that won't have me in tears.*

Finley continued, "I got Sri Lanka instead. Mainly Colombo."

"So, you can still see each other," Whitt exhaled and smiled to herself. *She has been missing him so much. Max has probably been going through the same. They are such a confusing couple.*

"Yeah, but I haven't told him the change of plans yet. I'll deal with it tonight." Finley would catch him before he headed to work, Delhi time, just after his run.

"As long as you can see each other, he'll be fine. And Colombo is just a short flight from Delhi."

"How's David?" Finley wondered whether he was sitting right there. He might be if she was working from home. "When do I get to see you guys?"

"He's fine. In a meeting downtown," Whitt said. "I was thinking, when you said Colombo, whether you wanted to exchange the trip to Uzbekistan for more time in Sri Lanka."

Whitt had given Finley a trip to Central Asia for her 30th birthday that she still hadn't taken. Finley loved her sister's taste in gifts—either really expensive pieces of jewelry or trips to faraway places. She loved both so the surprise was always there whatever Whitt chose. "We didn't have time to explore Galle or much of the south last trip." She continued.

"Can you get away on such short notice?" Finley asked. "I know you have the time accumulated, as hard as you work."

"I think I can. Just one small hurdle in the numbers."

"David coming too?"

"Nope, I'll leave him here," Whitt said lightly. "You know, absence makes the heart grow fonder and all of that."

Finley tensed. *That doesn't sound good. Wonder what's up? She's making a joke of it, but I don't think she thinks it's funny.* Her sister played the tough cookie as her public persona, but she was a softie who was pretty closed with her emotions. She could be bleeding inside and would make some cavalier comment that deflected the hurt. You never could tell for sure. Maybe it is time for some girl talk.

"Sure. Let me get this story out of the way and then we can have some fun."

"Where do you want to go?"

"Surprise me. Only request is that we do Yala again."

Whitt had planned the last trip to Sri Lanka, even though it had been Finley's graduation gift to her. There had been so many places that Whitt had wanted to see in the North and Central parts of the country that Yala was the only concession they made to the south. They had started in Colombo and then headed to Kandy to see the Temple of the Tooth before heading to Dambulla to wander the Buddha caves and a quick tour of Anuradhapura.

They hadn't gone further north to Jaffna, because of reports of political unrest. Instead, they had headed southwest to Polonnaruwa, an ancient city dating back thousands of years, with a quick stop in Sigiriya to climb Lion's Mountain. The panoramic view from the top of the 200-foot outcropping, that had purportedly served as both an old monastery and palace, had been surreal. Whitt said she could imagine a king looking out on this vista every morning and knowing that all that his eye could see was his kingdom. They had ended the trip in Yala for leopard spotting.

"Galle okay as our launch point?" Whitt asked. "Great gem shopping.

Finley smiled to herself. Whitt always had a nose for the best shopping in town and this trip would be no different. Without David there to carry packages, Finley knew she would serve the role of Sherpa. Thank goodness gems were small and light!

"Works for me. Got to go. Another call coming in, but I'll talk to you soon. Love you."

"Me too," was all she heard as the call dropped and Mooney's face appeared on her screen. Mooney Allen was one of her dearest friends. They had met in New York after Finley had returned from Tangier the first time. Mooney had been her lifeline back to the living during that time and had remained a trusted confidante ever since.

"Don't forget drinks tonight."

Finley screwed up her face and cursed under her breath. Mooney made it her job to be sure that all her friends got out and enjoyed the fabulous happenings in the city. She was especially mindful of Finley's tendency to pull on her sweats, order Thai or Lebanese food for delivery, and curl up with a book for days on end.

Mooney knew about Max and wanted to help Finley figure out what she wanted from that relationship, but she also hated for Finley to waste opportunities to see "what else was out there," as she was fond of saying. In particular, Mooney wanted Finley to at least consider Logan Reynolds, a very successful entrepreneur, a bit Finley's senior, who was attractive, rich, and above all, "FOF"— fond of Finley.

"You forgot," Mooney continued reproachfully. "That's why I called. In fact, I'll come pick you up in forty-five minutes."

Before Finley could protest, Mooney had clicked off. Finley sat looking at the phone. She stuck out her tongue at Mooney's picture before it faded and then put down her phone. *I don't want to go out. I don't have anything to wear.* She was glad she hadn't tried that excuse on Mooney. Mooney would have simply swooped in thirty minutes early and torn Finley's closet apart putting together killer outfits for tonight.

Finley moved to the closet to see what she could piece together for drinks. She didn't feel like getting dressed up, but if she didn't make an effort, she would have to deal with Mooney's mouth all weekend and into next week. And she wanted—needed—to focus on getting ready for Colombo, scoping out ideas and angles for her story, figuring out what to take. There, Mooney might be useful.

By the time Mooney arrived, Finley had rummaged the closet for an outfit and turned up with only a pair of black skinny jeans, a black cashmere turtleneck and some dressy black boots. Granted the boots were Jimmy Choo's from three seasons ago, but she had to admit that she could just as easily have gone grocery shopping at Dag's as gone to drinks at Cork in this. She grabbed a pair of large Berber earrings and some bangles just as the doorbell rang.

"I'm trying to decide if I like it or not," Mooney had stepped in the door and then held Finley at arm's length to determine whether she approved of what she was wearing.

"I haven't done my hair yet." Finley pulled at the hair tie that was holding her mass of curls back. She had kept it pixie short for almost four years but was now letting it slowly grow out. It wasn't to her waist as it had been years ago, but it was to her shoulder, thick and heavy.

She headed to the bathroom and finished her makeup before she started fingering through her curls. The hair around her temples and brow fell into soft tendrils that framed her face. She added a bit more blush to meet the delicate wisps that played close to her dark green eyes and then added a pop of brick red matte lipstick to break up the blackness of her clothes.

"You know, I love that on you," Mooney was standing at the bathroom door, watching as Finley put the final touches on her makeup. "It isn't me, but it is so understatedly you."

The contrast between them was indeed marked. Finley in her black on black, with her alligator green eyes and matte red lips providing the only flashes of color, and Mooney all brightness and light with her ash blond tresses catching the beams from the hall and reflecting it back in her crystalline blue eyes. Finley smiled at their yin-yang looks. She grabbed her long Kashmiri embroidered duster, cut the lights, and they were out of the door.

Cork was surprisingly quiet for a Friday night. Mooney had called ahead to reserve their normal high bar table toward the front window, but she really didn't need to, given the slow crowd that was there. It might have been the cold dampness in the air. It was February after all. *Goodness I will be glad for Colombo's warm weather. Humidity, I can take. Anything but this cold.*

Their table was starting to fill with friends from Mooney's work as well as Finley's former consulting firm. Even though many had left to go to other positions in the city, they had stayed tight friends and looked forward to catching up over drinks each week with people who knew them well enough to just enjoy their company without judgment. Finley had valued that when she had come back from Tangier the first time, licking her wounds.

"Love those earrings!" Lydia, Mooney's roommate and Finley's former classmate from law school, was reaching over the narrow table to hold the thick pendant dangles to the light. "Where'd you get them? And don't tell me some place exotic!"

Finley reached up to touch the etching on the earrings, trying to remember where and when she had gotten them. Her fingers traced the intricate hammer work on them and smiled, remembering well that they had come from Max and had been a gift from this last trip, when they were in Fes. Whitt and David had left, and Max had accompanied Finley to Fes to do her final segment of the Moroccan assignment. He had purchased them there without her knowing and then presented them to her as she was getting on the plane in Tangier to head home.

"Don't open this until you're in the air," he had said pressing a small woven bag into her hand as she stepped toward security.

She was well into the second hour of the flight before she loosened the black cord on the brocade pouch and unwrapped the earrings. They matched the silver beadwork on a necklace he had given her years ago, when they first met. The Berber symbols etched on both signified endless time.

"In Morocco," was all she said.

"Speaking of Morocco, I still owe you dinner." Someone had come up behind her, slipped his arm around her waist and kissed her cheek. It was Logan. "When you left for Morocco last year, I promised you a raincheck for dinner and you haven't called it in yet."

Mooney watched Finley's face to see how she was going to get out of this one. Finley and Logan had been out several times before Finley and Max reconnected. And they had continued to hang out together over drinks, like tonight, but Finley had put off his recent attempts to get her alone, especially over an intimate dinner. Much as she liked him as a friend, even if there had been no Max, she probably wouldn't have seriously dated him. But now, there was a Max.

"You do indeed," Finley acknowledged. She was going to have to handle this carefully since he was one of Mooney's clients.

Finley was saved from having to further commit by a former colleague who called her over to look at pictures of her baby. By the time, she returned to her stool, everyone was deciding where to go for dinner. Rocco's, a steakhouse in the Flatiron district, was the choice, and the group began piling into cabs for the short trip downtown. As fate would have it, Logan put Finley into a cab and then hopped in beside her.

"So where do you want to use your raincheck? The world is your oyster," Logan said as the cab entered the long line of traffic heading south on Fifth. "You name the place. Just the two of us. Anywhere in the world."

Finley knew that he meant it. If she had said she wanted steak frites, but in a Paris bistro in St. Germaine de Pres, or sushi in Tokyo's Ginza, Logan would have scheduled his plane and whisked her off for a dinner in France or Japan, even one that she could easily have gotten in New York. She smiled at the privileges that wealth could bring.

"I'm going to have to think on that for a while," Finley said. "I leave in a few days on another assignment, so I'll have a couple of long plane rides to contemplate where I want to go."

"You're leaving me again? Where to now?"

"Colombo for a couple of weeks. And then further south with my sister."

Logan turned to face her, smiling slightly. "Any other guy would think that you're trying to avoid me." He paused, "Are you?"

Finley returned his look and answered honestly. There was no point in not being direct, truthful. "No, I like your company. You're an exceedingly interesting man, but I think we both know that I'm not interested in you."

She straightened in her seat, turning her gaze forward and matching her smile to his. "And if you were truly honest, you would concede that it isn't me you want. It's the chase you like, not the catch!"

Logan opened his mouth to speak, shut it, sighed, and then burst into laughter, "You got me! Until you said it, I don't think I realized it myself. Touché!"

He lifted her gloved hand from her lap and held it in his. Theirs was going to be a long and complex friendship. The stuff of legends. They continued the rest of the trip in companionable silence. The cabbie glanced in his mirror a few times, shook his head, and turned up the radio.

Made in the USA
Middletown, DE
24 August 2022

70936388R00135